the VIRTUES *of* OXYGEN

ALSO BY SUSAN SCHOENBERGER
A Watershed Year

the
VIRTUES
of
OXYGEN

A NOVEL

susan
schoenberger

Published by

LAKE UNION
PUBLISHING

Published by Lake Union, Seattle.
www.apub.com

Amazon, the Amazon logo, and Lake Union are trademarks of Amazon.com, Inc., or its affiliates.

eISBN: 9781477872796
ISBN-10: 1477822798
ISBN-13: 9781477822791
LCCN: 2013922974

Cover design by Anna Curtis

For Kevin

CHAPTER 1

Vivian's Unaired Podcast #1

Brief bits of memory remain:
—Stiffness in my legs as I balanced on the second fence rail to feed the chickens.
—A too-bright sun searing my aching head.
—Clothes rough against fevered skin.
—Eyelids so heavy they pulled me into darkness.

~

I've been told that my sister, Darlene, found me on the ground and carried me into the house. My cheek must have been mashed against a button on her overalls, because I remember waking up and rubbing the welt on my face when she put me down on the davenport, but then my arm felt so tired I had to let it drop. That sensation—of strength draining out of me like water from a bathtub—has stayed with me all these years. The virus set in quickly, shutting down limbs that had just that morning propelled me into the spiraling oak in the backyard, the one I wasn't allowed to climb.

"You'll break your neck up there," my mother had said, little knowing that my arms and legs needed a challenge before they would be permanently decommissioned. She had walked back into the house yelling, "Why the Lord saddled me with two tomboys I'll never know."

Darlene was ten, four years older than me and therefore four times as smart, and so thoroughly a tomboy that she was sometimes mistaken for an actual boy. She refused to wear dresses except to church and she stomped around the farm in a pair of Daddy's old work boots. I admired everything about Darlene—how she had chopped her hair into a bob with a pair of rusty scissors in the shed; how she shrugged whenever my mother told her that boys didn't find dirty fingernails attractive; how she read extensively about airplanes and engineering and could take our old radio apart and put it back together. Daddy never seemed to mind her boyish ways, but my mother fretted about them endlessly. Darlene just had her own view of the world.

"Don't you feel like you could reach out and grab one?" Darlene said one summer night while we were lying on our backs on the hillside behind the farmhouse looking at the stars. She stretched her arms toward the sky and made little pincers with her thumb and forefinger around a star, so I did the same.

"Darlene?"

"That's my name. Don't wear it out."

"We'll always stay here, right? You, me, Mom, and Daddy."

"I'm going to fly airplanes when I grow up," she said. "But I guess I'll come back and sleep here when I'm done for the day."

"You promise?" It worried me to think about Darlene zooming around in the sky without the rest of us, dodging the stars, which she wouldn't be able to see in the daytime.

"I promise, Vivi. Now let's go inside before Mom has a conniption."

I remember Darlene crying before they took me to the hospital, which more than anything made me realize I was truly sick. The word "polio" had been mentioned in my presence during periodic quarantines, but I don't remember if I knew what it meant. I only knew that

I felt terrible—so terrible that I couldn't move, couldn't speak, couldn't cry. I didn't have the strength to worry about what was happening to me. I just wanted to escape from the pain in my back and my head; sleep seemed like the only release.

When I woke up in the hospital, my parents were hovering over me with looks of pure anguish on their faces. They told me the doctors were sending us to another hospital so that I could get better, and patted my hands and placed clammy palms on my burning forehead. I was already having trouble breathing. I remember hearing my mother pulling air audibly into her lungs as if she could compensate for my struggling.

I don't remember the ride to the polio ward in Syracuse, but I remember the moment they placed me into the iron lung, closing it around my slight body and fixing the rubber collar around my neck so that it made a seal. I couldn't see most of the machine, but I could feel the instant relief as I gave over the newly difficult work of breathing to a device much more capable than I was. It seemed miraculous. Weeks later—after we had slipped into a bizarre routine of daily visits and strange forms of physical therapy—my mother sat down next to my iron lung and put her hands on both of my cheeks.

"Vivian, sweetheart," my mother said, her eyes red from crying. "We have something very hard to tell you."

"What?" I said. In those weeks after I fell ill, my mother often looked like she had been crying, so I wasn't all that concerned.

"It's Darlene," she said, choking over my sister's name. "She didn't make it."

"But you said she could come to see me when I was better."

"No, Vivian," my mother said. "She had polio like you, except she's gone now. Gone to heaven."

My mother still had her hands on my cheeks. My father stood on the other side of me, one hand on the top of my head, as if they could somehow cushion the last part of me that still functioned on its own.

I don't know that I have ever felt worse, or more sorry for myself, than on that day.

Darlene, I later learned, contracted polio the day after I did. I could never ask my parents to give me the details of her illness, because I knew they couldn't relive them in the telling. They needed me to focus on surviving, because losing both of their children was inconceivable; even at six I knew that. I had to preserve whatever reason for living they had managed to retain.

And so I fought to resume the life I once led—albeit without Darlene. I couldn't wait to ride a bike, go on picnics, swim in the lake near our house, and catch fireflies again in the midsummer dusk. It was not all that uncommon for children with polio to regain their ability to breathe and move just before Jonas Salk's vaccine became widely available in the mid-1950s. Some were in wheelchairs, others in braces, but they still moved independently through the world. I had no doubt I would be one of them.

⌒

My favorite visitor—besides my parents—was Dr. Mitchell. He was tall, and young for a doctor, and had Clark Gable hair, and he always brought me a lollipop when he came to see me.

"Hiya, peaches," Dr. Mitchell said one day after my parents left for their lunch in the hospital cafeteria. He took the lollipop, which was cherry, and smashed it into pieces with a metal instrument on the rolling cart next to my lung. I couldn't manage a lollipop by myself, but I could suck on small pieces as long as someone was there to make sure I didn't choke. He placed a bit of the candy on my tongue.

"Are we going outside?" I asked him. The staff sometimes took groups of us out to the patio in nice weather, wheeling our bulky machines on their gurneys through the hospital's wide doors.

"It's raining, sweetheart," he said. "We can't take you out there today. You'd rust like the Tin Man."

I laughed and stuck out my tongue so that he could place another small piece of the lollipop on it.

"But I do have some news for you," he said. "We're going to give your lungs a chance to start working on their own again. Wouldn't you like to get out of this thing once in a while?"

I thought about it for a moment. I hated being trapped inside all the time, but whenever the nurses opened the lung to change my clothes or clean me or adjust the various tubes that handled bodily functions I no longer even thought about, I would battle for every breath. The muscles that once expanded and contracted without a conscious thought had atrophied. It was like trying to breathe underwater.

"I'm not sure," I told Dr. Mitchell. "What if I can't?"

Dr. Mitchell had been writing on my chart, but he looked back toward me, his face the picture of sincerity.

"We won't let anything bad happen to you, Vivian," he said. "I promise."

When Dr. Mitchell left, I remember wondering how anyone could promise such a thing. I understood from listening to my parents that no one even knew how polio was transmitted or why some people died from it while others were left relatively unscathed. Only years later was it clear that polio could travel from person to person through infected food or water, and that most people exposed to it didn't even show symptoms. Darlene and I somehow ended up in the small group for whom the virus destroyed motor neurons, causing paralysis and respiratory failure.

I could turn my head and see a long row of iron lungs just like my own in the special ward created for them, and it occurred to me that back in olden times I would have died instead of being placed inside a machine that did my breathing for me. Just as suddenly I realized that nothing had changed inside my brain. Even though I couldn't use my body, I could think and speak as clearly as I had before, and I wondered for the first time what I was missing in first grade.

A few days later I had my first session of independent breathing. The idea was to coax my muscles into remembering how to function and to increase the time I could spend without the lung breathing for me. Some patients learned to breathe on their own during the day and only had to sleep in the lung at night when they couldn't actively control their muscles. If I could breathe on my own for even short stretches of time, my parents might be able to take me home. Dr. Mitchell and a staff of nurses stood near my head and released the collar as an orderly unlocked the lung and slid the metal casing down.

The first minute or so wasn't difficult, because I had done it before—I could hold my breath at least that long—but beyond that I strained with my neck muscles to pull air into my mouth. I recall seeing the doctor's look of concern after I squeezed my eyes shut—the signal that I couldn't take much more. I sighed with relief when the lung began pumping again. In the weeks following I was able to breathe for up to five minutes on my own, mostly through sheer force of will, but I couldn't seem to get beyond that, and I began to dread those sessions, even if Dr. Mitchell came to cheer me on.

He later sat down with me and told me that the virus had destroyed my ability to breathe independently and that my condition was irreversible.

"So I won't get any better?" I asked him, truly surprised because of all the encouragement and attention I had received in the hospital.

Dr. Mitchell put his hand on the top of my head. "Your body won't get better," he said. I wanted his eyes to be bright with tears, the way they would have shown such a scene in the movies, but he was only solemn and subdued. "But that doesn't mean you can't have a good and productive life.

"This," he said, patting my head, "is not damaged at all. And this is where the world exists anyway. Don't ever forget that, Vivian."

I didn't forget it. I never could. Sometimes it was the only thing that kept me alive.

CHAPTER 2

As Holly ran the vacuum under Vivian's iron lung, she tried to imagine a hospital ward filled with long rows of them, their inhabitants breathing in and out with stunning regularity. She wondered how many of those patients, besides Vivian, were still alive so many decades after the wards had closed.

"Listen, you can't go wrong with cash for gold right now," Vivian said loudly enough to be heard over the vacuum. She turned her head, the only part of her that emerged from the machine. "You missed some crumbs . . . follow my eyes . . . right there . . . People need the extra cash, and they don't mind getting rid of broken earrings or bracelets. It's a public service in a way."

Classic Vivian, Holly thought as she vacuumed. Always assuming she knew how the ambulatory conducted their lives based on what she viewed on television.

She turned off the vacuum and wound up the cord. Vivian had had very little personal experience with jewelry, broken or otherwise, Holly thought, although she did sometimes ask one of her volunteers to put earrings on her for special occasions.

"You sound like a commercial," Holly said over one shoulder as she wheeled the vacuum to its home base in the hall closet. "And from experience I can tell you that cash is never extra. At least not in my house."

Vivian blew a stray hair away from her face. "I have a good feeling about this, and Bertram Corners needs a new business to perk up that miserable little downtown. This place will have a retail operation, too," Vivian said. "So you'll meet with him, right?"

Holly came back into the living room, tucked her hair behind her ears, folded her arms, and looked down at Vivian. She sighed. "What's his name again?"

"Racine," Vivian said. "Like the city in Wisconsin."

"Is that his real name?"

"I think so."

"I only ask because growing up I had a friend named Niagara whose parents thought it was cute to name their child after where she was conceived. If everyone did that, my name would be Bertram."

Vivian snorted. "Bertram, ha!"

Holly smiled, gratified as always when she made Vivian laugh. She picked up a hairbrush from a tray near the heavy steel gurney that supported Vivian's iron lung and brushed the hair around Vivian's face. Her blond highlights were growing out, revealing a band of white around the hairline, which, Holly thought, rimmed Vivian's face aptly, like a nun's wimple. Vivian's life-sustaining machine—though it looked more like a one-man space capsule than a lung and wasn't made of iron, as its name suggested—had cloistered her more effectively than any religious institution.

"You're assuming I'll do it," Holly said, knowing full well that she would agree. She couldn't say no to Vivian, with whom she shared a bond that went way beyond her volunteer status, though she couldn't quite name it. They weren't family, weren't the same age, or in remotely the same circumstances. They weren't colleagues either. But when Holly spent time with Vivian, she felt she was in the presence of a spirit akin to her own. They shared a peculiar mix of sentimentality and cynicism, as well as a mutual love for avocados.

"This is a rare opportunity, Holly. You'd be helping me out, and you can earn some extra money—I'll pay you for the time you put in. The boys will be ready for college before you know it."

"I help you because I'm your friend," Holly said. "You don't have to give me anything."

"But I worry about you."

Holly flinched at the irony of that statement coming from a sixty-three-year-old quadriplegic who hadn't been able to breathe on her own since she was a child. She picked up the water bottle with a straw that Vivian used to stay hydrated and took it to the kitchen to replace the tepid water with cold. She could see from the kitchen window that it had started to rain. When she returned, Vivian was still talking as if Holly hadn't left the room.

". . . and you know my track record," Vivian was saying. "I just need an extra set of eyes and ears—and maybe some working arms and legs—to watch over the store."

"I could do that without being paid," Holly said. "Just to help you out."

The rain began coming down so heavily that Holly had to raise her voice to be heard inside Vivian's small Cape. When the first clap of late-summer thunder hit, both Holly and Vivian, out of habit, looked toward the ceiling to see if the ancient brown water stain had grown, even though the roof had been fixed long ago. It troubled Holly that no one had ever painted over the stain, which was about the shape and size of a Frisbee.

"Of course I need to pay you. It may take a lot of your time on the weekends, especially right after the store opens," Vivian said. "Water, please."

"I'm not a lawyer or anything," Holly said as she held the straw up to Vivian's mouth. "Am I supposed to pretend I'm your assistant? Your accountant?"

Vivian took a long sip, then pushed the straw aside with her tongue. "You just make sure that Racine takes me on as an investor.

Then you handle the paperwork, help find a location, and supervise the operation. He'll be more on his toes if he thinks I've got someone watching out for me. It's the way of the world."

Holly put the water bottle on the tray, certain that Vivian knew less about the way of the world than she thought she did.

"I've always wanted some brick and mortar in my portfolio," she said. "And if it goes well, maybe I'll buy the whole shebang and put my name on the sign: Vivian's Gold Emporium. I can see it now."

Holly smiled at the thought of Vivian the gold tycoon, but she still wasn't sure she should take money from her, even for work. She didn't want a financial entanglement to change their friendship.

"I'm not saying I couldn't use a second job," Holly said, a sigh escaping involuntarily. "Chris would turn over in his grave if he saw the house. It's a wreck."

"It's not your fault, sweetie. Or Chris's. No one expects to die that early. Except for me. I expect to die every day, and then I surprise myself by staying alive."

Holly didn't think she'd last a day if she couldn't even drink water without assistance. Though she never said it out loud, it sometimes made her unbearably sad that Vivian could only see the world from her horizontal position inside the lung. She couldn't imagine how it would feel to be perpetually abed, forever parallel to the floor, unable to move anything except her head and neck, feeling nothing in her limbs or torso. The first time they met, Holly had been shocked by the sight of the massive machine with its stainless steel brackets and its yellow enamel cylinder, though now it seemed as normal to her as a couch or a refrigerator.

Thunder boomed overhead. Holly walked toward the living-room window to look at the rain, which was pummeling the sidewalk and creating puddles on the lawn. Whenever she moved around at Vivian's, she felt bizarrely conscious of the dexterity of her hands, the muscles in her legs, the rhythm of her unassisted breath. She went back to Vivian's side and positioned the water bottle at her lips again, and Vivian took another sip.

"You need to stay alive," Holly said. "Bertram Corners would lose ten points off its average IQ if you weren't around."

Vivian laughed and then coughed, a noise that always made Holly nervous.

"Are you okay?" Holly said, hovering over Vivian's face.

Vivian cleared her throat. "I'm fine. Do you mind turning on the TV? I think they're showing an old *American Gladiators* tournament. I'm thinking of using the show as a metaphor for the contraction of the American dream on my podcast this week."

Holly picked up the remote and turned on the television, then angled the screen positioned over Vivian's head so that she could see it. In the intermittent lightning flashes, the yellow enamel reflecting from the iron lung made Vivian's skin look even more sallow than usual.

"Do you ever wonder what it would be like to be me?" Vivian asked over the television commentary.

Holly sat down, surprised that Vivian had never asked that question before in the many years she had been among the volunteers who supplemented Vivian's medical team. Vivian could never be left alone, even when she was sleeping, because the slightest bit of mucus or phlegm could block her breathing.

"I think I would have given up a long time ago," Holly said, wondering, as she often did, how Vivian had survived as long as she had.

Vivian pressed her lips together, a private little smile that said Holly's answer was just what she knew it would be.

"You may think so, but the human will to live is primal. Think of the people who lived through the Holocaust, surviving on a bowl of soup a day, wasting away, the threat of death hanging over their heads every minute. If you were me, I think you'd be right where I am now, wondering if you'll get one more day, then watching the days add up to years, and the years add up to decades. And you just keep going, because what else can you do?"

Holly looked down at her pale, freckled hands—hands that merely typed and therefore revealed none of their labor—and realized that Vivian couldn't even see her own useless hands, had never turned the ignition of a car or touched the face of a lover.

"Do you ever wonder what it would be like to be me?" Holly asked. Her voice sounded tired even to her.

"You specifically? An overworked editor? A widow trying to raise two teenagers? A middle-aged woman who needs a dye job even more than I do? No, but I do wonder how my life would have been different outside the lung. If I had the use of my body . . ."

Vivian looked as though she had something to say but changed her mind. She sometimes caught herself before making one of her inarguable pronouncements, and Holly admired this immensely.

"I'd probably be watching this same show, only sitting upright and eating Doritos."

They both laughed, and Holly turned her attention again to the TV screen angled above Vivian's head. "Who's ahead?"

"Venom. The man is nothing but muscle. Look at him. He's a god."

He looked to Holly like one of those rubber action figures, distorted and overly shiny, but she nodded. "Whatever you say."

Another thunderclap echoed outside, and Vivian turned her head toward the window. "Could you check to make sure the light on my generator is on? I'll need it if the power goes out."

Holly followed a long cord from the iron lung to the generator. The light was flashing.

"The light's on," Holly said. "But it's blinking."

"Blinking is not good."

Another round of lightning illuminated the room like a flashbulb. Then every light, every electronic beep, every faint hum of current abruptly ceased.

"Vivian, oh my God," Holly said. "What do I do?"

"Don't panic," Vivian said, pushing out the words. "Call 911, then check the generator again. It should kick on automatically, but I don't hear it."

Holly pulled out her cell phone, dialed 911, and told the dispatcher to send help immediately. She knew that every policeman, firefighter, and paramedic in town would be at the door in a matter of minutes, but that didn't prevent the panic that gripped her chest. She ran back to the generator.

"The light's not even blinking now," Holly yelled.

"I'm losing pressure," Vivian said, her voice a step lower in pitch. "You'll have to hand-crank it."

"Where is it?" Holly said. "They showed me in training, but I've never had to use it."

Vivian nodded toward a device on the side of the lung, which Holly began to turn with as much strength as she had. The crank resisted her efforts. It felt to Holly as if the internal mechanisms had rusted.

"Keep turning," Vivian said, now in a loud whisper.

Holly leaned into the crank, using her weight to help her pull it down and then getting under it as much as she could to bring it back around. Vivian started to let out rasping noises that sounded as if she were breathing in repeatedly without breathing out. Holly felt her own breath getting more and more shallow. Sweat broke out under her arms.

"Hang in there, Vivian. They'll be here soon. Stay with me."

Vivian nodded weakly as sirens finally overtook the thunder outside. Two firefighters came through the door and went straight to the generator.

"Toggle the switch," Vivian said hoarsely, though Holly could barely hear her over the sirens and the thunder. "The on-off switch."

Two policemen came in next, and one took over from Holly on the hand crank while the firefighters banged, and swore at, the generator. Holly ran over and held Vivian's head in her hands, terrified that she wasn't getting enough oxygen to her brain. She was turning slightly blue around the mouth. Her eyes were closed and her breaths were weak, rattling versions of the robust and even ones her iron lung pumped out of her.

"We're losing her," Holly yelled at the firefighters, who had started arguing about the best way to fix the generator. "Do something!"

One of them tried toggling the switch again, and the lung sudden-ly let out a long hiss as though it had been holding its own breath. The machine began to pump away at Vivian's lungs like a bellows. In a few minutes, the blue faded from Vivian's lips, and her breathing became less strained. She said nothing, but Holly could see the relief in her eyes, which must have mirrored the relief in her own.

Even with Vivian breathing again, Holly's heart still beat in double time. She and all the volunteers lived in fear of being responsible for Vivian's death through inattention or incompetence. They didn't dis-cuss it, but each one knew that the town would despise anyone who botched the remarkable joint effort to keep Vivian alive.

When the electricity came back on, Holly let out a deep breath she didn't even know she had been holding. Her arms ached from turning the crank.

The firefighters began to shift in their heavy uniforms and gear, seemingly unsure of what to do, since the emergency appeared to be over. One policeman began writing a report as two others huddled around him.

Vivian looked as exhausted as Holly had ever seen her.

"I'm okay now," Vivian said in a small voice. "It's all over."

The firefighters soon ran out to another emergency, and the po-liceman writing the report made Vivian promise to get a new genera-tor. Eventually, the policemen said they would check on Vivian again before their shifts ended and left.

When Holly and Vivian were alone again, Holly found Vivian's eyes in her angled mirror. "We almost lost you," she said, an ache rising in her throat. "What if the generator hadn't kicked in?"

Vivian closed her eyes and sighed, then opened them. "I've proba-bly been that close or closer to dying a dozen or more times. It comes with the territory."

"You need to replace that generator," Holly said, still shaken. "And have the crank fixed."

"It's never been this stubborn. I'll have to call my technician, I guess, to order me a new one," Vivian said, sounding to Holly strangely calm and almost disappointed, as if she would miss a piece of machin-ery that looked like it came from the Roosevelt era.

"Tell him to get one today. I don't know about you, but I can't go through that again."

CHAPTER 3

It was someone's idea of a joke, Holly had always felt, to name the town Bertram Corners. There were few actual corners, because some early architect of the town streets apparently had an aversion to right angles. Instead, a map of the town showed arcs and curves, traffic circles and cul-de-sacs, with the exception of Main Street, which held the town up like a spine, running north to south. Such small hamlets in upstate New York could barely be associated with the city that shared the state's name, Holly thought, and yet they weren't all that far from the glass-heavy skyscrapers, the white-walled art galleries, or the punishing traffic and noise of the Big Apple.

Bertram Corners had its share of small-town small-mindedness, but Holly had had very little trouble convincing Chris that it was the best place for them to buy their first home. He had loved her stories about the Fourth of July bike parades, the annual fried pickle festival (now defunct), and the Main Street sidewalk sales during which the merchants handed out candy like it was Halloween. Holly's parents had wanted them to consider the exclusive neighborhood where Holly had grown up and even offered to help with the down payment, but Holly and Chris wanted the house to be theirs, not three-fifths theirs or two-thirds theirs. They wanted to pull off the grown-up act of buying a house all on their own.

They had looked at three inexpensive starter homes with trendy open floor plans, but Chris always knocked on the thin drywall and shook his head. He wanted plaster. He wanted crawl spaces and foundation stones and crown moldings and trees taller than the rooftop. He wanted generations-old dust to fill their lives and their lungs. He brought Holly into his quest for something grounded in the past.

"Otherwise, it's just us," he had told her as they drove out of yet another new development. "There should be layers of memory, you know? Doorknobs that have seen people live and die."

Holly remembered shaking her head, though, when they first toured the house they would eventually buy. It had doorknobs turned by many a generation, but it also had decrepit plumbing, rotting clapboards, and a kitchen with Depression-era appliances coated in rust.

"It's got great bones," Chris had said, though Holly thought he was referring to whatever might be buried under the dirt floor in the basement. What sold her was the china cabinet built into the corner of the dining room. They didn't own any china, but she couldn't stop thinking about the tiny windowpanes of that cabinet. A month later, after they had pulled together the down payment and figured out that the mortgage was only slightly higher than what they could reasonably afford, she found herself signing dozens of papers, committing herself to a relationship that felt almost as emotionally complicated as a marriage.

Within a year Chris had replaced the rotting clapboards and repaired the plumbing using a book from Home Depot. They bought a new refrigerator and stove, though they ran out of money before they could buy new countertops or install the tile backsplash they had spent months planning. Even with its imperfections, the house was loving and safe, chipped and charming. The house was them.

Now the house was her. Its endearing flaws had aged into liabilities. The plaster walls and ceilings had developed the same sorts of fine lines that had appeared on Holly's face. The speckled Formica countertops that had seemed so retro and cool now looked dated and worn;

she had scrubbed the speckles right out of them in spots just as her own childhood freckles had faded. And yet the roof still sheltered Holly and her boys. The house still embraced them as much as it possibly could. The doorknobs and the china cabinet and the creaking floors had witnessed their memories. She, Chris, and the boys were in the layers of paint and in the dust beneath the furniture. She never wanted to leave.

Holly had agreed to meet Racine, Vivian's cash-for-gold connection, in a coffee shop just down Main Street from the weekly newspaper she ran. As she walked toward the shop, she peered in the window of the pharmacy and saw a line already forming at the medication pickup window. The pharmacy seemed to be the one business in town that still thrived, and Holly assumed it was because it both indulged vices—cigarettes, fattening snack foods, sexual aids—and treated the medical issues they caused. Next door to the pharmacy was a liquor store that had a few customers at ten in the morning on a Monday. Past two empty storefronts was the coffee shop, which had a sign in the shape of a quaint whistling teakettle. The aroma of coffee and bacon greeted her as she opened the door. Nodding to the waitress, she found a seat in a booth by the big plate-glass window adjacent to the street.

When Racine walked in, almost everyone in the coffee shop turned to look, first because he was a stranger, and second because he wore jeans with a narrowly cut suit jacket—a combination rarely seen in Bertram Corners. He also had a leather messenger-type bag with a long strap that crossed his body, which told Holly that he either didn't care what other men thought about him or cared very much what certain other men thought about him. Even though they lived less than two hours away from one of the most clothing-obsessed cities on the planet, most of the men Holly knew were so afraid of looking fashionable that they erred on the side of flannel.

"Holly?" he said as she scooted her way out of the booth and stood up to shake his hand. He was slim and well dressed, and his curly hair was cropped close to his head. He had a wide, welcoming smile showing a line of exceptionally white, straight teeth. At the same time, his eyes kept Holly guessing. His lids were somewhat heavy and guarded, which gave Holly the impression that the welcome in his smile was conditional and possibly superficial. The conflict between two such essential parts of the face fascinated her.

"You must be Racine," Holly said, motioning for him to sit down. "I've been wondering how you got that name ever since I heard it from Vivian."

"Not that interesting, really," he said in an accent that Holly couldn't quite place. For the most part he sounded American, though not when he said certain words with long vowel sounds.

"I was born in Argentina, but my parents met in Racine, Wisconsin, when they were in college, and they liked the name, hence . . ."

"Hence," Holly repeated, extending a palm as if this explained everything. Nice-looking men always brought out her awkward side. She wished she had worn something chicer than a V-neck T-shirt and jeans.

"So Vivian tells me you're my contact for her investment," Racine said, running a hand lightly over his hair. "She recommended you highly."

"I'm at your service," Holly said, because she now believed Vivian, who had told her that Racine could sell milk to a dairy farmer or ice to Eskimos, or one of those. She could now picture everyone in town parading into the cash-for-gold store, clutching a handful of the pathetic gift-giving efforts of former husbands and wives, boyfriends and girlfriends: the thin gold chains that had broken in the first few months of devoted wear; the chunky earrings purchased from the sale rack because chunky earrings were out of style; the low-end tennis bracelets with diamonds so small they qualified as a vision test; the needlessly heavy class rings worn for a few months and then abandoned in a box of old souvenirs. These would be deposited with a smiling Racine, who would turn them into cash as cold and hard as the hearts of the men and women who sold their memories.

"Would you mind explaining to me how this works?" Holly asked. "It seems like these places are cropping up everywhere, but that must be because they make money, right?"

"Of course," Racine said. He took a white binder out of his messenger bag and put it in front of Holly. "This should have everything you need to know, but basically we set up the shop for a minimal outlay. If gold dips too low for an extended period of time, we close up and move on, but right now we're looking at a significant profit for every ounce we collect. Gold is a much safer investment than the real estate market these days."

"Do you have some kind of a track record with this?"

"I do, actually. I've set up four of these shops in Lower Manhattan, two in Brooklyn, and five more in Connecticut. Right now we're looking for small towns in New York State that don't have a lot of competitors. Once it's set up, the business kind of runs itself. It's really all about the initial capital and a good location, and when the investors are from the community, we tend to have a better outcome. It gives us more eyes and ears on the street. Speaking of which, I'm looking for a spot on Main Street, if you know of any. Vivian said you might be able to help me with that."

"You shouldn't have a problem, with all the empty storefronts," Holly told him. "I can give you the name of a real estate agent. She should be able to track down the landlords."

"Perfect," he said, taking a pen out of his messenger bag. "So I have Vivian down for a hundred and twenty thousand. Is she still comfortable with that?"

"That's her commitment," Holly said, wondering even as she said it how Vivian could have that much money to spare for an uncertain investment.

"Excellent," he said, clicking the pen a few times. "What about you? I could squeeze in another investor if you're interested."

Holly looked down at her menu and suppressed an urge to write Racine a check that would bounce higher than the Empire State Building. She wanted, for some reason, to make him think that money meant nothing to her.

"I don't think that's in the cards," she said, feeling her cheeks grow slightly warm.

A waitress Holly had known for years approached the table. "Hi, folks, can I start you with some coffee?"

"Thanks, Helen," Holly said, nodding.

"Nothing for me," Racine said, standing up from the booth. "Unfortunately, I need to get back to the city. Here's my card. I'll call you when I have the papers ready for Vivian."

Holly took the card—noting that he hadn't tried very hard to talk her into investing. He ran a hand over his hair again, which Holly noticed was just on the verge of receding, and slung the messenger bag back over one shoulder as he left the restaurant. Through the plate-glass window, Holly could see him getting into a small white sports car.

"That's a Jag," Helen said, sitting down with the coffee pot where Racine had been just moments before. "He's driving a Jag."

"He must be doing okay then," Holly said, now convinced that Vivian knew what she was doing and grateful for a small second paycheck that might allow her to reduce her reliance on her mother, who had been helping her with her mortgage for the last year. A little breathing room was all she wanted. After Helen filled her coffee cup, Holly sat up a little straighter, pushed her hair behind her ears, and opened the white binder. It wasn't about driving a Jag for her. It was about fixing the garage door, which had been stuck halfway down for more than a year. It was about finally paying for the long-overdue service on the ancient furnace. But mostly it was about Marshall and Connor, who deserved to stay in their own home, the only one they had ever known.

She flipped through the binder. Maybe this was just a start.

CHAPTER 4

A week after her meeting with Racine, Holly found herself with her brother and sister in a funeral home. They had been charged with choosing a casket after their great-aunt Muriel died.

"I seem to recall that Aunt Muriel had a walnut dining-room set," Holly's brother, Henderson, said as he flipped through the casket catalogue in the funeral director's overstuffed office, which smelled of stale tea bags. "Her living-room furniture was walnut too, wasn't it?"

"Walnut is the Hyundai of coffins," Holly told him, taking the catalogue and opening it across her knees on the couch where she sat with Henderson. "We could at least spring for cherry."

"I have a friend who has a Hyundai," said Holly's sister, Desdemona, who could have chosen a chair but instead sat on a low circular ottoman covered in some kind of pink flowery fabric. "He says it's a great value."

Henderson sighed and looked out the window, as though he couldn't be bothered to follow the conversation.

"How about an unfinished pine box?" Desdemona said in a low voice almost drowned out by the funeral home's air-conditioning unit. "What kind of car would that be?"

"That's a beater with two hundred thousand miles on it," Holly said, smiling at her own comment.

Holly expected Henderson to make a snide remark about Hyundais or unfinished pine boxes, but instead he loosened his tie and unfastened the top button of his pressed white shirt. Holly noticed a few broken blood vessels dotting Henderson's eyelids. His forehead was still relatively smooth, but the masculine thrust of his chin was losing a battle to the slack skin on his neck, which clearly wanted to spread its insolence, like a sullen teenager. She found herself uncharacteristically worried about him but then remembered how often he faked illness as a child. He was forever climbing on their mother's lap, feigning a fever after pressing his forehead against the radiator in the bathroom.

"Let's just pick one and get out of here," Henderson said. "I'm suffocating with all this ancient upholstery. The dust mites are everywhere. I swear I can feel them crawling on me."

The funeral director—stocky, balding, solicitous in the manner of a waiter—came back into the room. "Are we ready? I can give you a few more minutes if you need it."

Henderson took the catalogue back from Holly, flipped a few pages, and pointed to a cherry casket with ivory silk lining. He had chosen it just as he would a bottle of wine: not the most expensive, but in the upper tier.

"That one," he said.

"Very good, sir," the funeral director said. "Excellent choice. I think you'll be pleased."

When the papers were signed, the three of them stood on the funeral home's wide porch, which looked out over a stand of birch trees that seemed, to Holly, to symbolize aging—the bark so fragile, layers shedding from year to year exposing the imperfections in the once-sturdy trunks. The small, blue-collar city of Newburgh, New York, was where their mother had grown up and where Muriel, sister of their maternal grandfather, had lived her whole life. Muriel had never married, but as far as any of them knew, she had been content inside her small circle of cat-loving, sweater-making, churchgoing friends.

"I'm worried about Mom," Desdemona said, twisting her gauzy scarf into a knot. "She must be feeling even worse than she says to skip being here for Aunt Muriel."

"We've reached that stage," Holly said, succumbing to the mood of resignation that permeates funeral homes. "We're standing at the precipice as the previous generation crumbles away."

"Uh-huh, the edge of oblivion," Henderson added casually, looking at his watch as if it might tell him the date and time of his own death.

"Dad couldn't stand Aunt Muriel," Holly said. "He did nothing but complain when she came to visit. Don't you remember? He said she smelled like a wet sheep."

"All that knitting," Henderson said. "Incidentally, we'll have to get the money from Mom to pay for the casket, because I am essentially broke." He delivered the last part with a tone of accomplishment, as if he had defied the odds and managed to pull off a feat no one had expected of him.

"You don't know what broke is," Holly said, rolling her eyes. "You drive an Audi. You wear expensive suits, and you go abroad twice a year. You're the one who pays for things when Desdemona and I can't afford them. In fact, I thought you were paying for the casket."

"You think there's some law of economics that prevents me from going broke just because the two of you are poor? I'm telling you the facts. My business went under. Nobody wants a financial adviser when they have no finances left to advise." He ran a hand over his face and avoided their eyes. "I'm filing for Chapter 11."

Holly stared at Henderson as if she could see into his brain if she tried hard enough. A chill ran down her back.

Then Desdemona voiced what Holly was thinking: "Are you really broke? As broke as the two of us?"

"Holly's not broke, she's just in a low-income bracket," Henderson said to Desdemona, kicking a small rock off the porch into the rhododendrons. "And dancers never make any money. There's a difference."

Desdemona pulled a hand through her long dark hair, which she usually wore in a ponytail or bun. Having it out of its restraints seemed to make her nervous.

"We can't afford the casket you picked out if we have to split the cost," Holly said. "Or we'll at least have to make sure it's okay with Mom."

"Maybe we should go back in and pick a cheaper one," Desdemona said. "Aunt Muriel would understand."

Henderson shook his head. "I need to find the restroom," he said, and his sisters followed him back inside into a large oak-paneled viewing room, where he clutched his chest and let out a plaintive "Ow," which gave Holly a startling twinge inside her own chest. Then she remembered it was Henderson. In response to the noise, the funeral home's cadre of dark-suited men seemed to materialize from the paneling and practically wrestled Henderson to the shiny wood floor.

"Stretch him out," one of them said. "You need a hard, flat surface for CPR."

Henderson tried to sit up once, then swooned back. Two of the men eased his shoulders down to the floor as the third called 911, speaking with urgency.

"I just need some air," Henderson said weakly, as if everyone else in the room were taking more than his or her fair share. It was the kind of stunt he had pulled when they were kids, Holly thought, and their mother wanted him to clean up his room.

"We'll take him outside," Holly said, wanting to suppress the panic rising in the room around her. She didn't want a repeat of her episode with Vivian, which had left her depleted for days. "I'm sure he'll be fine in a few minutes."

"We can't take a chance with chest pains," one of the funeral employees said. "It's best to be conservative."

While they waited for the ambulance, the men in suits hovered around Henderson, checking and rechecking his pulse so compulsively that Holly began to wonder if they expected him to die, accustomed as they were to corpses.

After the cavalry came and took Henderson away in the ambulance, Desdemona and Holly followed them to the hospital in Holly's car.

"I'm sure he's okay," Desdemona said as Holly pulled out of the funeral-home parking lot. "This is just one of his stunts, right?"

"Of course it is," Holly said, though she suddenly felt a dull ache in her left arm. "He's pulled this a million times. Remember? Every time Mom asked him to take out the garbage he'd suddenly develop a migraine or abdominal pains. He did the same thing to Wendy, which is probably why she divorced him."

As Holly searched for a place to park at the hospital, that nagging 1 percent of doubt began to creep in, and she started to wonder if Henderson might really be sick. But by the time Holly and Desdemona were allowed to see Henderson in his curtained emergency room bay, the doctors had determined that his chest pains were caused by indigestion. They gave him some Prilosec and told him to go home.

Desdemona sat in the back as Holly drove them to the funeral home so Henderson could pick up his Audi. When Holly turned off the motor, they all listened to the ping and hiss of her old Subaru giving voice to its chronic exhaustion. All three got out of the Subaru and walked toward Henderson's Audi, then Desdemona and Holly watched Henderson fold his six-foot-one frame into the tidy leathered nook of the driver's seat. For some reason they all looked back toward the funeral home, which had the ivied air of a business that prints money, death being such a dependable commodity. Holly thought about the wood floor—Henderson's CPR staging area—its gleaming planks hammered down with grief and polyeurethaned with the tears of countless grieving relatives.

Holly gave Henderson a long hug, half out of smugness that she had been right about his exaggerated pains and half out of true sympathy for his financial plight. She knew his sense of self-worth was tied to his bank balance. Poor Hen, she thought.

When Henderson drove off, heading to an expensive apartment in Boston he doubtless could no longer afford, Desdemona and Holly walked back to the Subaru so that Holly could drive to the station, where Desdemona would catch a train back to the city. Desdemona stepped toward the car with a dancer's unconscious extension of limbs, her toe skimming the ground before the rest of her followed.

"I'm used to scraping by," Desdemona said over the top of the car as Holly walked around to the driver's side. "But I never worried about it when Henderson and Mom were there for backup. Not that I would ask, but . . ."

"I know exactly what you mean."

Once inside, they both stared straight ahead through the windshield, and the car—mobile confessional that it was—allowed Holly to tell Desdemona something she'd been keeping from her.

"Mom has been helping me and the boys lately so we could keep up the house payments," Holly said. "But I always assumed I could go to Henderson for help if I got desperate. He was my cushion."

"Are you?"

"Am I what?"

"Desperate."

"More like predesperate."

"Didn't Chris have life insurance?"

"Who expects to drop dead at his age? He had a little insurance through work, but I ran through that years ago. I just never thought I'd come this far down the ladder, you know?"

Desdemona nodded as they left for the train station. "I do know," she said quietly.

"But I have a second job now, so maybe I'll finally be able to save a little," Holly said. "I know I can't ask Mom to help me forever."

Desdemona didn't seem to hear her. She continued to look out the window as the broad, slate-colored Hudson River came into view.

"When Dad died, I thought we'd have a reprieve from funerals," Holly said as they drove through the city's crumbling downtown, absorbing its sadness. "I thought Mom would be next, but ten or twenty years down the road. Instead, it was Chris and then Aunt Muriel, who I thought would be knitting cat clothes until she was a hundred and ten. People shouldn't die in the wrong order. It's so much harder."

When she got home, Holly took out her cell phone and dialed her mother's number. She was exhausted from the driving, the casket shopping, the news about Henderson's bankruptcy, the trip to the ER, all of it, but she couldn't go to sleep without hearing her mother's reassurance that it would all be okay.

"Hi, Mom, it's Holly," she said. "Just checking on you. Feeling any better?"

"Hi, sweetie. Yes, I'm just fine," Celia said. "Still a little tired, but I'm sure I'll shake it soon."

Holly thought she detected a note of false bravado in her mother's voice, but she attributed it to a bad connection.

"So did you hear all this about Henderson? About his business?"

"Oh goodness. He told you? I heard yesterday, but I thought maybe he'd keep it to himself until after Aunt Muriel's funeral."

"Well, he did keep it to himself until after we picked out a fairly expensive casket."

"Don't you worry about that," she said. "I'll take care of it. Muriel didn't have anyone but me."

Holly felt a knot in her neck loosen just a bit. Her mother had a way of taking a heavy burden without complaint. She was the family's financial and emotional Sherpa.

"And speaking of not worrying," Celia went on, "I'm going to send you this month's check. I'll put it in the mail tomorrow when I pay my bills."

Holly nodded, as though her mother could see her. "Thank you, Mom," she said. "I know I say this all the time, but you're my savior. I know it's just a house, but it's our security. It's all we have."

"Say no more, Holly. It's really nothing . . . but I think I should go now. I can't seem to keep my head up."

"Okay then. I'll call you tomorrow."

Holly hung up and went to bed, but she didn't fall asleep for hours. She kept parsing the conversation, trying to sort out whether her mother had sounded all right or not quite herself.

⟿

When the call came the next day, Holly knew. The phone number on her cell was that of her mother's next-door neighbor, who wouldn't be calling her for anything other than an emergency. All her worst fears were confirmed. Her mother had suffered a stroke the night before, probably around the same time Holly had tossed and turned in bed worrying about her.

Holly sat completely still on the hard wooden pew for Aunt Muriel's funeral, internally reassessing everything she knew about her life. Her mother was sick and might not recover. She, Desdemona, and Henderson would now be the ones who talked to the doctors, who made decisions, who sorted through brittle, decades-old documents to find out what their mother would have wanted. Holly was numb with shock.

The three of them were the only mourners besides Aunt Muriel's even more ancient next-door neighbor and the woman who sold Muriel knitting supplies. Holly tried to pay attention as a minister who looked like a bullfrog, his bulging neck wider than his head, gave a stock eulogy. She studied the casket, its fine wood grain shining in the amber light filtering through the stained glass, and briefly wondered who, in the end, would pay for it.

On the drive home from the funeral, Holly's thoughts returned to the mail and the check she was expecting. She felt guilty worrying about money when her mother was lying in a hospital bed, but *the house.* The mortgage. She had never missed a payment, even after Chris's life insurance ran out. She realized for the first time that she could, in fact, lose the house, and that terminology had her imagining the futile drive around Bertram Corners looking for it on empty lots and behind supermarkets.

What if the check wasn't in the mail today?

She wondered if she had anything of value to sell besides her car—which she needed for work—just for this month, just until she could figure things out. But there was nothing except her wedding ring—a plain gold band that resided in a sacred corner of her otherwise pathetic jewelry box. No. She could never part with the ring, even if it might cover the shortfall for this month's mortgage. She clung to the idea that her mother could have sent the check. Maybe their phone conversation had prompted her to tuck it in the mailbox early. If she had, it would probably be in today's mail.

She pulled into the driveway and got out of the car, her heart pounding. But when she looked into the mailbox and pulled out the collection of pointless catalogues and more bills, she found nothing else. She rifled through the mail again, even shaking out some of the catalogues. When the truth descended on her, she looked up at the house, which at least was still there, and murmured an apology.

CHAPTER 5

Vivian's Unaired Podcast #2

In 1957 it had been five years since I'd left the hospital. My parents had paid for the front door of the farmhouse to be widened and a ramp built so my machine would fit inside, but without an extensive remodel—which they couldn't afford—the gurney could go no farther than the living room. I was no better or worse physically. The paralysis below the neck was indeed permanent, but my unfeeling body continued to grow and function as long as the iron lung kept the oxygen circulating.

There had been a few close calls. Once when I had a bad cold, my parents stayed up in shifts for five days straight because I kept choking on the phlegm in my throat. They had to aspirate my nose and mouth with a bulb syringe like they did for babies.

Another time the power went out, and the lung stopped working. My father used the hand crank for three hours, until the fire department could secure a generator. That's when we realized we couldn't live without one, and my parents had to sell a dairy cow to buy it.

When I was ten, I got it into my head that I could breathe again if they gave me a chance. I had had a dream about being outside the lung, and it felt so real that I was convinced I had been miraculously cured. My parents wouldn't let me try breathing on my own for more than the short amount of time it took to change my clothes and clean me, so I convinced a visiting friend to help me while my mother was in the kitchen getting us some lemonade. As soon as April undid the metal latch that created a seal around my throat, I felt the release that I always felt, along with a giddy sense that breathing on my own would be even more wonderful and life changing than walking again.

I tried to use my neck muscles, but they were out of practice, and I began to asphyxiate after just a few minutes. My mother came back into the room as April was trying to reseal the collar. She managed to get the lung pumping again before I caused myself any brain damage. After that, she would call out "Marco" when she was out of the room for more than a minute or two, and if I didn't call back "Polo" right away, she'd come running.

By the time I was twelve, I had begun to realize that my mother's life revolved almost exclusively around keeping me alive. My father worked the farm and took a shift with me late at night so that my mother could get a few hours' sleep, but she rarely even left the room except when the hospital's visiting nurse came once a week, at which time she ran out for groceries, to the bank, and to do all her other errands. She had friends who would occasionally relieve her, but I often complained that they didn't know how to angle the spoon correctly or didn't fix my books at the right angle in the metal frame that held them in front of my face. They would also get distracted by a magazine or, if they came in a pair, by their own conversation, and I'd have to ask them repeatedly to turn the page for me.

The doctors' prediction that I wouldn't live long had caused my parents to spoil me terribly. I'm sure they assumed that any lifelong lessons about patience or charity or how you get more flies with honey than vinegar would be wasted. As a consequence, I had become a bit of a tyrant.

"Why can't we get a color television?" I remember asking my mother in those days. "Janet says they got one, and it doesn't have all the lines and static like ours does. I could watch it through my mirror, and then I wouldn't be so bored all the time."

"We're saving up," my mother told me. "We'll get one as soon as we can."

"If we got one, then Timmy Gallagher might come over to see me again."

My mother paused at that pronouncement. "So you like Timmy Gallagher?" she said. Despite her efforts to mask it, I could hear the caution in her voice, even the disappointment she anticipated for me.

"He makes me laugh," I said, fairly certain that if I hounded her long enough, I would get the color television that would bring the neighborhood kids around again. They had all flocked to my side in the year after I came home—all my school friends and Darlene's friends and the dutiful sons and daughters of my parents, who had dragged their kids along to "play" with me. But now the visitors had dwindled down to a hardy few who could tolerate doing word games and puzzles and being around someone alive but trapped like a fly in tree sap. Looking back, I realize that nobody likes to be reminded of the fragility of the human condition. Yes, they all admired my parents and my ability to continue with my schooling and my mental development, but they also pitied our family for being so devoid of choices.

"I'll talk to Dad about it," my mother said, and I noticed her wiping away a tear. I knew she was worried that I hadn't yet accepted my future. There would never be a boyfriend for me—no first kiss, no prom, no necking (not enough accessible neck), no wedding night, no marriage, no babies. She seemed to think I hadn't come to terms with those things, but I had realized that my life would have to have a purpose outside the realm of normal existence. It wasn't that I didn't want the life every girl of my generation hoped to lead. But I had already had five years with nothing to do but think, and after studying literature and learning about all those women who pined away for men they couldn't have, and all those men tempted into adultery by younger, prettier versions of their wives, I had decided I wasn't missing out on all that much. That conclusion changed as I got older—I have spent years grieving the life that was lost to me—but at twelve, I thought I had it all figured out.

A few weeks after that, our new color television arrived, and we threw a party. I'm not sure how my parents paid for that TV—we surely couldn't afford it—but maybe they realized that it would provide me with hours of entertainment and maybe even a little time off from turning my pages or reading to me when I was too tired to read on my own. All our neighbors and their children—yes, even Timmy Gallagher—came to gather around the set for *The Ed Sullivan Show*. My mother made cookies and finger sandwiches, and we all laughed at the girls swooning in their seats over Elvis Presley.

"He's set for life," I said from my position in the center of the room. "You can't buy that kind of publicity."

The room erupted in laughter, and everyone looked at my parents with a mixture of sadness and pride. Timmy Gallagher wandered over when the show ended. He was the boy from school I missed most, because we had never felt awkward around each other.

"I gotta hand it to you, Vivian," he said. "You're something else."

"What else am I?" I asked, blinking at him with eyes as wide as they would open.

Timmy laughed and bumped his shoulder against my iron lung, the equivalent, I supposed, of a friendly punch in the arm.

"What's this thing made out of anyway?" he said. "Kryptonite?"

"You guessed it," I said. "I could take down Superman."

Just then Timmy's mother came over and told him they were leaving.

"So nice to see how well you're doing, Vivian," she said, showing me her teeth in the most insincere smile I had ever seen, and I had already seen many.

"Thanks, Mrs. Gallagher," I said, fake-smiling back. "Come over anytime."

She put both hands on Timmy's shoulders and steered him toward the door like she was pushing a lawnmower. Before he left, he glanced back to give me a nod, and that was the last time I ever saw him.

CHAPTER 6

The stroke had been catastrophic, but Holly still assumed that her mother would fight her way back to health, until the doctors finally admitted that in her mother's case "rehab" was simply death in the slowest of motions. Within a week it was clear that Celia's cognitive ability wouldn't return and that she could no longer communicate and might not even recognize her own children. The sense of loss was palpable, even though some fragment of Celia remained. Holly felt sick at the notion that her mother—the fixer, the decider, the stopper of gaps—could no longer do the job she was born to do. She missed her terribly, often thinking incoherently that she needed her mother's advice to cope with her mother's illness.

"Ready?" Holly said.

"I guess so," Desdemona replied. They left the car reluctantly and walked slowly to the lobby of the rehab hospital, where they each nodded to the front desk clerk, then took the elevator to the fourth floor.

Celia was propped up against a nest of pillows with her hair splayed out around her head. At seventy-six, she still dyed her hair black, which provided a stark contrast with the white mask of a face that only approximated the face of the mother Holly remembered. The stroke had shut down her left side, which made one side of her mouth and her left eye droop.

Holly looked at Desdemona, who looked as pale as one of their mother's hospital sheets.

"You look wonderful, Mom," Desdemona said.

"You do," Holly said, turning back to her mother. "You have more color than the last time we saw you."

Desdemona went to one side of the bed and took her mother's hand. "How are you feeling?"

Celia looked at Desdemona, then at Holly, but without any sign of recognition. Holly counted it a blessing that Celia didn't seem to understand what she had lost. Desdemona looked as if she wanted to cry, and Holly stepped around to the other side of the bed to pat her sister on the back even as she wanted to cry herself.

"Marshall and Connor miss you, Mom," Holly said. "They've both been so busy with band, Marshall especially."

Holly went on for a while, offering short vignettes about the boys and the newspaper, until her mother's eyes closed. When it looked as if Celia was asleep, Holly walked over to the window and looked out at the parking lot below. The cars turned into a blurred mosaic of colors.

"She sleeps a lot, doesn't she?" she said. "I wonder if they have her too drugged-up."

"She does seem tired," Desdemona said, still holding her mother's hand.

Holly picked up a handmade card from Connor that she had propped on her mother's windowsill. As much as she hated to accept the role, she had to be the fixer now. Desdemona was too passive and Henderson too tied up with his own problems.

"Eventually, you know, she'll max out her time at this rehab," she said. "Then one of us will have to take care of her at home, or we'll have to find a nursing home."

Desdemona put a hand on her forehead, as if checking her own temperature.

"I don't think I could take her in my studio. You're already pulled in a dozen different directions, and Henderson certainly couldn't do it."

"Why couldn't Henderson do it?" Holly said. "He's not working right now."

Desdemona got up from Celia's bed and stood near Holly at the window, crossing her thin arms.

"He doesn't have the right temperament. He'd be impatient with her. Don't you think?"

Holly put an arm around Desdemona's narrow shoulders, barely finding a place to hold on. Desdemona's frailty sometimes bothered her more than Henderson's bluster.

"You're right," Holly said. Her head felt heavy and fogged up, as if she were getting a cold. "I'm not sure any of us could handle it, frankly. She has some savings anyway. That will get her in somewhere."

Celia stirred and mumbled something, and they both ran back over to her bedside, almost tripping over each other on the way. Holly wanted Celia to wake up, to show the doctors that they had been wrong and that she would fight her way back. But by the time they reached her, her eyes were closed, her body quiet again.

"I think we should go," Holly told Desdemona, who had started patting Celia's withered hands.

"Hey, where are her rings?" Desdemona said, placing Celia's hand on the bedcovers and looking around the nightstand. "She's not wearing them."

"I don't know," Holly said, ducking her head under the bed. "I'm pretty sure she had them on last time we were here. Maybe they had to take them off for a procedure or something. Look in her purse."

Desdemona pulled a neat envelope-style leather purse out of the nightstand near Celia's bed and rummaged around. "Nothing," she said.

Holly looked around at the stark, gray semigloss walls, the clean linoleum floor, and the expensive monitors hooked up via wires and tubes. How long might Celia need full-time nursing care? Holly could already see the inevitable sucking away of a lifetime of gathering, earning, and saving into the insatiable void of the health-care industry.

Her mother's rings seemed to have been pulled into the same terrifying vortex.

On the way out, Holly and Desdemona stopped by the nurses' station. A plump young woman wearing blue scrubs stood at the desk tapping away at a computer.

"Hi," Holly said. "We're. . ."

The nurse held up a chubby finger to stop her, then spoke into a headset Holly hadn't noticed.

"Dr. Miller won't be in until Wednesday," she said. "I would suggest you call back then."

The nurse typed for another full minute, her nails clicking on the keyboard, before looking up at Holly and Desdemona and offering a disingenuous smile.

"I'm sorry," Holly said, who felt like she was always apologizing for existing in the cluttered and complex world and taking precious time from someone else's day. "Our mother is Celia Fenton in room 236, and we were wondering if you knew where her wedding and engagement rings were. She never took them off."

The nurse looked at them as if they were in need of medical attention.

"It clearly states in the admission papers that valuables should be left at home," she said. "We can't be responsible for them."

Holly squinted at the nurse, then looked at Desdemona, who was already beginning to tear up. She tried again.

"But, as I said, she never took them off. I'm not sure she could get them over her knuckles. The engagement ring was very distinctive—a two-karat diamond with emeralds on each side. What could have happened to them?"

The nurse pursed her lips, as though Holly and Desdemona were accusing her of stealing the rings herself.

"I'll write a note on her chart to have the orderlies look for them," she said curtly. "I'm sure they'll turn up."

Holly murmured an obligatory thank-you as Desdemona dabbed at her eyes with a tissue. Holly knew the rings were most likely gone for good, which probably didn't matter to her mother anymore but mattered to her family because of what they represented.

"Maybe we should go back and look again," Desdemona said. "Maybe they fell off because she's gotten so thin in the last few weeks."

Holly nodded, and they went back to the room, where Celia was sleeping. Desdemona crawled under the bed but found nothing. Holly scoured the top of the nightstand, its small drawer, and the tray table that pulled up to the bed.

"They're gone," Holly said. "Just gone."

Desdemona looked at Holly with eyes that registered her complete disillusionment with humanity. "Someone probably sold them for the gold," she said. "To one of those horrible cash-for-gold places. They're sprouting up all over the city now."

Holly nodded her head, appalled that Desdemona was probably right and that she herself was helping Vivian establish just such a place in Bertram Corners. The business hinged on people gathering up their gold—any gold they could get their hands on—and sending it through the spinning machine to make hay, the opposite of Rumplestiltskin.

"What would Dad say if he were still alive?" Desdemona said, crying now. "It's like we've let him down."

"We didn't know," Holly said. "Did you read the fine print when she was admitted? I was a little preoccupied with her survival." Holly put her arm around Desdemona. "C'mon. Let's go."

Together, they walked down the hallway. Nurses and visitors glanced at them with expressions of sympathy, probably assuming they had just lost a relative, which, in a sense, they had.

CHAPTER 7

Portia Kim, Holly's youngest and most productive reporter, was the only one in the *Chronicle* office when Holly arrived.

"Where is everyone?" Holly asked.

"Town Hall," Portia said. "There's a truck handing out free samples of some new kind of Hot Pockets."

"Did someone bring a camera?"

"Les did. He's going to write it up for a front-page feature."

"Why aren't you there?"

"I'm on a diet," Portia said, looking down at the small roll of fat just above the belt on her black jeans. "It's really my mother's fault. She still treats me like I'm five. I get the look if I don't eat everything on my plate."

Holly sat on Portia's desk, sensing this would be a longer conversation than she initially thought. "Any chance of liberation this year?" she asked.

"Not really. I still have to do their books because their English isn't good enough, and another cousin just came over from Korea, so he's in training. It takes him an hour to do a manicure."

"Well, I'm pulling for you. Any daily would be lucky to have you," Holly said, though she knew that most daily newspapers were laying off reporters. The economics of the industry barely sustained the actual gathering of news anymore.

"Thanks," Portia said. "You're the reason I don't beat my head against the wall wondering why I went to Vassar. I mean, you moved back to Bertram Corners, and you've never regretted it, right?"

Holly picked up a rubber band from Portia's desk and began to twist it around her fingers. "Do you know how old my husband was when he died?"

"I know he was young."

Holly had wrapped the rubber band around the tips of two fingers, which were now turning white. "Thirty-seven. Marshall was nine, and Connor was six. He kissed me good-bye one morning, left for work, and had an aneurism when he got to the office. It took me a full year—a full year—to stop waking up in the morning and looking to Chris's side of the bed, absolutely sure it was all a nightmare. Even now, seven years later, I have nights like that."

Portia lowered her head. "I'm so sorry you had to go through that. And your poor kids."

Holly pulled the rubber band off her fingers and let the blood flow back. "I know," she said, taking a deep breath. "But to answer your question, I don't regret coming back, because this town came together for me after Chris died. Marshall and Connor had a lot of support, especially in those first few years. I know that everyone in town is looking out for them, like we all look out for Vivian. That's what we do."

Holly knew forty or fifty e-mails awaited her, bristling with false urgency, but she paused, putting her hands under her thighs as she sat on Portia's desk. Her impulse to warn Portia that life could pivot drastically without warning needed a little tempering.

"You know that you'll be fine, right?" Holly said. "You're smart and you're resourceful, and you'll make your own way, if not in this business then in another one. I'm completely confident about that."

"I hope you're right."

"I am right," Holly said, jumping off Portia's desk. "If I'm right about nothing else, I'm right about that."

Back in her office, Holly looked at the large paper calendar on the wall, a gift from the bank. She had just sent a check to the very same bank for half of her mortgage with a handwritten note on a Post-it saying she would make up the difference as soon as possible. It wasn't a complete lie, even if "possible" might actually be "never." But as her eyes swept across the perfectly boxed days and the neat rows of weeks, she realized that the next month's mortgage would be due in just a few weeks. And just four weeks after that another check would be due, and another after that. The fear of losing her house consumed her. It felt like she had gone too far underwater and couldn't be sure she'd have enough air to make it to the surface.

She pulled her eyes from the calendar and tried to breathe slowly and evenly by imagining herself inside an iron lung that did the breathing for her.

⌒

"Mom, I'll be late for school."

Holly could sense Marshall standing over her even before he started prodding her in the shoulder and shining the bright red digital numbers of the alarm clock in her face. She had been up until two in the morning putting the paper to bed, as she did every Tuesday night before Wednesday's press run.

"It's six forty-seven, and I have to be there by seven fifteen. C'mon. I made you some coffee."

Holly got up, pulled on some sweatpants, and shoved her feet into an old pair of untied running shoes. She felt her way down the stairs, rubbing her eyes as she entered the unnatural glow of the kitchen. Marshall put a cup of coffee into her hand.

"This is the last day I can bring in the money for the band trip."

Holly fished around in the bill drawer for an envelope with the money she had saved for the trip and counted out two hundred and eighty dollars in twenties into Marshall's open hand. She had a feeling the money for this band trip was just the beginning of all the cash she would be asked to shell out during his junior year in high school.

"It should be three forty," he said. "Where's the rest?"

She counted the money again. Two hundred and eighty, despite her fervent wish that at least a few of the twenties had been stuck together.

"It has to be here," she said. "I've been putting a twenty away every week."

"Did you take any out?"

She paused, remembering an emergency pizza night a few weeks ago, before the mortgage mess, when she had borrowed from the band fund, intending to pay it back. There may have been a few other emergencies as well.

"I may have accidentally used some of it," Holly said. An ugly knot of guilt traveled from one internal organ to the next like a pinball as she realized she hadn't been vigilant enough with her saving. "But," she quickly added, "I'll get it today. Just bring this in and tell them you'll have the rest tomorrow."

Marshall looked at the twenties as if they were unclean or some kind of pitiful ransom. "Why don't you just write me a check for the whole thing?"

"When did we all start looking down on legal tender?" she said, taking a long sip of coffee to avoid explaining to Marshall that her checking account could not accommodate his request until her next paycheck hit. It would be worse to bounce a check and have to pay a penalty. "Go get Connor while I start the car."

Marshall, who played the trumpet, tightened his lips the way trumpet players habitually do and put the cash in his pocket, then headed back upstairs to find his brother. Holly stepped out onto the wet lawn, worried because the Subaru sometimes had trouble starting on the kind of high-humidity days they often had when school was just starting. She got in the car and turned the key, leaning forward in her seat as if that might give the car momentum. The engine sputtered but eventually caught. A few minutes later, Marshall emerged with his backpack slung over one shoulder, and Connor followed, still groggy, eating a slice of bread with peanut butter on it. Marshall's hair dangled in his eyes so annoyingly that Holly brushed back her own, clearing her forehead. At the same time she promised herself that she would let it go because it wasn't worth starting the day with an argument. The boys climbed into the car.

"You seriously need a haircut," Holly said, the words out of her mouth before she could stop them.

"We're late, Mom."

"How can you see? It's like a blindfold."

Holly backed out of the driveway, cautious of the traffic on the street, now the main access road to a new subdivision of homes for those craving a bonus room and a three-car garage. The new lots hugged the hill behind the Showalter house, which looked like a historic homestead, with its stone foundation and its wide front porch, its peeling paint and its tiny dormer windows. Holly wanted to take the house to dinner and buy it expensive new clothes, but she couldn't afford to make any improvements. Instead, the ceiling in the kitchen leaked from the shower stall above, the wallpaper in the hall had faded in areas that saw the sunlight, and patches of gray showed through the white exterior paint that Chris had used to change the house color after they bought it. He had always wanted a white house.

"Don't forget to hold the door handle," Holly told Connor, who was in the backseat. "I don't want you flying out this morning."

"I miss Dad," Connor said, surprising all of them.

"Me, too," Marshall said.

"Oh my boys," Holly said, blindsided once again. A grief counselor had warned Holly that her children would have to reprocess their father's death at every stage of their development, but the counselor hadn't addressed how helpless Holly would feel every time it resurfaced. She cleared her throat so that her voice wouldn't break. "Me, three."

A few days later, Racine blew into the newspaper office like a fresh breeze off the ocean, and Darla, the lifestyles reporter and calendar editor, spotted him before Holly could run out from her office.

"And how may we help you?" Darla said, coming out from behind the desk where she was presumably writing the weekly community theater roundup Holly had asked for that morning.

"I'm looking for Holly Showalter," he said, turning around as if he might be in the wrong place. The newspaper office looked like the home of a hoarder, with boxes and papers stacked on every conceivable surface, the sight lines obscured by shelving units full of obsolete phone books. Clearing it out would have qualified as an archeological dig.

Darla, who at barely five feet couldn't even see over the bookcases, stroked the uppermost of her three chins. "She's here somewhere," she said.

Holly could see Darla smiling in a slightly inappropriate way as she took in the whole scene from her office, which had a door she rarely closed and glass walls above waist height. Holly enjoyed seeing Racine from a distance, where she could study his fine bone structure without being self-conscious about her own features.

"May I say who's asking for her?" Darla asked.

Racine extended a hand to Darla, who looked delighted to take it. "Tell her it's Racine."

"Racine," Darla repeated. "Now doesn't that sound like an exotic travel destination."

Holly emerged from her office to cut off whatever Darla might say next. "Hey, there," she said. "I'm glad you stopped by. I have Vivian's check for you."

"Excellent," he said, running a hand lightly over his hair. "And I was looking for your advice on the storefronts. Could we take a walk?"

"Sure. Just have to finish answering an e-mail. Be right back."

Racine stayed in the main newsroom, looking around with an amused expression, perhaps at its quaintness, as Darla followed Holly into her office.

"Where do I get one of those?" Darla said in a low voice.

"He's just someone I'm doing business with," Holly said as she typed and hit "Send."

"Doing business. Is that what you kids are calling it now?"

Staring down Darla's smirk, Holly left her office and led Racine through the warren of the newsroom and out the door. He was wearing some sort of sneaker-shoes with visible stitching that made small squeaking noises with each step, though he didn't seem to notice.

"I like this town," he said, glancing into the window of a second-hand sporting goods store a few doors down from the newspaper. "It's not too pretentious, solidly middle class, which puts it right in the sweet spot of our target market. Any place too upscale means people won't be seen walking into a place like ours. Too down-and-out means they have nothing of value they haven't already hocked."

He said all this with a detachment that both troubled and fascinated Holly. They kept walking.

"It doesn't bother you," she said, "that places like this make money because other people are struggling?"

"We provide a needed service. We convert unused assets into something you can buy groceries with. It's a win-win, really."

"And you give people a fair price?"

"Absolutely. We're more generous than the mail-order gold mills, maybe a little less than an established pawn shop, but most people feel uncomfortable walking into a pawn shop. Bottom line, gold has no value sitting in your old jewelry box, so whatever we offer is a net gain."

Holly nodded, because her own Internet research had confirmed what Racine said. She wasn't overjoyed to be comparing Vivian's investment unfavorably to a pawn shop, but then again the gold shop wasn't a charity. Racine stopped near an empty storefront about half a block from the newspaper office. It had an iron gate on the front windows—unusual for Bertram Corners—and a brick exterior. His Jaguar was parked in front.

"This is the place I like," he said. "It gives off that solid, respectable vibe, but it's not ostentatious. What do you think?"

Holly stood back and looked at the shop in the context of its neighbors, a failing video store and a Dunkin' Donuts.

"The Dunkin' Donuts will bring in traffic," she said.

"Exactly my thought," he said, knocking lightly on the wood frame around the front doorway. "The price is right, too. About a quarter of the rent we're paying in Brooklyn."

"I'm not surprised," Holly told him. "The downtown's been teetering since the day they opened the mall back in 1986, and then it took another hit with the outlets, which are now killing the mall. It's amazing any of these places have held on this long."

"What about your newspaper?" Racine said. "How does that hold on? I thought they were all disappearing."

Holly paused to look down the street at the assortment of storefronts, which included a dental office, a nail salon, a Chinese restaurant, and a dry cleaner, interspersed with empty buildings that once housed a tailor, a shoe repair shop, a candy store, and a jeweler. She couldn't deny that the mammoth chain clothing stores, fast-food joints, and ubiquitous purveyors of bitter coffee that banded together in ugly strip malls had sucked the vibrancy right out of Bertram Corners. But the newspaper kept chugging along, even as it reported on the town's disintegration.

"We're holding our own," she said, though she wasn't completely sure about the latest advertising figures. "We have loyal readers."

"You're lucky then. So we're good on the location?"

"It's fine with me. Did you ask Vivian?"

"She told me to ask you," Racine said, laughing. "She said you know the town better than anyone. I tried to talk her into walking me around, because she's one of my biggest investors in this location, but she made some excuse."

Holly stopped on the sidewalk in front of the courthouse. "You don't know?"

"Know what?"

"About Vivian."

"What about her?"

"She's got . . . some medical issues," she said, stopping there.

"She sounds fine on the phone."

"She holds her own, barring weather mishaps . . ."

Holly was mumbling now, fairly sure that she should stop talking before she said anything she would regret. And yet she wanted to tell Racine something he didn't know—to bring him inside the loop—because he seemed like a perpetual traveler who kept a polite distance, never quite feeling at home.

"That's a relief," Racine said. "Want a lift back to the office?"

"I should stop by Town Hall and chat up the clerk. If I buy her a Diet Coke once a week, she stays on my good side. If I forget, the real estate transactions are late. Oh, here's that check for you."

She reached into her purse, pulled out her wallet, and found the check Vivian's accountant had prepared.

"Be good to it," Holly meant to say, but it came out "Be good to me." She stood in the middle of the sidewalk, reddening, as Racine bestowed a radiant smile upon her.

"I will," he said, and walked away.

CHAPTER 8

Holly walked into Vivian's living room to find her with Marveen Langdon, the *Chronicle*'s bookkeeper, who was retouching Vivian's highlights with a dye kit from the grocery store.

"So I say to him, I say, 'You're crazy,'" Marveen said. "No one pays full price for movies anymore. You get your discount tickets from AAA. It's a no-brainer."

"Hi, Holly," Vivian said, smiling from the halo of foil that framed her face. "Marveen is giving me the treatment."

"I can see that," Holly said, wondering if Marveen could be talked into cutting and highlighting her hair. She hadn't been to the salon in a year and had taken to trimming her own hair with the same pair of scissors she used to cut coupons.

"Do you buy AAA discount movie tickets?" Vivian asked Holly. "Marveen seems to think everyone does."

"Do people still go to the movies? I can't remember the last movie I saw."

Vivian and Marveen exchanged a brief glance conveying that Holly was always strapped for cash and was, therefore, an object of pity, even a source of frustration, as though she should get on the stick and make more money so others wouldn't have to feel guilty about their own spending in her presence. Vivian had a hefty bank balance because her parents had left her their house, disability insurance covered most of her medical expenses, and she was known to be something of a wizard with her investments. She also had no need to spend money on travel or clothing or furniture or anything else besides the technology that kept her connected to the world.

Marveen made a small salary as the newspaper's part-time book-keeper, but her husband was a wealthy executive. She only worked because it provided her with more people to gossip about. Holly hated that her income—or lack thereof—so circumscribed her life, and even more that no one wanted to talk about it, preferring to pretend that money didn't matter. If it didn't buy happiness, it bought, she had decided, at least some measure of comfort. The philanthropist and investor Harold Bertram, for whom Bertram Corners had been named, had put it in a rather grotesque way that Holly nevertheless admired: "Worship not penury, for it is but a noose."

"Are you planning to stay?" Marveen asked.

"I can stay," Holly said. "When does your shift end?"

"Just another half hour, and then the nurse comes in, but if I can make it to the drugstore today, I won't have to stop after work. I need a new curling iron."

Vivian gave Holly a wink as Marveen picked up her purse. The wink referred to their joint opinion that Marveen's devotion to her hair bordered on the religious. On a daily basis, she straightened it, then curled it, then teased it into a froth that made her three inches taller, and she was tall to start.

Marveen, who was a languid hugger, gave Holly a long, tepid squeeze and then kissed Vivian on the cheek.

"Bye, ladies," Marveen said as she and her hair left through the front door.

"I'm the first person to admit that I spend way too much time on my hair," Vivian said once Marveen was gone. "But look at me. What else do I have to fuss about?"

"She must burn through a curling iron every few weeks," Holly said. "Hey, I need to ask you something. Are you sure you don't want me to tell Racine about your condition? He'll hear about it eventually anyway."

Vivian rolled her eyes. "You're used to me, Holly. You know my brain hasn't been affected. But I learned the hard way not to tell business partners that I'm in an iron lung. They can't wrap their minds around it. If they do find out, they start talking to me like I'm frail and elderly, and eventually they find a way to get out of the deal."

"So how do you get around it?"

"Usually I give the impression that I'm constantly traveling or too busy to meet in person. It makes me seem important."

"And you are," Holly said. "As important as they come."

Vivian smiled. "My financial adviser takes care of most of my investments anyway, but this one was different because Racine's company wanted local investors with a hands-on approach. His group doesn't want to be one of those fly-by-night gold operations, which is smart in my book. I didn't want to scare him away."

Holly forgot sometimes that most people under fifty had never heard of an iron lung and would have been shocked to find that any were still in use. Bertram Corners had grown so used to Vivian's unique situation that the town had lost sight of how the rest of the world might regard it. If it weren't for Vivian, Holly realized, her kids wouldn't have known that iron lungs had ever existed.

"I gave Racine the check, by the way," Holly said. "I hope it pays off."

"I'm sure it will," she said. "And maybe things will get easier for you with a little extra coming in. Maybe you can save up a bit and invest some of it in the store."

Holly nodded. It was nice to imagine having enough of a nest egg to put some money toward the service of making more money. She considered telling Vivian the full extent of her cash-flow problems now that her mother wasn't sending a monthly check. The bank wouldn't let her stay in her house indefinitely if she couldn't make her mortgage payments, and even with the checks Vivian's accountant sent her each week, she was still behind and likely to make another partial payment for the upcoming month. She instantly imagined the boys curled into sleeping bags in the back of her car. But she decided against telling Vivian. Not voicing the extent of her problems made them feel less dire. At least she still had a job. However small the salary, she had an income and health benefits, which was more than some people could say. If she could cut back on her expenses a little more and work more weekends for Vivian, maybe she could make her own investment.

When she left Vivian's, she was tempted to stop at the gas station to buy a lottery ticket, but she stopped herself. Every dollar she didn't spend was a dollar she might one day invest.

⌐∽

A few hours later, Holly remembered with a start, then a sigh, that she still needed to pay the remainder for Marshall's band trip. When she ran into Marveen in the parking lot behind the *Chronicle*, she decided on the spot that she was the right person to ask for a loan, since she reported to the publisher and not to Holly. Marveen always had cash in her wallet, because her husband didn't believe in using credit cards.

"Hi, Marveen," Holly said, as though she hadn't seen her in ages. "Nice hair. You must have gotten that new curling iron."

"Well, thanks," she said, giving Holly another hug as if she hadn't seen her in months. "I did touch it up before coming over."

"Hey," Holly said. "I hope you don't mind if I ask you something kind of personal."

Marveen pulled her tote bag out of the backseat of her BMW. "Did you want me to do some highlights? Like I did for Vivian?"

Holly did want the highlights, but Marshall's trip was a higher priority. She shifted from one foot to the other. Asking Marveen for a loan was like standing on the roof with a megaphone to announce that she couldn't manage her own finances, but Marshall had to go on that trip.

"This is kind of embarrassing, but I'm a little short for Marshall's band trip, and I was wondering if I could get a small loan from you until we get paid next week. I hate asking, but I'm pretty much out of options."

"Really," Marveen said, squinting at Holly as though she were a child caught in a fib. "Because I heard you met with that cash-for-gold guy. How are you talking to him if you can't pay for your son's field trip?"

Holly could have told her that Vivian had hired her to meet with Racine, but she thought Marveen might be upset that Vivian hadn't chosen her, with her bookkeeping experience and her love of bright and shiny things.

"It's a cash-flow problem," Holly said, feeling the blood creep up her neck. "Never mind, though. Forget I asked. I'll figure it out."

"Don't be silly," Marveen said, reaching into her purse for her wallet. "I'm happy to help. I just wish you had told me about the gold place. I might have wanted in on it. How much do you need?"

Holly couldn't meet Marveen's eyes. "Sixty," she said, looking down.

"Is that all?" Marveen said, handing over three crisp twenties as if they were singles. Holly was jealous of how Marveen treated money. It reminded Holly of the days when her mother used to carry a hundred dollars in cash for emergencies, which seemed to come up every time she passed a shoe store.

"Thank you," Holly said, putting the twenties in her purse. "I really appreciate it."

"No problem. Though you can do me one teensy favor."

Holly sighed, knowing she should have expected to pay a price for Marveen's generosity. "What's that?"

"Introduce me to this guy Racine. I'm hoping he'll let me in on his next store."

～

Within two weeks, Racine had the cash-for-gold store, now called The Gold Depot, up and running. A crew of workmen had gutted the small storefront and put up drywall, then hauled in some glass cases for the resale items and built a few cubbies with chairs along the back wall, where prospective clients would hand over their gold for an estimate of its value.

Holly walked over from the newspaper for the grand opening. A single white balloon floated from the handle on the front door, which was propped open, but no one was inside except for two bearded men wearing green visors, who sat on the other side of the cubbies, presumably waiting for the cascade of gold soon to come their way.

When Holly walked in, Racine was pouring a bag of wrapped peppermint candies into a large glass bowl on one of the front counters. He looked up and smiled at Holly.

"What do you think?" he said, looking around.

"It's exciting," Holly said, running a hand along the glass counter. "The opening of a new business is big news in this town. One of my reporters is writing a feature story for this week's paper. I'd do it myself, but it's a conflict of interest."

Racine set the bowl of candy in the middle of the counter, then moved it over to the right a few inches. Holly noticed that the glass cases were filled with jewelry, watches, pins, letter openers, and comb and brush sets. Each item had been buffed and cleaned, but they all looked a little dated and fatigued, as though they were housed in the retail equivalent of a nursing home.

"Where did all this come from?" she said.

Racine took a bottle of glass cleaner from behind the counter and began wiping it down, even though it already looked clean. She noticed as Racine turned to one side that he had a bump near the bridge of his nose, a slight flaw that made him more likeable. She still sensed the conflict between his welcoming smile and the caution in his eyes, but she couldn't begin to guess what might have caused it.

"We buy out estate sales. People don't want to see their neighbors parading around in their grandmother's old brooches, so we try to mix it up among stores."

"I see," Holly said, finding it surprising that any sensitivity at all went into the store's operation. She nodded toward the visored men in the back. "Where'd you find them?"

"They're on loan from one of our New York stores for the opening. They'll work here for a month or two, get us established, then we'll hire some appraisers of our own. It's a growing field."

"I imagine it is," Holly said. One of the men in the back was polishing a small eyeglass, and the other was adjusting the strap on his visor.

Just then their first customer walked through the door. Holly recognized her as a Stop & Shop cashier, though she didn't know the woman's name. She was in her late sixties, small boned and slightly stooped, and she wore the kind of putty-colored orthopedic shoes that Holly associated with giving up on life.

Racine gave her the full force of his smile. "Hello, ma'am. So glad you could come in on opening day," he said. "How may we help you?"

The woman opened the clasp on her purse and took out a plastic sandwich bag with some tangled jewelry in it. "I thought I'd come in and see what this is worth," she said with a self-conscious smile. "I never wear it anymore."

"Right this way," Racine said, leading her to a chair at one of the cubbies.

The store was small enough that Holly couldn't help but witness the transaction. The visored man sitting on the opposite side of the table took the baggy and emptied it into a tray lined with black velvet.

"Thanks for coming in today," he said, looking at the jewelry and not at the woman in front of him. He sorted it quickly, viewing some of the items through an eyepiece. He examined a small pocket watch several times, turning it over and opening its engraved cover. He weighed each broken hoop and each bracelet fragment, adding numbers on a calculator. The appraiser looked up briefly, and Holly turned away so that she wouldn't appear to be eavesdropping, though she could hear everything he said.

"These two aren't real gold," he said, handing the woman a thin bracelet and one of the earrings. "And the pocket watch is an amalgam, so we can't take that, except for resale. The clasp is broken, so that would be fifteen dollars."

The woman shook her head slowly and took back the pocket watch. The appraiser piled the small handful of jewelry left onto a tiny scale and wrote down a number on a small white pad, which he then turned toward the woman, who nodded meekly. The appraiser swept the tokens of her past into a plastic bowl and counted out the cash. He placed the money in a white paper envelope, and the woman took it without changing her expression. She walked slowly past the glass cases, pretending to look inside them, as if she might spend the cash she had just received on someone else's discarded trinkets.

When she passed Racine, he gave her another smile, to which she responded with a smile of her own that said, *At least a nice-looking man acknowledged my presence today.*

"Thank you for your business," Racine said, bowing slightly. "Come again."

The woman nodded vaguely and left, which was Holly's cue to leave as well. She glanced at the men in the back, then turned to Racine.

"Looks like you have everything under control," Holly said.

"Business will pick up in a few days. It takes a while for the word to get out. Actually, I was thinking about putting out some flyers."

"My boys could help you with the flyers," Holly said, brightening at the thought of being helpful in a concrete way.

"Sure. Have them come by."

"I will. Take care."

She hurried out the door and walked right into the path of the Sister Sisters—the town's elderly sibling nuns—who were strolling down the street in the long black habits they wore long after the Catholic church stopped requiring nuns to be identifiable from a block away. They were carrying a basket between them.

"Is that Holly?" one of them said. Their names were Sister Eileen and Sister Eleanor, but no one ever knew which was which. The sister closest to the door of the gold shop looked up at the sign.

"Are you investigating?" she said, raising her eyebrows.

"Investigating what?"

"These gold places. They take your treasures and give you a fraction of what they're worth," the nun said. "It's all over the Interwebs."

"You two have a computer?" Holly asked the sister who spoke.

"Vivian gave us very good instructions about how to use one at the library," she said. "We check our e-mail every week."

"What are you up to today?" Holly asked them, intent on changing the subject. Talking them out of their misconceptions about the gold business would have taken too much time.

"We're on our way to . . . where are we going, Sister?"

The other sister put a hand in the pocket of her habit and pulled out a small scrap of paper ripped from a notebook.

"Ellen Crandall," the other sister said. "She tore her ACL playing basketball, so we're bringing muffins."

"How wonderful," Holly said. "Well, have a good day, Sisters."

Halfway down the sidewalk, Holly looked back to see the sisters still standing in front of the gold shop. One of them was peering in, her nose right to the glass.

CHAPTER 9

Vivian's Unaired Podcast #3

The placid acceptance I had displayed at twelve eventually morphed into a simmering rage that I wasn't a) dead and glorified as a martyr, or b) the beneficiary of some amazing medical breakthrough that made it possible for me to escape the iron lung. I had given up worrying about my body—I was so detached from it that I felt no shame or embarrassment when doctors and nurses fussed around it. I couldn't feel it anyway. I just let them take care of the business end of things. But I knew from watching television that people in wheelchairs could travel just about anywhere. If I could breathe on my own or even use a portable apparatus, I would be able to attend movies, concerts, plays, or just sit in the park on a sunny afternoon feeling the wind caress my face. I missed being outside, where I felt closest to Darlene.

My parents tried their best to take me out as often as possible, but it was such a production. Several grown men were needed to set up the ramp, take the door off the hinges, and wheel me into a special medical van with restraints to prevent my lung from banging around. Other than two or three hospital visits each year, I saw the outdoors maybe once a month or so.

By seventeen I was old enough to realize that the doctors had been completely wrong about my prognosis—which was discussed in whispers and asides that I had no trouble overhearing—and clearly had miscalculated my parents' ability to survive without sleep. I became aware that I could live for a very long time. That revelation made me all the more furious that I couldn't be a part of the world—couldn't visit other places, couldn't go to college, couldn't see much of anything outside the room that was my prison. I was about to graduate from high school—I took all my tests orally or dictated to my mother—and I had excelled. I was near the top of my class, and yet I couldn't contemplate a career or anything besides lying in the same room as my parents wore themselves frail and thin caring for me.

Just before graduation, my mother's friend dropped off some cookies for the high school picnic that followed the ceremony. My parents had gone to a lot of trouble to get the school to accommodate my iron lung. They had moved the graduation outside so that I could be wheeled on a gurney behind my classmates and could receive my diploma with them.

"Are you excited about graduating, Vivian?" my mother's friend said in a voice more appropriate for a five-year-old.

"Thrilled," I said deadpan. "I can't wait to see what life has in store."

"Vivian," my mother said. "Please."

"Please what?" I said, oblivious to her friend or to her feelings. "Am I supposed to be grateful for whatever you call this? Because it's not a life. I'm like some weird science experiment. I shouldn't even be alive."

"Don't say that," my mother said. "You are an amazing person, and you have so much to contribute."

"How do I contribute when I can't do anything for myself? I can't even blow my own nose. Do you know how humiliating that is?"

My mother turned to her friend with a look of apology and showed her to the door. After the wretched woman left, I finally said what I had wanted to say for months.

"I can't take it anymore. Just turn off the machine and let me die."

My mother looked distraught. "You're in a phase. Everyone goes through it at your age. You want to get away from your parents and make your own decisions, and you will someday, but this is not the day."

The misplaced anger I felt at that moment would have taken my breath away if the iron lung didn't force my respiration.

"You can't possibly understand," I said, yelling loud enough now to bring my father on the run. "I am trapped in this goddamned machine forever. How could you let this happen to me? Why didn't you keep me inside that summer? I was only six. I didn't even know what polio was."

My father stepped into the room just as I said those words.

"That's enough, Vivian," he said in a tone I had never heard him use with me before. "That is more than enough."

He came and put an arm around my mother, who was trembling and crying in the chair next to my iron lung. I knew it was wrong, but I thought I would explode if I couldn't blame someone for my misery, and my parents were the easiest targets. I began to turn my head rapidly from side to side, which was one of the few ways I could release frustration. When I had exhausted myself, my mother rose from her chair and put her hands on either side of my head, squeezing just a little too hard.

"You are not done yet," she said through clenched teeth. "I won't let you be done . . . Just tell me what you want, and if it's in my power, I will try my best to get it for you."

"That's the problem," I said, turning my head away, out of her grasp. "It's not in your power at all."

⤸

After graduation, I sank into a depression that seemed to have no bottom. I spent many of my waking hours trying to figure out how to sabotage my own medical care. I couldn't hold my breath, because the lung forced me to breathe. I couldn't choke on food, because someone was always there to clear my airway. I began to fantasize about death and about how it would release me from Shakespeare's "mortal coil," which I pictured literally as a giant metal spring wrapped around my inert body inside the machine.

I knew that if I stopped eating altogether the doctors would insert a feeding tube in my abdomen, so I saw only one path. I would eat less and less until I wasted away. I thought if I did it gradually enough, it might be too late for anyone to intervene.

Naturally, my mother noticed almost immediately, but instead of coaxing me to eat my peas like a toddler, she tried a different approach. She brought in Professor Harold Margolis from the community college in Albany, which I looked down on because my grades would have qualified me to go to a much better school. The professor knew that. He knew so much about me that I suspected my mother had been badgering him for months.

"So Vivian," he said, "I've been asking your mother if she would consider loaning you out to us on an occasional basis."

"Spare parts for your heating system?"

Professor Margolis laughed and looked at me with either appreciation or bemusement—I couldn't tell which.

"Not exactly," he said. "We're developing a computer program, and we need good minds to help us see the patterns—connect the dots, as it were. You'd visit us once a month to work in the computer lab, and in exchange we'd offer you some classes at home. You could get your associate's degree, and it won't cost your parents a dime."

I'm embarrassed to say that I thought too highly of myself—even as I wallowed in depression—to want an associate's degree from Albany Community College, but I was intrigued by the idea of working in a computer lab, even just seeing one.

"Who would teach me?" I asked him.

"That depends on what courses you'd like to take."

On the spot, it occurred to me that I wanted to learn about business. I had always been a math whiz, probably because I couldn't use a slide rule, or even a pencil and paper, and had to do all my calculations in my head. I loved listening to news reports about the economy and about the new businesses cropping up as the world remade itself into a modern and interconnected place.

"Business," I said. "Economics and business."

"Then business it shall be," the professor said, nodding at my mother. "I'll work something out with our business department: You'll be hearing from us soon."

My mother walked Professor Margolis to the door, and I could hear them speaking in low voices, something that infuriated me, which my mother well knew. When the professor left, I turned my venomous tongue on her.

"So you think you can buy me off with a few days outside this god-forsaken house? Do you think I don't know he just feels sorry for me?"

My mother, normally quick to placate me, instead kicked the otto-man my father used to put his feet up after dinner and tipped it over.

"I've had it, Vivian," she said, tears streaming. "It took me three months to get him to come out here. Well, here's how I see it: you can either drown in your misery, or you can decide to live your life. Not the one you wish you had, but the one God gave you."

With that, maybe the longest speech my mother had ever made to me, she left the room. A minute went by, then two. I wondered if she had finally given up on me. As two minutes ticked into three, I realized that I truly did want to learn about business and spend time in a computer lab, if only to get out from under the same ceiling I had been staring at for years and years. Just as I began to panic that my mother had left the house, I heard her from the kitchen.

"Mar-co," she said, her voice still shaking.

"Po-lo," I called without hesitation.

CHAPTER 10

Holly dialed Desdemona's cell phone number.

"I'm thinking about going to see Mom again this weekend," Holly said.

"Do you want me to come?" Desdemona said.

"Do you think you could get away?"

Holly could hear the crowd noise on the streets of the East Village, where Desdemona had a studio apartment the size of the walk-in closets in the development near Holly's house. As Desdemona paused, Holly could hear shouts and car horns and bicycle bells in the distance—the never-ending soundtrack of the city.

"Sorry," Desdemona said finally. "I had to get around one of those knockoff purse vendors. They always clog up the sidewalk. I have rehearsal on Saturday, but if you go on Sunday, I can meet you there. We can look for her rings again."

Holly wanted to tell Desdemona that their mother's rings were long gone, probably melted and turned into a new ring, maybe even an engagement ring that would stay on someone else's finger until it withered, and the ring fell off in a nursing home fifty or sixty years from now. But she said none of it.

"I'll call you tomorrow and we'll set it up. Should I see if Henderson wants to come?"

"Do you think he'd drive down from Boston?"

"He's not working right now, so why wouldn't he?"

Holly remembered Henderson's indigestion fiasco at the funeral home and briefly wondered what might happen this time. She pictured him needing the Heimlich maneuver in the hospital cafeteria.

"Sure, then," Desdemona said. "It would be nice to see how he's getting along. Maybe he could bring Phoebe. I haven't seen her in ages, and she's probably changed so much."

"Middle school will do that to a girl. I'm not sure if he has her this weekend, but I'll ask. Bye, Des."

"Bye, Holly. See you soon."

⌣

They entered the room in birth order—Henderson first, then Holly, then Desdemona—and each kissed Celia's wrinkled forehead.

"Hi, Mom," Henderson said in a voice overly animated for the occasion. "Here we are. Your children. We came to visit you."

"Why are you talking like that?" Holly said.

"I'm just trying to be upbeat," Henderson said.

Desdemona, who was standing on the side of the bed opposite Holly and Henderson, picked up her mother's hand. "Still no rings," she said. "I was kind of hoping they'd just reappear."

Henderson let out a string of profanities. "Somebody walked in here in broad daylight and robbed her," he said. "Because she's helpless. Look at her. She couldn't do a damn thing about it."

"We don't know that," Desdemona said, still reluctant to think the worst. "Maybe there's some other explanation."

Holly and Henderson looked at each other as if they pitied their sister's faith in humanity.

"Look," Holly said, "we don't know what happened, but we know the rings are gone, so let's start with that and decide what to do. We've already reported it to the hospital, and they claim they're not responsible. They blame us for letting her wear them in here, so we're dead in the water there. Is it worth it to call the police?"

"I doubt it," Henderson said. "We can't prove she even came in with them."

Holly sat down in a straight-backed chair near the bed. She rubbed the fourth finger of her left hand, which still had faint indentations from the years she had worn her own wedding rings.

"What about insurance?" she said. "We could file a claim."

"She didn't have a jewelry rider," Henderson said. "I already checked."

Desdemona picked up her mother's left hand again. "I still think they might turn up. Remember how Dad wanted to buy her an even bigger diamond, but she refused? She said the one she had was enough."

Holly got up and rifled through the side table again but came up empty. Celia stirred and put one hand to her white throat. All three moved toward the small plastic pitcher on Celia's bed table. Holly got there first and poured some water into a plastic cup.

"Here, Mom," she said. "Here's some water. It's Holly, Mom."

Holly held her mother's head and tilted it toward the cup. Celia took a small, feeble sip.

Henderson moved toward the bed. "It's Henderson, Mom. I came down from Boston to see you."

Celia turned her head toward him, though she seemed to be looking through him, as if he were a window. Henderson let out a sob.

"Oh, Hen, it's all right," Desdemona said. "She's not herself."

"I can't help it. Think of what we've lost. I should have videotaped her years ago so that Phoebe would remember her like she used to be. I can't bring her to visit now. She'll be traumatized."

"Don't say that," Holly said. "She's still Phoebe's grandmother."

"But why did this happen to her?" Henderson said. He found a box of tissues and blew his nose. "Some people are fine into the triple digits. She's only seventy-six. She could have had twenty more good years, and now there's nothing but scraps. Scraps aren't enough. And she could live like this for years and years. And for what?"

While everything Henderson said was true, Holly wanted to pinch him—her weapon of choice in elementary school—for sounding like a whining child.

She turned to face him. "You're acting like she had a choice. She didn't. She's here, and she's hanging on to whatever's left, even if it doesn't seem like much. What's the alternative, Hen?"

Henderson said nothing, only folded his arms and walked over to the window. Desdemona kissed her mother on the forehead again and smoothed back her hair.

"Maybe I could take care of her," Desdemona said. "I could take a leave of absence from the company. My bunion's inflamed anyway. My podiatrist says I should rest it."

Henderson turned back toward them. "In that crappy little studio? It's a fifth-floor walk-up. How would you even get her up there? That's ridiculous."

"Now wait a minute. It's not like I want to live in a 'crappy little studio.'"

"Don't even think about it," Henderson said, finishing his original statement. "Holly at least has a bedroom on the first floor."

"Hold on," Holly said, amazed that Henderson knew so little about her life that he could suggest such a thing. "You're not even working right now, and you have an elevator in your building."

"I'm not even working?" Henderson said. "Don't you think I'm working my ass off to find a job? I'm working more than I ever have. And Phoebe's going to live with me for a while because the bankruptcy court suspended my child-support payments. I had to take Phoebe so Wendy could go work for her father, who is the only person who would ever hire her."

Desdemona stroked her mother's hair, which seemed to relax her and allow her eyes to close again. "We can't fight about this," she said softly. "We need to figure out what to do if they decide she doesn't belong here anymore."

Holly regretted getting upset with Henderson, falling back into ancient rivalries. She knew that Henderson, like her, only wanted the mother he remembered back.

Holly flipped through some paperwork they had given her on the way in. "If she improves significantly, they'll release her. Same goes for if she declines significantly. The only way she stays here—and Medicare pays for it—is if she shows very gradual improvement. Otherwise, she'll either go to one of us or to a nursing home."

Celia's eyes fluttered for a moment, and Desdemona moved to the bedside and patted her hand.

"She looks agitated," Desdemona said. "Her eyes were moving. I saw it."

But now that all three of them were staring at her, Celia was completely still.

Maybe it would be better if she died, Holly thought, immediately reprimanding herself for letting such a thought run through her head while simultaneously recognizing it as the unfortunate truth.

⤳

Marveen wore a low-cut blouse with a statement necklace that featured a large enameled daisy. Holly thought she was even more overdone than usual—her hair was especially inflated—but she wasn't going to argue, since Marveen had agreed to forgive her sixty-dollar debt in exchange for a personal introduction to Racine. Marveen had learned all about Holly's second job through Vivian, and it seemed not to bother her at all.

They walked over from the newspaper office, where they had met on a Saturday, with Marveen stopping every thirty or forty feet to adjust her toes in the strappy stiletto sandals that held her feet like the strained casings of overfilled knockwursts.

"I don't know why you wore those shoes," Holly said. "You'll tower over him. Men don't like to feel short."

"Oh, you're right," Marveen said, stopping to pull at one of the straps. "But it's too late now. I'll just have to make the best of it."

As they moved on, Holly caught Marveen looking at her reflection in the plate-glass window of an empty storefront. The next three storefronts were empty as well, which left Holly wondering if Bertram Corners' downtown would ever bounce back from the devastating effects of the outlet mall. The outlets attracted shoppers from as far away as Syracuse, but they never seemed to venture beyond the pale gray moat of its vast parking lot.

"We should do another update on the downtown development committee," Holly said. "I don't think they've had a meeting for a year. We could shame them into doing something, even if it's just repainting these trash barrels."

"You can do all the stories you want about this miserable downtown," Marveen said. "The ad revenue has dried up. If it wasn't for the outlets, the paper would have no income at all. I say we admit defeat and move Town Hall into the outlet food court."

Holly couldn't argue with Marveen's logic, but it seemed sad that the town's former economic engine had been usurped by the insatiable desire for cheap tube socks and discount leather goods. She liked a bargain as much as the next person, but the unintended consequences of the "buy cheap" mentality were in front of her every day. As the downtown shops floundered because they didn't have the economies of scale or the access to second-quality goods, their owners and families couldn't even afford to support each other anymore. Now everyone needed cheap tube socks.

Marveen looked at her reflection again as they passed Dunkin' Donuts, and Holly wondered if they should stop and get coffee so that her hands had a job to do when they stopped in to The Gold Depot. When Holly's hands were empty, they tended to travel through space in ways that she herself did not expect, especially around a nice-looking man. But Marveen had charged ahead and held the door to the shop open for Holly.

"You first," she said, smiling broadly. "Remember what you're supposed to say."

Holly edged around Marveen and walked into the gold shop, which had two customers. One was looking in the cases that held old rings, watches, and bracelets, while the other sat at the back with one of the visor-wearing gold appraisers. Both looked up when Holly and Marveen entered, and the woman selling her gold registered a flash of embarrassment at being found there.

"Where is he?" Marveen said. "I thought you said he'd be here."

Holly peeked around the display case but saw no one. "He's got to be around. The boys met him here this morning to work on putting up some flyers."

Just then Racine came in the front door, with Marshall and Connor behind him. Racine had a smile on his face, but both boys looked hot and tired.

"Hi, Holly," Racine said, surprising her with a kiss on the cheek. "You've got some hardworking boys here. I had them all over town."

The kiss threw Holly so much that she stood there without introducing Marveen, who stepped forward with her hand out.

"Hi there, Racine. I'm Holly's friend Marveen. Marveen Langdon. I just wanted to tell you that I'm interested in investing in your next shop. Very interested."

Marveen said all this with the sort of smile on her face that would have made a less confident man blush.

"Nice to meet you, Marveen," he said, shaking her hand. "I'll definitely keep that in mind. Right now I'm focused on getting this place up and running. The traffic's a little slow, but I think the flyers should help."

Holly left Marveen talking to Racine and approached the boys, who had gathered up their backpacks and stood in a corner waiting for someone to transport them somewhere.

"You look exhausted," she said, brushing the hair off Connor's damp forehead. "Did he have you climbing telephone poles or something?"

Marshall gave her his impatient face and pulled on the strap of his backpack. "Can we just go?" he said. "I have band practice later, and I need to learn a part."

"Sure. Let me just tell Marveen."

Once she made sure Marveen didn't mind walking back to the office by herself, Holly ushered the boys out the door.

"I'm wiped," Marshall said as they headed down the street. "He had us go into every store at the outlets and try to talk them into putting up a flyer."

"He was nice, though. And he did buy us Cokes," Connor said.

"Yeah, two Cokes," Marshall said. "Big spender. I was hoping he'd give us a few bucks so I could go to the movies tonight."

Holly was disappointed that Racine had viewed her boys as free labor. She tried to remember whether she had anything in her wallet besides coupons and spare change.

"We could rent a movie," she said, needing to offer something. "You could invite your friends over."

"It's okay, Mom," Marshall said. "I'm tired anyway."

Just as they were about to turn the corner, Racine came running up from behind them.

"Boys, I forgot to pay you," he said, breathing loudly. He handed each one a twenty-dollar bill. "Thanks again for your help today."

"Anytime," Marshall said, glancing at Holly as if to acknowledge that Racine had redeemed himself.

"Thanks!" Connor said, folding his bill and tucking it into his back pocket.

As they walked away, Holly turned her head and caught Racine turning his head to watch them as well. She smiled and she waved and she wondered.

∽

The next weekend, Holly told the boys they were driving to Connecticut to see Celia. Marshall didn't want to go, but Holly convinced him that his grandmother had been missing out by not hearing him play the trumpet for at least a year.

"You want me to bring my trumpet?"

"Of course," she said. "Old people love brass instruments."

Marshall was the best trumpet player in his high school, and he loved his instrument as much—or even more—than his cousin Phoebe loved her trombone. She knew he couldn't pass up a chance to show off.

About halfway to the rehab hospital, Connor leaned toward the front seat. "Where are we going again?"

Connor followed Marshall so blindly that Holly worried he might find himself standing in Marshall's first college dorm room—if she could find a way to send him to college—under the impression that he would be living there, too. Holly's theory was that Connor forced his feet into Marshall's footprints because his father wasn't there to help him set his own course. Connor rode Marshall's old bike and took the same courses he did. He wore his hair the same way—too long—and used the same speech patterns. The exception was the trumpet, which Connor dropped after a year of agonizing lessons. Now he played the clarinet instead.

Holly wondered what Chris would say if he could see them now. She imagined him coming home one day—as if he had been on a long vacation—and noticing the torn wallpaper and the chipped paint, then seeing his boys, practically grown, looking so much like him. Would he fault Holly for their circumstances, or would he understand that she had tried to do her best? Would he worry that his boys didn't have a strong male role model, or would he see as clearly as she did that they were turning out nicely anyway?

Holly filled up the Subaru using a new gas credit card that was approved despite the growing weight of her unpaid debt. The less responsible she was about paying off her credit cards, the more the offers flooded her mailbox: sample drugs for junkies. But sometimes she just didn't question it. When the pump accepted the card, she felt the fear clutching her chest loosen just enough to smile at the boys as they entered the highway on a spectacularly fine day, all azure sky and verdant hills and a smooth ride with the gas tank full.

The wind from the malfunctioning window in the backseat kept them from talking much. A rip in the upholstery left a little cave in the back of the front passenger seat, providing Connor with a place to store the plastic bag of randomly assorted crackers he had found in the bread box. Marshall sat in the front, noodling around on his trumpet, until Holly told him that it sounded too much like a car horn. Along the way they ate the peanut butter and jelly sandwiches Holly had packed and drank apple juice from some miniature boxes she had found in the back of the pantry.

The rehab hospital was in a semirural Connecticut town, and Holly had to drive down a long, steep hill before the closest intersection.

"You shouldn't ride the brakes," Marshall said as they started down the hill. Holly hadn't come up with the money for driver's ed, but ever since Marshall's friends had started driving he'd been correcting her with all the information he picked up from them. "You need to downshift."

"It's an automatic, Marshall."

"But you'll put less wear on the brakes if you put it into the lower gear."

Holly kept heading down the hill, thinking about how much Chris would have loved teaching Marshall to drive.

"What are you going to play for Grandma and her friends?"

"You should be in the lower gear, Mom."

"I've been driving a lot longer than you have."

"But sometimes I know stuff you don't know."

Holly knew this to be true, but she wasn't in the mood to let Marshall tell her what to do.

"How about a John Philip Sousa march? They'd love it."

"I was thinking Cole Porter or maybe Gershwin."

It sometimes surprised Holly that Marshall had knowledge in his head that she herself hadn't provided. At such times she would look at him and see a young man she wasn't sure she knew very well. She could only imagine the stew of images, needs, desires, and impulses simmering in his teenage brain.

"One of Grandma's favorites is a Cole Porter song. 'You're the Top.'"

Marshall picked up his trumpet and began playing "You're the Top" in a plaintive, jazzy variation that made Holly wonder how he spent his afternoons when she was at work.

As they negotiated the last segment of the hill, they could see the more active rehab residents gathered on the porch, all lined up and staring toward the intersection as though they were watching a TV show. The green light turned to yellow before Holly passed through the intersection, but she couldn't stop in time, so she kept going, narrowly missing a car that had been waiting to turn left as the light turned red. Marshall had been right. She should have downshifted.

Holly parked, and they walked toward the main building. As they navigated the maze of wheelchairs on the front porch, Marshall kept his face in a frozen smile, while Connor stared at an old woman who was gumming her own hand. Holly poked Connor in the side.

Marshall and Connor knew that their grandmother, whom they loved, would never be the same after her stroke. Holly didn't want them to be left with a sunken, medicated version that replaced the old Grandma—the one who had pushed them on swings and taken them swimming in cold lake water she called "bracing"—but she felt they were old enough to face her decline. Vivian, Holly thought, would have had a lot to say about medical advances that kept people alive when they might not want to be, given a choice. Holly entered first and straightened out her mother's bedclothes as Marshall and Connor filed in and stood heavily to one side, looking down at their large and ungainly feet. Marshall held his trumpet with one hand, and Holly thought it might slip out of his grasp. He looked upset.

"Say hi to Grandma," she prompted, and both boys came shuffling over to give Celia a loose and tentative hug.

The most significant change in Celia's appearance was the downturn of her mouth on the left side. It gave her face a half-sad, half-confused look, as if the two sides were battling each other for the dominant emotion.

"Pffbbt," Celia said, which Holly sensed was some sort of attempt to acknowledge their presence.

Marshall lifted his gaze, and Holly could tell he was trying to access an inner adult to meet the changes in his grandmother with maturity.

"Hi, Grandma," he said. "I thought I'd play you some Cole Porter."

Marshall lifted the trumpet to his mouth and blew a few practice notes. Within seconds a nurse came running in the door.

"It's naptime for a lot of folks," she said. "Do you mind taking that into the activity room?"

Marshall reddened and lowered his trumpet.

Holly turned to the nurse. "Can we move my mother to a place where Marshall can play?"

The nurse agreed—though Holly thought she was somewhat less than enthusiastic—to put Celia in a wheelchair and bring her to the activity room, which was a large open space filled with tables and chairs, some of them occupied by elderly card players. In one corner a group of women sat in straight-backed chairs and did arm exercises, though their dappled, loose-skinned limbs didn't look strong enough to pick up a bag of groceries. They were led by a middle-aged woman in vintage Jane Fonda attire. Holly could hear her over the recording of Rod Stewart's "Do Ya Think I'm Sexy?" shouting, "Stretch . . . and reach . . . punch left . . . then right . . . and left . . . and right . . . and left . . . and right."

"You can play when the class is over," the nurse said. "They should be finished in a few minutes."

Marshall put his trumpet to his lips and pressed the keys rapidly, though he didn't make a sound. He looked nervous.

When the class ended, everyone in the room turned toward Marshall, whose face was now the color of a bing cherry. He'd performed solos before, but always with the backing of a band that could cover for him if he made a mistake.

Marshall put his horn to his lips and let out a few blahts and bleats to warm up. He was the rare child who connected with an instrument the way some people connect with animals. He spoke its language; he saw it as an extension of himself and practiced without nagging. Holly knew he loved the trumpet, but even she didn't realize how much until he played for his grandmother.

A few crumpled crones in the back were whispering to each other when Marshall hit those long notes in a minor key that signal the beginning of "Summertime." The crones stopped talking and looked up just as Marshall began channeling a grizzled old blues man from Mississippi. He played with authority, filtering the piece through some inner sadness that caught Holly by surprise. He stretched out the low notes creatively and shortened the high notes, giving them unexpected punch. Celia closed her eyes, and the nurse, who was standing behind her, started to hum, not loudly enough to draw everyone's attention, but softly and deeply—driven by some inner vibration. Holly inflated with the pride that every mother feels when her child does something extraordinary. She told herself she wouldn't nag Marshall for a week about his long hair.

When the last solemn notes fell on the crowd, a full second of silence elapsed before the applause. All the spectators smiled, turning and congratulating each other on their mutual good fortune to be awake for such a performance, when Marshall, charged up by the applause, launched into "You're the Top." They all looked toward him again, nodding their feeble heads on necks so reed thin they looked as if they might snap. The music seemed to energize them for a moment, infusing their sallow, sagging skin with pinkish tones. Holly looked around and saw glimmers of memory on each dried-potato face. And then it ended, with the last loud notes of "But if, baby, I'm the bottom, You're the top."

They applauded just as loudly after the second piece, but they seemed a little deflated, as if they couldn't sustain the effort of an extended trip down memory lane. Then Marshall, oblivious to the shifting mood of the audience, dove into a Cole Porter medley. The crowd had been pleased to hear one song and enjoyed the second but now wanted out. They had not been warned that this might be a full-fledged concert. As Marshall busted his way through "I Get a Kick Out of You," one shuffling old man actually left the room with the help of a walker, and Holly could see a few others follow him with jealous eyes.

Holly tried to signal to Marshall that he should wrap it up, but he had his eyes closed, blissfully one with the music. The medley went on for six or seven minutes, significantly past the time an audience starts to resent a musician for enjoying himself so much. When Marshall finished, Holly applauded loudly, but everyone else just nodded and scattered before he could start again.

As the room emptied, Marshall sat down at a nearby card table and played with the spit valve on his trumpet while Connor picked up a throw pillow from a stained couch and swung it a few times, making light-saber noises.

Celia had her eyes closed, and Holly couldn't tell whether she was reliving the performance or had fallen asleep. As they followed the nurse and the wheelchair back to Celia's room, Holly wondered how much longer her mother would exist in this abbreviated state. Would the boys know her longer this way than in her former incarnation as an active member of society? For how many years would they visit her out of obligation before her body let go of its automated functioning? Celia might end up as Vivian's opposite, an inert brain trapped inside a body that wouldn't stop breathing.

On the way home, Holly noticed that Connor was exceptionally quiet in the backseat.

"Everything okay back there?" she said over one shoulder.

"Not really," Connor said.

"I know it's hard seeing Grandma that way, boys. But it's important that she knows we care about her."

"Could she get better?" Connor asked.

Holly didn't know how to answer him. If this was the most they could expect, Celia would have another month or two in the rehab and then be moved to a nursing home to live out her days. Holly didn't know if that was what her mother would have wanted, but since Celia didn't need extraordinary measures to stay alive, they had no choice but to watch and wait.

CHAPTER 11

Holly peered into the windows of The Gold Depot at ten fifteen on a Saturday morning and wondered why the door was locked. She had worked up enough courage to approach Racine about how business was going so she could report back to Vivian, and now she would have to start all over again. A few inches of snow had fallen the night before, so she killed a few minutes making impressions with the waffle bottom of her snow boot while deciding whether or not to splurge on a small coffee at Dunkin' Donuts. Lately, she had been buying Maxwell House instant, which was like drinking hot water that only aspired to be coffee.

Just as she decided to skip the coffee and stop by Vivian's on her way home, Racine came around the corner.

"Holly," he said. "What are you doing here?"

"Just checking on Vivian's investment," she said with an awkward smile. "Don't we open at ten?"

"Totally my fault," Racine said. He opened the door with his key and motioned for her to go inside as he held it. "I drove in from the city this morning and hit some unexpected traffic."

"Do you drive back and forth every day?"

"I usually stay over a few nights at the Homewood Suites, so it's not too bad."

Holly put her purse down on one of the gleaming glass counters. She had to give Racine credit for keeping the store clean and welcoming inside, though she knew many people in town would never cross the threshold to find out. There was still something mildly shameful and moderately humiliating about trading jewelry for cash. As if to dispute her assumption, Narina Patel, the wife of the high school principal, came in the door behind her.

"Hi, Holly," she said. "What are you doing here?"

"I'm helping Vivian. She's one of the store's investors, so she asked me to help get it launched."

"Well, I, for one, think we're long overdue for this place," Narina said. "My relatives keep sending me their broken jewelry to get the best exchange rate, and I've been driving into the city with it. This feels a little safer to me."

Narina took a silk pouch from her purse and spilled its contents on the counter. Heavy gold bangles and hoop earrings chimed on the glass surface.

"Let me help you with that," Racine said, gathering up the jewelry and taking it to one of the booths in the back, where a visored gentleman had suddenly appeared without Holly noticing. As Narina sat down, Racine motioned for Holly to follow him into the rear office, which she did.

"So are you satisfied that we're on the up-and-up?" Racine said, gesturing toward a chair in front of the small office desk. Racine sat on the edge of the desk, which meant that Holly could see the fine weave of the socks he wore with his European shoes.

"I wasn't . . . I mean, I'm sure you're on the up-and-up," Holly said, feeling her cheeks warm.

"But you're wondering—or Vivian is wondering—when she'll see her first dividends," Racine said. He crossed one leg over the other, as if he had all the time in the world for her. This was his gift: to make women of any age feel as if they mattered.

"How old are you, Racine?" Holly asked. "I can't tell. You could be a mature thirty-two or a very well-preserved forty-nine."

"Closer to that second one," he said. "I just turned forty-two."

"Oh good."

"Why is that good?"

Holly thought for a moment. It was good because had he been forty-nine, she might have felt compelled to flirt with him. Even if there were no good foreseeable outcome, she would have given herself the pep talk about diving back into the dating pool—a mental tic that surfaced at the sighting of the rare available man. But since he was her age and no doubt dated women ten or fifteen years younger, she could just keep her fantasies to herself. No harm done.

"It just means that you have some experience in life," she said.

"I do," he said. "Which is why I can tell you that the store is settling in nicely. A few more customers like Mrs. Patel, and we'll be well on our way."

"That's nice to hear," Holly said, though the "well on our way" could mean anything from tomorrow to next year. She avoided looking into his eyes, which were so dark brown that she couldn't distinguish the pupils from the irises.

"No, I mean it," he said. "I know this is important to Vivian, and I'm sure it's important to you as well. I won't let you down."

Holly nodded solemnly. She sensed that Racine had the mistaken impression she would get more out of the gold shop's success than the fee Vivian paid her, but she did nothing to disabuse him of that notion. She had felt lately that the universe didn't much care if her family had a roof over its head or food on the table—maybe the universe was even conspiring to bring her down from the peg to which she had already fallen—so she accepted Racine's concern and pocketed it as insurance for the next truly bad day.

On the way back to her car, Holly stopped at the ATM across the street to view her balance. She was worried a check she had just written to the dentist might have bounced if she hadn't balanced her checkbook to the penny. The machine spit out the receipt showing her balance: $0.00. No more or less. Her eyes remained on the figure. The zeroes reproached her with their clean and final emptiness.

Every dollar of her next paycheck was already assigned to a bill she had yet to pay or a fee she owed for the kids. Again, she came back to the wedding ring in her jewelry box. Selling it might give her a tiny bit of the breathing room she so craved. But again, she couldn't do it. She couldn't imagine herself walking into the gold store and facing the men in the green visors, or leaving the symbol of her marriage behind, destined for the melting pot. She looked at the receipt again and sighed. At least it wasn't less than zero.

Holly opened Vivian's door with her key, then wondered why Vivian even bothered keeping it locked when half the town had keys. Gretchen Carlsbad, who was holding a cell phone near Vivian's mouth, switched hands to wave to Holly as she came in.

"She's talking to my graduate school adviser," Gretchen said in a whisper. "He couldn't believe some of the things I've told him about her."

"Yes, I did graduate from high school," Vivian was saying. "College, too. I have a business degree, which I use every day."

"She's amazing," Gretchen said to Holly. "There's no one like her."

"I know," Holly said, gathering up some used tissues and napkins from the rolling tray near Vivian's head. She had found that the younger the companion, the less likely they were to pick up Vivian's surroundings.

"So that's about all there is to say," Vivian said into the phone. "If you'll excuse me, I'm a little fatigued right now. It's been delightful chatting with you, though."

Vivian closed her eyes as Gretchen put away her phone and picked up her coat and purse.

"I'd love to come again, Vivian," Gretchen said. "You'll let me know if you have any openings on your schedule, right?"

"Of course, dear," Vivian said. "You'll be the first one I call."

Gretchen let herself out as Holly finished cleaning up and brought Vivian some fresh water.

"If she ever comes in here again, I will find a way to pull the plug on this machine with my teeth," Vivian said. "What a bore. And she kept me on the phone with her professor for almost an hour. As if I have nothing better to do. She's trying to squeeze me for information."

Holly looked at the iron lung. "And you're not easy to squeeze."

Vivian's face relaxed. "Of course I am," she said, winking. "I'm full of lemony goodness . . . with very little pulp."

Holly laughed. She knew that Vivian loved to tell her story but loved even more to pretend that it was an imposition.

"So I stopped by the gold place and had a chat with Racine today," Holly said. "He seemed to think you'll be seeing a return on your investment fairly soon."

"Really?" Vivian said. "I wasn't expecting anything right away. I assumed he'd need some time to recoup what he spent on the renovations."

Holly wondered again how Vivian could tie up a significant amount of money without any certainty as to when it would pay off.

"What's the podcast about this week?" Holly asked, hoping to be distracted.

Vivian lifted her eyebrows. "Are you ready for this?"

"I'm ready."

"It's about how even Ivy League graduates don't know when to use 'who' or 'whom.' With all the texting and e-mailing, we judge people more by their grammar now than we ever did before. When you lose the copy editors, you strip naked the power elite. Blockbuster, huh? I'm expecting quite a reaction."

"I like it, but it won't bring back my copy editors," Holly said. "They're a luxury now."

"My point is that the powerbrokers can't hide behind them anymore. People don't come out and say it, but they look down their noses at anyone who breaks a grammatical rule that they happen to know or spells something wrong that they know how to spell. There's no hiding it now, unless you hire someone to proof all your tweets and Facebook posts. Autocorrect doesn't fix everything."

Holly had a Facebook account but rarely looked at it, and she barely knew how to use Twitter, but Vivian was a master of social media. Thousands listened to her weekly podcast.

"Did you see my new generator?" Vivian said, turning her head in the direction of a bright red box about the size of an air conditioner. "I'm told it will keep me going through a Category 4 hurricane that knocks out the power for a week."

"What happens in a Category 5?"

"That was my question. I was told that we've never had one in this part of New York, but I still worry that I'm tempting fate."

"If a Category 5 hurricane hits this town, the only thing left standing will be your house."

"You could be right. Back in the '90s, a tree fell on a transformer and burned three houses to the ground, including the one next door. I remember watching from the window as my parents hosed down the front of the house. I still miss them, Holly. They kept me going through some dark times."

Dark times. Listening to Vivian always made Holly realize that her lot in life, while no red-carpet walk in recent years, could not compare to what Vivian had endured—and risen above. She sat down in the chair closest to Vivian, who had closed her eyes in preparation for one of her epic memories.

"I was seven when they moved my lung back home," she began, her eyes still shut. "My parents took turns at night, each one sleeping for a few hours while the other one sat with me in case my airway had to be cleared. I had chronic bronchitis back then, and all my food had to be pureed so that I wouldn't choke while eating. I was awful sometimes, spitting out mashed peas and sticking my tongue out at my mother when I didn't like something. I remember one time that my mother got fed up with me and threw her dishcloth right over my face. I didn't even try to shake it off; I just cried into it, Holly. It wasn't her fault what happened to me, but I was a miserable piece of work back then. If I had been her, I probably would have strangled me a hundred times over . . . I'm so tired all of a sudden. Can I have my little pillow now?"

Holly placed a flattened water-filled pad under Vivian's head—it prevented bedsores—and put a hand on Vivian's forehead as she closed her eyes. She left her hand there until she saw Vivian's mouth fall open slightly. Because of the iron lung's forced and even respiration, it was sometimes hard to tell when Vivian was asleep, but Holly knew the signs.

As Vivian slept, Holly checked her calendar and saw that Marshall had a rehearsal later that night in preparation for the band's visit to Disney World. She couldn't afford her mortgage or her loans or the car repairs that surely lurked in her not-distant future, but at least she had been able to scrape together the money for Marshall to go on his trip. She would wait as long as possible to tell her sons that their lean existence might get even leaner. If Vivian could live with uncertainty every day, then so could she. She would have to.

CHAPTER 12

Vivian's Unaired Podcast #4

As the country awoke to a wave of radical thinking about civil rights in the early 1960s, I had a revelation myself: I decided that I didn't have to spend my entire life in the same room. With my mother's help, I had enrolled in the community college and attended classes once a week. It was still a huge production to move my iron lung, but the college assisted by paying for a van and staff to move me around and by scheduling classes in places that were accessible to my bulky machine.

Professor Margolis had increased my hours in the computer lab, so with my classes I managed to get out of the house twice a week. My mother fussed and fretted about the jarring trips to and from the van and into the buildings, but that didn't bother me at all. It was freedom, and freedom was all the rage.

The computer lab work I had started at seventeen had tripped some wire in my brain that allowed me to process vast amounts of information and to help the technicians see where the computer—which filled a room on campus—had gone wrong. The machine, of course, was never actually wrong. Programming errors were always to blame, but these could be difficult to spot. My job was to scan hundreds of punch cards—which my mother would place before me in batches of ten—and try to identify the mistake. I loved it. It was like an elaborate game to me, and finding a mistake that could set the computer back on the right path was like winning a prize. I found these only once a month or so, but when I did, Professor Margolis would shout for joy, and the programmers would applaud.

It was exciting work, and I only wished that I could be in the lab every day, but my mother grew weary of the dull job of placing the punch cards in front of my face and moving them when I told her I was ready for another batch. The college couldn't afford to use one of their own employees to watch over me, so my "job" was not much more than an excuse to engage my brain in something greater than self-pity.

At first the college sent a teacher to our house to work with me on my business courses. My mother would listen and take notes and then review them with me before tests and quizzes. She also took dictation if I had to write a paper. But it was taking too long for me to complete just one or two courses, and I wanted more, so I finally convinced my mother to let me line up my classes during one long day of lectures. She still sat with me and took occasional notes, but I had become adept at memorizing information after hearing it only once. It was during this time that my mother took up needlepoint and made elaborate Christmas stockings for every relative we had.

On the first day of my on-campus classes, I brought the entire place to a standstill as my van wheeled up to the door and some college custodians arrived to place a temporary ramp across the stairs to the building. My machine and I were wheeled in through double doors, and I was positioned so that I could see the professor through my angled mirror. My portable generator made a lot of noise, so they parked me toward the back of the lecture hall, which meant that I had very little interaction with students—until one finally approached me in Macroeconomics class.

Her name was Sandy. She was a petite, brown-haired sophomore with glasses that seemed too large for her delicate features. She came up to my mother after class one day and asked my name.

"How kind," my mother said. "This is Vivian."

I smiled at Sandy, but only politely. It had been my experience that curiosity seekers or dare takers would approach me for a lark—let's see if she can talk like a normal person—but they never returned once their curiosity had been satisfied or the dare met. But Sandy wasn't one of those.

"Hi, Vivian," she said to me. "I'm Sandy. Are you enjoying the class? What do you think of Professor Simpson?"

"I'm glad I'm not sitting in the front row," I said, rolling my eyes. "I can see him spitting from back here."

Sandy laughed and looked at my mother as if she needed her permission to keep talking. My mother nodded.

"He's definitely a sprayer," Sandy said. "I have one of those for Shakespeare, too."

"Are you an English major?"

"I think so. I'm still deciding between English and history, but I know I should take some business classes, too. Most of my friends are secretaries."

"I thought about that, too," I said, giving my genuine smile so that she knew I could joke about my own condition. "But I'm a terrible typist."

She laughed again, and I felt triumphant, as I always did when I managed to make someone reasonably comfortable in my shocking presence. But just as quickly, I found myself wishing once again that I could behave like a normal college student—maybe go out for coffee or dinner with people my own age instead of having my mother stuck to my iron lung like a human-sized magnet. The resentment I felt toward her at seventeen had not completely subsided.

"Mother," I said, and I never called her "mother." "Would you get me some cold water?"

My mother hesitated but finally went off to fill up my cup from a water fountain.

"So what's this really like?" Sandy said, tapping the iron lung. "Can you feel anything in there? Your arms? Your toes?"

"Nada. Crazy, huh? But this happened when I was six, so I'm used to it."

"It's such a trip. You're so normal."

"Most of what makes a person a person is upstairs anyway. It took me a long time to understand that."

"Hey, a bunch of us are going to form a study group for this class. Want to come?"

I hesitated. I couldn't ask my mother to cart me to the college more than twice a week; my travel days were taxing her as it was.

"What day do you meet?"

"We'll start next week. Right after this class."

"That could work. But it depends on where you're meeting, too. I don't fit through most doors."

"I'll see what we can work out. We'll talk again next week."

"Sounds good," I said, almost unable to believe that a college student could be so kind as to include me—the horizontal freak—in any kind of group. But when my mother returned with my water, I didn't mention Sandy's invitation. Better to let it slip when she couldn't do much about it.

A week later, I could barely listen to the professor in Macroeconomics as I schemed about how I could get my mother to leave me with a group of strangers. I knew she would want to go home right after class, but I also knew she would cave if I pressed her hard enough. On top of that, I worried that Sandy would forget her offer or that the other study group members would object to having me along.

But when the class was over, Sandy came straight over and said the group had decided to meet right in the lecture hall. Four other students came up behind her and took seats near my iron lung. My mother looked at me with concern, but I gave her my prepared speech.

"Mom, Sandy just offered to let me join her study group. Why don't you go to the cafeteria and relax while we study? You can come back for me in an hour, and we'll head home."

I had expected resistance, but my mother clearly couldn't believe that these students would see past my machine and allow me to mix with them.

She leaned down, her lips to my ear. "Vivian, are you sure?"

"I'm sure, Mom," I said. "Let me try."

So she left me that first day, and I became a valuable member of the study group—valuable mostly because I understood the material without even looking at it twice, and some in the group seemed to be math-challenged. I would often clarify points for them that the professor had "sprayed" in a particularly confusing way. By the end of the semester, we had all become familiar enough to know each other's stories on top of knowing a little more about economics.

After the final, we had a little party in the lecture hall, and my mother left as usual to drink her Coke and do needlepoint in the cafeteria. Ian, one of the study group members, pulled out a bottle of vodka half a second after my mother left the room. He also had some plastic cups and a couple bags of chips.

The study group members dug into the chips and passed around the bottle of vodka until each had a small plastic cup about halfway full.

"What about me?" I said. "Don't I get any?"

I don't know what made me say it except that I so badly wanted them to keep thinking of me as a friend. I had never had alcohol before; a normal teenager would have found a way to test the waters, but I couldn't even drink water without help.

"I don't think that's a good idea, Vivian," Sandy said. "What would your mother say?"

"It's fine," I lied. "I drink all the time. They give me vodka to help me sleep."

They bought it, and someone ran to the cafeteria for a straw. Sandy put a small amount of vodka in a glass and put the straw into my mouth. I pulled on it a little too quickly and flooded my mouth with what tasted like turpentine to my virginal taste buds. I coughed and choked.

"Oh my God, Vivian," Sandy said. "Should we get your mother?"

I shook my head and through sheer force of will stopped coughing.

"I'm fine. I want another sip," I said, now that I could feel a sudden warmth traveling down my esophagus and radiating, or so I imagined, through my internal organs. It seemed like a miracle that alcohol—which my parents didn't allow in their home—could connect me to my inert body in such a profound way.

Sandy held the straw to my lips, and I took a smaller drink this time, feeling the chemical rush as it rose through the top of my head. I thought I might never have the chance to drink again, so I nodded toward the glass, and Sandy held it up again, though reluctantly.

"Be careful, Vivian," she said. "This stuff will get you looped in no time."

"I don't care," I said as the vodka gave me courage and bent my perception of time. The consequences seemed far away, which made them appear smaller.

An hour later, my mother returned to load me back into the van. As soon as she walked in the door, all the other students scattered, with the exception of Sandy, who, even in an inebriated state, wouldn't have left me to face the music alone.

"Hel-lo, muvver," I said.

My mother knew instantly what had happened and gave Sandy a look that might have stopped a freight train.

"Young lady," she said, her voice shaking. "I counted on you to look after Vivian. What could you have been thinking?"

Sandy could have told her how I lied about my drinking habits, but she was too nice for that. She simply hung her head and apologized before slinking off behind her friends. She never spoke to me again.

After that, I wasn't allowed to meet with other students without my mother present, which meant that no student ever approached me again. I went to my classes, did my job, and eventually graduated with an associate's degree in business. For what, I had no idea.

CHAPTER 13

The *Chronicle* hit mailboxes each Thursday, which meant that Fridays were usually a light day, but Holly didn't have time to visit the gold shop. She had to pick up Desdemona at the train station before meeting Henderson at the rehab hospital. They all needed to sit down together to review their mother's situation, since the hospital had determined that her progress had plateaued.

Holly arrived at the station a few minutes early, so she called home to make sure Connor had remembered to take the bus home. He sometimes forgot what day of the week it was.

"Hello?"

"Hi, Connor, it's Mom. Just wanted to make sure you got home okay."

"Yeah, I'm here. Hey, what did we have for dinner last night? I can't remember, and I have to write it down for Health."

Holly hated these assignments, which felt expressly designed to make her feel like a bad mother. They always seemed to fall on weeks when she couldn't get to the grocery store and resorted to cheese quesadillas or spaghetti with sauce from a jar. She imagined that the mothers of her sons' friends cooked only grass-fed beef, quinoa, and organic vegetables, or soy-based imitations of real food: tofurkey and veggie burgers. These were the mothers who shopped at Trader Joe's and

Whole Foods and frowned at the cupcakes at school events as if they were poison.

"Write down that we had chicken, brown rice, and broccoli," Holly said.

"But we—"

"Just write that down. I'll cook tonight, so it won't be fibbing. I'll be back after I see Grandma, okay?"

"Sure, but I don't think I like brown—"

"Bye, hon," Holly said as the train pulled into the station.

Desdemona was invisible in the rush of people who got off the train, until they dispersed like gas molecules and she emerged, a waifish figure holding an oversized tote bag and blinking in the fading light. Holly, who had been circling the no-parking zone, opened the window and waved until Desdemona noticed her and came toward the car.

"Hi," Desdemona said, climbing in. Neither one spoke much on the way to the rehab hospital. Holly quietly wondered if Henderson, who had taken it upon himself to retrieve Celia's checkbook and bank statements, would be upset that their mother had been helping Holly with her mortgage for the past year. The well-off version of Henderson she had always known wouldn't have begrudged her, but she didn't know how the bankrupt Henderson might react.

When Holly and Desdemona arrived, Henderson was already waiting in the lobby. He led them to a small conference room that had surely been used many times for the same conversation among siblings. Henderson said little as he laid out several folders and a spreadsheet on the table.

"So here's the bottom line," he said, adjusting the papers and folders so they were at right angles with the edge of the table. "Mom qualifies to move to a nursing home after the rehab stint, but she'll have to pay out of pocket until she empties her savings. But once she's in, she'll be covered until she dies."

It wasn't that Holly was surprised by this news, because she knew from her friends how the insurance system worked. But she was startled to hear Henderson—the momma's boy—say "until she dies" in such a flat and unemotional way.

"Oh," Desdemona said, putting a hand over her mouth.

"Is there anything else we can do?" Holly asked. Her neck felt stiff, and her finger joints ached, as if she had become elderly that instant, taking her mother's place in the world.

"Unless one of us wants to care for her at home—and that would mean paying for outside nursing care—we really don't have a choice," Henderson said.

"So there's nothing?" Desdemona said. "Nothing left?"

Holly knew what she meant. Their parents had been wealthy, but unless their mother died before the funds were depleted, none of them would see a dime. It was another step in acknowledging that she alone was responsible for keeping her small family afloat.

"What's left will go to Mom's care in all likelihood," Henderson said, his voice growing thick. "Dad built a business and worked like crazy for forty years, all so a bunch of strangers can keep Mom's body functioning for the next ten while her brain barely registers that she's alive. It doesn't make sense."

"No, it doesn't," Desdemona said, swallowing audibly. "I guess I always thought I'd be able to move out of that dinky apartment some-day. Not that I was waiting for an inheritance, but it seemed like they had plenty saved."

"They did, although some of us took a little inheritance before all this happened," Henderson said, giving Holly a look. She felt the recrimination right down to her core.

"I'm sorry I didn't tell you about it," Holly said. "I never thought we'd be in this situation."

It had never occurred to her that her siblings would one day resent her mother's generosity.

"I get that you must have needed it, Holly, but Des and I won't get the same kind of help, even though we both need it."

"I know that now, but you didn't need it until recently," Holly said, feeling sick to her stomach. "And as far as I knew, neither did Desdemona. I just assumed she was happy with her small apartment."

"Well, now you know," Desdemona said, her voice even smaller than usual. "I wake up every night when my upstairs neighbor flushes his toilet. Think about where we grew up, Holly."

Silence flooded the space around them as Holly remembered her parents' formal dining room and circular driveway, their father's paneled den, and the family playroom. It all seemed impossibly posh and warm and out of reach. She was now the same age as her father when he bought his first Mercedes, and she couldn't even keep up with the mortgage on a small, rundown house.

Then again she had few friends who lived the kind of life she had once known. Financial security seemed like something that existed for a few decades after World War II and then evaporated even as people continued to believe they could attain it. She dated her disillusionment to the second year after Chris's death, when his life insurance was dwindling and she realized she would always be just one step ahead of the debt collectors and might remain there until the lid closed on her, just as it had on Aunt Muriel in her unpaid-for casket. She had applied for countless better-paying jobs and never got anywhere. Her chosen profession had been slashed and burned until it was unrecognizable, and yet she had no other skills or experience, so she held on like a polar bear clinging to a shrinking ice floe. She realized, too, that she had reached that stage of maturity where she knew she could survive on very little. But her boys and their future were a different story.

"It sucks, girls," Henderson said finally, putting his spreadsheet back into one of the folders. "We are the victims of an economic rout and some very bad timing."

"How are you holding up?" Desdemona asked him. "How's Phoebe?"

"She asked me if I was poor the other day," he said, leaning back in his chair with a small smile. "Not if 'we' were poor, but if 'I' was poor, because she knows her mother has family money."

"What did you say?" Holly asked. "I've been dreading that same conversation with the boys."

"I told her that I had hit a rough patch, but that I would bounce back as soon as I could. And she told me she appreciated my candor. A twelve-year-old used the word 'candor.'"

"She's always had a big vocabulary," Desdemona said.

"Then she asked me if she could still take private trombone lessons. That killed me right there, I'm not gonna lie. It's like forty bucks an hour."

"So what did you say?" Holly asked.

"I told her we'd find a way to pay for her lessons."

Desdemona and Holly both nodded in sympathy, knowing that was what he would say.

"Then I had to call my ex-father-in-law and practically beg for the money," Henderson said, his chin quivering. "I *hate* this. And I hate that Mom is in that bed. That she can't talk to us. That she can't keep living her life."

"We know you do, Hen," Holly said. "And if I could pay back that money I borrowed from Mom, you know I would. Right?"

Desdemona nodded. Henderson sighed and ran his fingers hard across his eyebrows, then rubbed his temples.

"I'll sign the papers," Henderson said, standing up to go. "They're moving her next week."

CHAPTER 14

On Saturday, Holly let the boys sleep in and drove downtown to The Gold Depot. Inside were two middle-aged men in running pants and windbreakers looking like they had taken a detour while jogging; an elderly woman clutching a canvas bag to her chest while she waited for an appraisal; and the Sister Sisters, who were each unwrapping a butterscotch candy.

"Holly, dear," one of the sisters said, waving her over. "Vivian assured us that this business is not one of those scammers. She told us she's an investor and that you're helping with it. So we're here to cash in our trinkets. We realized we could send the money to a mission in Africa."

"What a lovely thing to do," Holly said. "But I hope you're not giving up anything special. Once it's gone, it's gone, you know. They melt most of it down."

One of the sisters pulled a plastic bag out of her purse and showed Holly a tangle of thin chains and gold crosses of various sizes.

"People give us crosses all the time, and we can only wear one," said the sister holding the bag. "We each picked our favorite, and now we can turn these into something useful. We're hoping we can buy a cow."

Holly had written enough about the charities that supplied animals to poor families to know that they could afford a scraggly flock of chickens, maybe a goat, but she said nothing. Racine, who was behind the counter showing a watch to one of the joggers, caught her eye and nodded toward the back office.

Holly went to the office and examined her cuticles as she waited for Racine, who came in about five minutes later. When he saw Holly, he ran a hand over his hair and smiled.

"That was our opening rush," he said. "I've had customers waiting for me to unlock the doors for the last few days. I guess the word is getting out."

"If the Sister Sisters are here, you're in," Holly said. "They talk to everyone. And their cash is going to charity, so maybe you can give them an extra good price."

Racine went out and spoke into the ear of the appraiser sifting through the sisters' gold, then came back into the office.

"We'll take care of them," he said. "They look like sweet old ladies."

"Don't let their looks fool you," Holly said. "They've been on missions all over the world. I heard that one of them worked with Mother Teresa in Calcutta."

Racine shook his head, smiling. "I really like this town. You all look out for each other."

"We do," Holly said, a bit surprised that Racine would even notice how the town functioned outside the doors of the gold store.

"Hey, I notice you haven't traded in any gold since we opened. We'd definitely give you a good price."

Holly didn't want to admit that she had traded in her small stash of jewelry long before Racine's shop had opened in town. The total take had been seventy-eight dollars. She thought about the wedding ring again, wondering what it would actually bring in, but she pushed the thought away.

"So business is picking up then?"

"No question," Racine said. "We're in a great spot, and the price of gold has been climbing steadily since we opened. In a few months, I'll probably hire a store manager and open another store. These upstate New York towns have a lot of potential."

Holly felt a little let down. Not that she expected Racine to stick around Bertram Corners, but she didn't realize he would be gone so soon.

"You look disappointed," he said, laughing. "It's good news for Vivian that things are going so well."

"No, of course," she said quickly, trying to sound upbeat. "She'll be glad to hear that."

Just then the front door opened, and a couple came inside with a shopping bag that looked heavy, containing perhaps a tea set or a candelabra.

"Back to work," Racine said, heading back out the door. He turned around, though, and leaned his head against the doorframe. His hand came up toward his hair, but he put it down again.

"Hey, would you like to have dinner with me?" he said, flashing the smile that no doubt was responsible for half the customers in the store, maybe even the joggers.

"Oh," Holly said, completely unprepared for the question, though Racine appeared to assume she meant "yes."

"Today's out because I have a meeting back in the city later," he said. "But how about Friday?"

She did a mental inventory of her closet and almost said no because she had nothing to wear but then realized she could borrow something from Marveen.

"Sure," she said, exiting the office behind him. "So Friday then."

She looked back on her way out of the shop, but Racine was already deep in conversation with the heavy bag couple, and so she couldn't ask him what time on Friday or where they should meet, but she supposed that such details could be worked out later. Her social skills predated her marriage and were therefore primitive by modern standards. Of course, she thought, he would e-mail or text or call her with the particulars, which meant she would be waiting all week and worrying about a date that he would most likely cancel if a better offer came along.

In the years since Chris died, Holly had gone on a few dates—mostly blind ones arranged by well-meaning friends—but had remained more or less alone. At first there was simply too much grief, and then there were too many obligations, but as the boys got older, she felt even more constrained. In part, she didn't see too many opportunities in a small town where most of the men in her acceptable age range were either married or so obviously undateable that they were out of the question. But mainly she worried that the boys would find it upsetting to see her dating someone, attempting to replace their father with some inevitably inferior model. In the boys' minds, their father was something of a tragic hero who had died before he could fulfill all his good intentions of playing ball with them and teaching them how to drive. She bore some responsibility for the deification, because she often pointed out what their father might have said or done had he been alive.

"Dad would have been so proud of you tonight," she told Marshall at his last band concert. "He loved the trumpet."

Chris had loved the trumpet no more than he had loved the oboe or the saxophone—he could tolerate jazz but hated classical music—but she somehow couldn't help herself from creating this custom-made persona for the benefit of her boys, since Chris would never be around to dispute it. All of that meant that any man she dated or married would never live up to the über-Chris, even perhaps in her own mind.

But Racine was different. He wasn't a real person in the Bertram Corners sense. He didn't have dirt under his fingernails or drive a pickup, and he didn't worship at the altar of chicken wings. Holly saw him as the modern-day version of the charming traveling salesman who wouldn't be around long enough to complicate her life or the life of her children. She imagined, based on nothing more than their few interactions, that he was the kind of person who didn't know what he wanted but knew what he didn't want: commitment, tradition, sticky-handed family gatherings. At another time in her life, she would have shied away from him, but she decided that even a temporary respite from her troubles could be almost like joy itself. And if that was asking too much, at least she'd get a good meal out of it.

⌒

That afternoon, Holly received her first call from the bank. The loan officer was Vince Romano, whom she had known since high school.

"We're a little concerned," Vince said, "that you only sent in half your mortgage payment, and the rest is quite late."

"I know, Vince. I'm so sorry about that. I'm having a little cash-flow problem, but I'll work it out."

"You understand that you'll be hit with a penalty, right, Holly? That'll make it even harder to pay next month."

"I get it, Vince, but I just don't have the money right now. If I did, believe me you would have a check in your hand."

Vince paused for a moment, and Holly could hear him shuffling some papers.

"I see that you also took out a small home equity loan a while back," he said.

"Yes, and I paid the interest on it this month. I remember sending that check."

"If you can't pay the mortgage, you might want to delay any improvements you were planning. Housing prices have been falling recently, and you might want to keep those funds liquid so you don't lose the house."

Those words. *Lose the house.*

Holly bent over, unable to keep her head balanced on her shoulders. She felt dizzy. "Are you telling me you're going to foreclose when I'm late to pay just one time, Vince?" Holly said, because the home equity loan money had been used long ago to pay down some of her credit card debt. "Is that what you're telling me?"

This time she pictured the boys under an overpass, shivering in their garbage-bag raincoats. She would not allow it.

"Not right away. But if you go another few months without a mortgage payment, we'll have to start foreclosure proceedings. This is a bank, Holly, not a charity."

It stunned her that people now used the word "charity" in an almost pejorative sense, as in, we can't afford to give our money away like those sloppily managed organizations that toss it out like bubble-gum at a parade.

"I can't lose the house, Vince. I'll do everything I can to catch up."

Holly hung up the phone with a trembling hand, wondering what to do. She went upstairs to her bedroom, opened her jewelry box and pawed through it, teary eyed, only to realize what she already knew. There was nothing of value left except for the plain gold wedding band. She took out the ring, laid it on her palm, and examined the dull yellow gold and the inscription inside. "Chris and Holly. 1990." Was this the only thing standing between her and stalling foreclosure? When Holly was a teenager and a college student, her goals were ethereal, though she didn't know it then. She wanted to make the world a better place by writing about it, telling its stories with what one of her journalism professors had called her gift of writing with great sensitivity toward her subjects. She wore, for example, her frumpiest and least attractive coat when covering a story at the homeless shelter, where the residents were so frail, almost boneless, that they looked as if they had been filleted from their skeletons.

Now, her goals had become crude and basic. To maintain their home. To stay out of said homeless shelter. To keep her boys from being filleted and boneless. To prevent her children from knowing just how poor they might become.

Connor walked in the open door as she was wiping her eyes and shutting the ring in the box once more, though he didn't seem to notice.

"I have a cold, Mom," he said, sitting down on the bed. At thirteen, he was still on that fulcrum between boyhood and manhood during which sickness easily tipped him toward the former. She smoothed back the bangs on his forehead to check for a fever and felt the cool expanse of his unblemished skin—a blank canvas for all the acne and misery that would surely visit him in the next few years.

"Poor baby," she said. "Get into bed, and I'll bring you some tea."

"I'm not that sick," he said, suddenly shaking off the boy to her regret. "I'm going to Jason's this afternoon. He's got a new game."

"Okay, hon. Hope you feel better. Is Marshall still asleep?"

"No, he's been gone for a while. He had band practice, I think."

Connor headed back out the door. Holly didn't know that Marshall had band practice, although she had admittedly fallen a little behind on her son's complicated schedule. In addition to the trip to Disney World, he had to prepare for the SATs, practice driving with his friend's father so he could get his license when she had the money for his state-mandated classes and insurance, and start looking at colleges. Connor, of course, was right behind him. Every check she wrote for Marshall would have to be written again a few years later.

In the spirit of spending as little as possible on herself when her boys needed so much, Holly dug through her underwear drawer until she found a decent black bra that was too small to be comfortable but could be forced into service, and a pair of underwear with a navy-blue pattern that could read as black in a dark room. Now she was set for even the most unlikely outcome of her date and hadn't spent a penny.

CHAPTER 15
Vivian's Unaired Podcast #5

In 1970 we moved from the farm into Bertram Corners—a Podunk town, but a town nonetheless. My father's arthritis had worsened, and he could no longer farm. My mother wanted to be closer to church so that she could attend on Sundays without leaving me for too long, but I think she also had an ulterior motive: she wanted the church and its doers of good deeds to be closer to me.

My parents sold the farm to a developer looking to put forty houses on the fields where several generations had grown corn and pastured cows. When I was young, my father would say he'd never sell, that the land was his legacy, and that it shouldn't be carved up into a bunch of identical lots and paved over with macadam, that its value and its majesty was in its openness and all those things that farmers who make a living wage can afford to say. But as he aged, those ideals receded with his hairline. He had no one to leave the farm to anyway.

The little Cape house my parents bought in Bertram Corners had to be modified for my iron lung—the doors widened, a ramp built, the electrical system updated for my generator. I know my father missed his arms-wide-open-width view of green fields and distant, blue rolling hills, but I loved being able to see the neighbors walk by on the sidewalk outside the living-room window. I felt less isolated, even if few people in town knew I was lying there behind the white clapboards, alive only because a machine forced my lungs to expand and contract.

Within weeks of our move, my mother became a much more active member of St John the Apostle Church and volunteered our house as a staging area for a clothing drive. That was her way of getting some church members over to meet me without it seeming like she was asking for something.

I was, as before, the unavoidable centerpiece of the living room. The door to the biggest bedroom had been widened, but there seemed little point in wheeling my heavy machine to and from the bedroom to create the pretense of privacy. On the closing day of the clothing drive, my mother and father pushed my gurney a little closer toward the window so that the church ladies would be able to sort through the donated clothes on the floor.

"We'll have some company," my mother said that morning before the church ladies arrived. "Won't that be nice?"

I wondered why this would be nice for me. I couldn't help sort clothes, couldn't lug bags or boxes, couldn't drink the pink lemonade my mother had made unless someone thought to bring it to me with a straw. Though it took some effort, I tried to sound positive anyway.

"Sure, it'll be nice," I said.

My mother brightened so visibly that I became painfully aware of how rarely I made the conscious choice to behave kindly toward her. I felt a jolt of guilt that my mother's whole life had been spent catering to someone who had to make a special effort just to be agreeable in her presence.

When the women arrived with their bags and boxes of donated clothing, they all appeared to have been warned in advance about my condition, though one put a hand to her mouth when she first laid eyes on my iron lung. Being women of the church, they all tried to be charitable.

"So Vivian," said the youngest one, who was wearing a pink minidress that was not flattering to her thighs, "how do you like our little town?"

I looked over at my mother. She usually rescued me from boneheaded attempts to pretend that I was normal, but she was busy setting up a system to categorize the donated clothes.

"From what I've been able to see, I like it just fine," I told Thunder Thighs, thinking my mother would be proud that I had harnessed my sarcasm.

"I know it's small," she said, "but we do have a movie theater and some nice little diners, and you should see the town picnic we have on Memorial Day."

As I looked toward the ceiling—it was so hard for me to get out of a conversation—another woman came over. She was about my mother's age and wore a light blue pantsuit with matching light blue eye shadow.

"Hi, Vivian," she said, standing just in the right place so that I could see her face through my mirror. "I see you've met Bernadette. I'm Charlotte. I'm in charge of the lay ministry at the church. Bernadette, why don't you help with the sorting?"

Bernadette waddled off, leaving me with the pastel-enrobed Charlotte, who looked like she had something to say.

"Your mother has been telling me that you're a bit isolated here," she said. "How would you feel about joining our Bible study group? We could meet at your house so it wouldn't require transporting you to the church."

Everything I knew about the Bible came from the children's version my mother used to read to me when everyone assumed I'd never need the adult version anyway. I was mildly curious about the "fire and brimstone" sections I'd heard about, but I hadn't bothered to read them for myself.

"Sure," I said. "I'd like to learn more about the Bible, and I'm sure my mother would love the company."

"That's wonderful," Charlotte said, waving my mother over. "Vivian has agreed to study the Bible with us. I'm so pleased."

My mother looked as if she'd swallowed a hard candy whole.

"Well," she said. "That's just . . ."

She looked as if she could not come up with a suitable word. Charlotte plunged ahead.

"It's all settled," she said. "Do Thursdays work for you? Seven?"

My mother nodded her head and went back to her sorting, giving me sideways glances every now and again.

I'd had a rocky relationship with God, who naturally had been petitioned, summoned, bargained with, and, frankly, begged to make me better, all to no avail. My parents fell to their knees every night before bed, and whole churches had been asked to remember me in their prayers, but I had seen no evidence that God deemed me worthy of his attention. Still, I hadn't quite given up. I guess some small part of me wanted to think that God, if He chose, could step in and perform the miracle that would take me out of the machine forever—or even for five minutes. If there was some secret code in the Bible that allowed one to jump to the front of the miracle line, I wanted to find out what it was.

⌒

The Bible study group—Charlotte and about a half dozen other women—showed up at the appointed hour on Thursday. My mother had arranged some chairs into a semicircle, with my lung completing the loop. Charlotte introduced the other women, whose names I promptly forgot, and then opened her Bible and announced that we would be discussing a passage from the Gospel of John. She read aloud:

"For God so loved the world, that he gave his only begotten Son, that whosoever believeth in him should not perish, but have everlasting life. For God sent not his Son

into the world to condemn the world; but that the world
through him might be saved."

"Let's start with Vivian," Charlotte said. "What does this verse mean to you?"

I glanced at my mother, who looked liked she wanted to dive under the couch in case I tossed a grenade and blew up her nice little gathering. But the passage didn't bring out my cynical side. It gave me pause.

"I'd like to think that this means something more than, literally, if you don't believe in Jesus, you're doomed," I said. "I think it's more like God saying, 'I was willing to give up my own child, I loved the world that much.'"

"Beautifully said, Vivian," Charlotte said.

I nodded, and then the pious women of Bertram Corners talked about how devoted they were to believing in Jesus and snagging a piece of that everlasting pie. They didn't use those words, of course, but it seemed to me that one was trying to out-Jesus the other.

Despite my suspicions about the Bible group's motivations, I felt the sudden light of what I can only describe as a religious insight coming over me. I could love Jesus, too, I thought. I could convince myself that God sent his only son to the world to be tortured and killed as a way of saving humanity. And if I did this throughout the years left ahead of me, maybe I could step right up to an eternal life that did not require a generator and pureed food. Everlasting was a long time—a time that would make this life, my aborted existence, seem like the flash of a camera bulb.

When the women left, I toyed with the idea of turning myself over to Jesus, who had, after all, cured the sick, made the blind see, fed a multitude with just a few fish and a few loaves of bread. He taught humankind that the lowliest among us would have the best seats in the house once this blip of a life was over. I found solace in that thought. Maybe suffering—and who else suffered more than I did?—was just a ticket to the VIP lounge in heaven.

This beatific mood lasted into the next day, during which my mother kept taking my temperature because she couldn't understand why I was so quiet and cooperative. She finally asked me if anything was bothering me.

"I don't know, Mom," I said quietly. "I guess I'm willing to look into the whole Jesus thing. I want to believe that I can live another life. This one has been so hard."

My mother put down the thermometer on my tray and laid her hand across my forehead. "Darling girl," she said.

In that moment, I was her darling girl again. I was the toddler who followed Darlene into the barn to watch her swing on the rope tied to the distant rafters; I was the four-year-old who demanded that my father take the training wheels off my bike so I could ride like my sister; I was the child who fell asleep in my mother's arms as she read to me. No matter how sharply my life had diverged from the one that darling girl had been expected to live, she hadn't disappeared completely.

My baby steps toward Christ lasted right up until I asked my mother to let me read the Bible in preparation for the next meeting. I asked her to randomly flip through the pages and to fix the Bible in the overhead frame that held my books. When she did, I came upon this passage in Deuteronomy:

> *The Consequences of Disobedience*
>
> *But it shall come to pass, if thou wilt not hearken unto the voice of the LORD thy God, to observe to do all his commandments and his statutes which I command thee this day; that all these curses shall come upon thee, and overtake thee:*
>
> *Cursed shalt thou be in the city, and cursed shalt thou be in the field.*
>
> *Cursed shall be thy basket and thy store.*
>
> *Cursed shall be the fruit of thy body, and the fruit of thy land, and the increase of thy kine, and the flocks of thy sheep.*

Cursed shalt thou be when thou comest in, and
cursed shalt thou be when thou goest out.

I brought it up when the group met on Thursday night, asking whether or not the vindictive Old Testament God could be reconciled with the forgiving New Testament God.

"I'm confused. This seems to be saying that if you slip once on 'Honor thy father and mother,' you're cursed for life," I said. "That seems a little harsh to me. Wouldn't most of us already be doomed?"

Charlotte looked around the circle but no one ventured to say anything.

"The commandments are pretty clear and basic," Charlotte finally said. "This is just reinforcement for doing the right thing."

"But what if you violate 'Thou shalt not steal' because your kids are starving?" I said. "Isn't there some kind of flexibility there?"

"Jesus is love," ventured a soft-spoken woman I'd never noticed before, but Charlotte jumped in before she could continue.

"We don't generally dip into the Old Testament, Vivian," she said.

"But it's the majority of the Bible," I said. "Don't you have to study the whole thing?"

"The New Testament is more relevant to Father's sermons. He usually tells us what he's reading for the next week's Mass, and we follow along. It helps us get more out of the service."

My mother excused herself to get more lemonade as I thought about whether or not it was worth arguing. The lightness that had filled my heart drained out of me just as quickly as it had entered. I continued to read the Bible on my own, but my mother had to tell the study circle that I was no longer interested in joining them. Maybe I gave up too fast, but something told me that "studying" the Bible wasn't compatible with asking questions, and so I let the devout women of St. John the Apostle move on to another charity case.

CHAPTER 16

Holly was fairly sure that her date with Racine would be a disaster. For one thing, their names were incompatible. Hers was solidly American and redolent of Christmas, while his seemed foreign and risky, with no trace of the Midwestern city from whence it came. She couldn't see it on a party invitation: "Let's watch the Super Bowl together—Holly and Racine." They were like bologna and foie gras. But she had borrowed a dress from Marveen for the occasion—a simple black A-line that was probably the most boring thing Marveen owned—which meant that Marveen wouldn't hear of it when Holly mentioned in the office that she might cancel.

"Oh no you don't," Marveen said. "He might be a player, but if you don't go I will never let you forget it."

"I haven't had a date in so long," Holly said, groaning. "I don't even know how to act. Am I supposed to offer to pay for dinner? Half?"

Portia, who had come up behind them, offered her perspective as a young single woman. "If he asked you out, then he pays," she said as though this were common knowledge. "Especially on a first date."

Holly was relieved, since she didn't think any of her credit cards were below their limits, and she had nothing in her wallet but some change.

Late in the afternoon, Marveen came into her office with a box of hair dye and a tote bag full of hair-related electric appliances.

"This is an intervention," Marveen said. "You cannot go on a date with your hair like that. You have some grays that have been driving me crazy for a year now, so I'm helping both of us."

Holly put a hand to the top of her head. "I know it's bad, but I can't afford the hairdresser anymore. I cut it myself when it gets too long."

Marveen dropped the tote bag. "Christ, Holly," she said, "that is indefensible."

An hour and a half later, Holly's shoulder-length hair was dyed an even, dark brown, trimmed of its split ends, blow-dried, flat-ironed, curled, teased, and tousled to look as if she just woke up that way. Then the whole elaborate illusion was locked into place with industrial-strength hairspray. She almost didn't recognize herself.

"You're good, Marveen," she said into the small mirror in the office bathroom. "You could open your own shop."

"I just had the same thought," Marveen said, gazing at her handiwork. "You look like a million bucks right now."

And Holly felt, if not like a million bucks, then at least like a hundred grand. She put on the dress Marveen had loaned her, black tights, heels, and some silver-toned hoop earrings she had found in her jewelry box while rooting around for gold. She was thinner than she'd ever been, due to obsessive fretting, which ironically may have been one of the reasons Racine found her attractive.

She felt put together but not beautiful, although she could remember two other days in her life during which she had embodied that coveted adjective. One was during college when she had left her dorm room in a new blue T-shirt that brought out the color of her eyes. Her hair had been freshly washed and dried, long and straight and shining, and she had just had her teeth cleaned the day before—the coffee and Tab stains polished away. She remembered turning into the sunlight on her way to an art history class, smiling at no one and for no reason except that she felt she had never looked better—a realization that arrived with the knowledge that she would likely never look that good again, except maybe on her wedding day, when a whole team of experts would be brought in to assist.

But she did, in fact, look even better on a particular day ten years later when she was a young mother on a trip to the Bronx Zoo with Marshall's preschool. She had lost her baby weight from Connor and had the postpartum boost in hair thickness. Both boys had slept through the night, giving her a burst of energy. They had stopped to look at the elephants when a photographer started snapping her picture with them. She looked toward the clicking noise, and he caught her eye. He said nothing, only smiled and nodded, but in that nod she knew that she had attained—in that moment, at that angle, in that particular light—some measure of loveliness that only visited normal people on rare occasions. She remembered wondering what it might feel like—the magic and the burden—of being beautiful all the time.

"If Racine wasn't taking you out, I'd date you myself," Marveen said, stepping back to take in the whole picture. "Knock 'em dead, Holly."

⤺

They met at the Bertram Corners Inn, which was housed in a historic home that dated back to 1789. Each room had a fireplace and a different damask wallpaper. Holly couldn't remember the last time she had eaten there, though it had been her father's favorite place. She ordered the salmon en croûte in his honor.

"I can get a little spoiled sometimes by all the choices in the city, but it's this kind of place that never dies," Racine said, looking around. "Solid and reliable."

Holly wondered if "solid" and "reliable" really qualified as compliments, but she gave Racine credit for trying. She was finally starting to relax a bit around him as she discovered that he wasn't as pretentious as a man with his looks might believe he had a right to be.

"Tell me about your boys," Racine said as dinner neared an end and they both began pushing food around on the overly large plates. "What are they like?"

Holly smoothed her napkin across her lap, wondering if this was just a polite question or he really wanted to know. She decided to give him the capsule version.

"Marshall's a junior. He's a pretty serious trumpet player, which means he's always at band practice or on band trips or marching in a parade. I guess you could say he's a band geek, but he's just in love with his instrument."

"Good for him," Racine said. "Girls love a musician."

Holly nodded, not wanting to hear what else Racine knew about what girls loved. She went on. "Connor's in eighth grade. He'd play video games all day if he could, but he's a sweetheart. He even lets me hug him once in a while. He's the one who seems to miss my husband the most, maybe because they're so much alike."

Holly hadn't meant to raise the specter of her dead husband in the middle of the Bertram Corners Inn, but there he was, hovering above them in the dusty draperies. Racine looked down at his plate.

"I'm sorry," she said. "I didn't mean to bring that up."

"Don't be sorry," he said quietly. "I feel sorry for your boys. My father traveled all the time, but he was very important to me. A little distant, but important."

It was Holly's turn to look down at her plate. She tried not to think about what her boys were missing, because it could start a spiral of regret. "Thanks," she said. "They're strong kids. They'll be okay in the end."

And yet, even as she said it, she realized that there was no "end" until they carried you out in a box like the purloined casket that housed Aunt Muriel. Maybe her boys would be more than okay during some adult phases of life and less than okay in others, just as she had been and was now. Much less than okay. She suddenly felt like she might vomit all over the white linen tablecloth.

"I'm sorry," she said. "I'm not feeling all that well. Do you mind if we leave?"

"You look white as a sheet. I'll get the check," Racine said, concern etched on his face. He signaled the waiter.

"I think it's the rich food," Holly said, and it was true that she had not eaten so much butter and cream in years. She wondered vaguely whether the rich had more sophisticated digestive systems so they could break down their overly complicated meals.

Racine walked Holly to her car. "Are you sure you're okay to drive?" he said. "I could take you home."

Holly, who was focused on keeping her dinner in her stomach, looked up for a moment.

"I'm fine," she said, not wanting Racine to see the exterior of her rundown house. "I mean I'll be fine."

Racine gave her a chaste kiss on the forehead. "Go rest and feel better."

Holly drove home and went to bed, feeling that Racine would simply cross her off his list and move on to the next option, which upset her more than she thought it would.

⌐

Holly's boss, Stan, was sitting in her office when she came in on Monday morning. Stan was middle-aged, a shrug of a man who wore a good toupee, though it wasn't good enough to avoid looking like a toupee. Darla used to joke with Holly that she liked to run her fingers through Stan's hair—even when he wasn't around.

"The news is not good, Lois Lane," Stan said as Holly stowed her purse under the desk and took her seat behind it. Stan had called her Lois Lane from the moment she had started working for him, and she called him Clark Kent, although the joke, as they both aged, was wearing thin.

"What's wrong?" Holly asked. "Did we have a typo on the front page again? I told you we shouldn't have laid off the copy editor."

"It's not that, Holly," he said. "It's the ad revenue. It's gone down so much in the last few months. I'm not sure how long we can keep publishing. They're talking about closing down some of the weeklies, if not the whole chain."

Holly felt as if Stan were telling her that some mutual friend had died. Newspapers were never just a business. They were democracy's lifeblood—even small operations like theirs that devoted a whole page every week to the school lunch menu.

"But what's changed? We're at every school board meeting, every pumpkin-carving contest, every high school football game. What more can we do?"

"That's just it," he said, gripping his knees. "The news we print is not the issue. It's the economy—layoffs, housing prices. Businesses are scared to spend a dime even to bring in more business. And that includes the outlets, which have been keeping us going for years."

Somewhere inside Holly the tiny flame of hope that she could find a way to pay the mortgage, her bills, maybe even save some money, went out. She felt dull and hollow. Then she looked through her office window at Darla, who was on the phone laughing and talking as she took notes. She couldn't see Portia or Marveen, and Les was almost always out covering a game or school event, but she knew they would be devastated.

"I don't have a timeframe," Stan said. "The owners are meeting next week. Maybe they'll only close one or two. Nothing's been decided, so don't say anything."

"I won't," Holly said, even as she had already decided to tell them right away. They needed to know in case they had to make plans.

After Stan left, Holly found Darla, Marveen, and Portia, and learned that Les was out covering a mock disaster drill at the high school. She brought them all into her office.

"I'm not going to sugarcoat this," she said. "The paper's in trouble."

The three of them looked at each other, their faces grim, then back at Holly, as if they had been expecting the news.

"I can't say I'm all that surprised, since I do the books," Marveen said, crossing her arms. "The revenue's way, way down."

"Stan didn't want me to tell you, but you're my friends, and if you have any connections I would completely understand if you want to start job hunting," Holly said. "You can use me as a reference."

Portia cleared her throat. "I think I speak for all of us when I say I'm more worried about you, Holly," she said.

Darla and Marveen nodded as if they had all discussed this before.

"C'mon, I'll be fine. It's not like I can't find another job."

Even as the words came out of her mouth, Holly saw herself surrounded by even more bills she couldn't pay. A future without a paycheck looked like a dark, open maw into which she would pour all her worldly possessions—tossing in tablecloths and Christmas ornaments and dining-room chairs until there was nothing left. And what about her boys? Who would give them a future? Even if they went to community colleges, the cost would eat her alive if she didn't have a paycheck and benefits. It was bad enough as it was. Darla, Marveen, and Portia were all looking at her as if she had announced she had a terminal illness. She couldn't bear their pity, so she transitioned into boss mode.

"So who's covering homecoming tomorrow night?" Holly said. "We need a big photo gallery."

After the meeting, Holly allowed herself a few moments at her desk to brood about Racine. He hadn't called her over the weekend, and she hadn't called him to thank him for dinner. Marveen came back into her office just as she was starting to dial his number.

"So, let's talk about something far more interesting than all this doom and gloom," Marveen said, sitting down in the chair in front of her desk. "How did your date go?"

Holly knew Marveen's real motivation in coordinating her date night makeover. It was to give her leverage in insisting that Holly spill when it was over.

"We had a nice time," Holly said, not wanting to admit how sadly her date had ended after Marveen's Herculean efforts.

"That's it? That's all I get? It was 'nice.' Jesus, Holly, we're not in high school. Did you or did you not sleep with him?"

"No, Marveen," she said, looking up at the ceiling, defeated. "I did not sleep with him. In fact, I thought I was going to throw up, so I went home early. I didn't even enjoy my dinner."

"All that work for nothing," Marveen said, slapping a hand on the desk. "Well, get him to ask you again. You deserve a little fun in your life."

"He hasn't called me, and I'm not sure if I should call him or what."

"Under no circumstances should you call him. That'll look desperate. You have to wait for him to come around, like a prize marlin. You have to let out the line to reel him in."

"Are you seriously comparing him to a fish?"

"Look, Holly, this is no reflection on you, but he probably has a woman in every town with one of these gold joints. If you want him to stay interested, he has to think you're not interested."

"See, this is why I don't date. It's way too complicated."

Marveen stood up to go. "It's always been complicated, Holly, from time immemorial—which I date to about 1976 and my first movie with a boy. I was afraid my hand would be clammy if he tried to hold it, so I kept eating popcorn one kernel at a time. He never called me again, and it still hurts."

CHAPTER 17

Vivian's Unaired Podcast #6

During the years that most of my former schoolmates started careers, got married, had children, and bought their own homes, I existed. There's not much more to it than that. I slept, I ate, I watched television, and read; my breath went in and out; my heart pumped. I endured countless doctors and medical procedures, and I lived for the days when my parents could muster up the energy to take my iron lung outside for a few hours so that I could see the trees, smell the perfume of the lilacs in our yard, and gaze at the sky, which changed so beautifully, unlike the living-room ceiling.

I existed.

Toward the end of what I would later come to call, ironically, the Endless Years, I became aware of another person who had been in an iron lung for about the same amount of time that I had. His name was Lance, and he had almost my identical diagnosis.

I was thirty-three years old when I saw Lance on a television program about polio that displayed him smiling at the screen from a lung that looked almost exactly like mine, down to the yellow enamel. They didn't interview him, but I deduced from his face that he was intelligent and kind and just as frustrated by his circumstances as I was. I began to lay the groundwork to get my mother to arrange a meeting.

Lance lived in Pennsylvania, so I asked my mother if I could be brought to New York City for my thirty-fourth birthday, which was in April.

"I know it's a lot, Mom," I said. "But I've always wanted to see New York. We could just drive around, and I could look out the windows."

"Oh, Vivian," she said. "Where would we stay? I'm not sure a hotel would even allow it or if they could get you inside a room."

"It's less than two hours away," I told her. "We could leave early in the morning and come back at night. You and Dad could take turns driving. Please, Mom. I don't ask for much, and it might be my last chance."

I had long since stopped feeling ashamed for the way I could manipulate my mother. It was nonsense that I didn't ask for much—I asked for things all the time—but in the context of my narrow existence, it wasn't like asking to walk again. I knew that, if she could, she would try to give me anything I wanted.

So we planned a trip to New York, picked a date the week after my birthday, and once it was all on the calendar, I told my mother that I wanted her to write to Lance. I had some movie-of-the-week transcript of how it would all go in my head, but I needed my mother's help to make it happen.

"Remember that man we saw on the TV program about polio, the one who's been in an iron lung all his life?" I said one day.

"I remember," my mother said cautiously.

"It turns out that his home hospital is New York-Presbyterian. Maybe we could meet up with him while we're in New York."

"And you just thought of this," she said, smiling.

I think it made her happy to know I had come up with a scheme to relieve my own boredom.

My mother managed to track down Lance's address in Pennsylvania, and she sent him a letter that I dictated to her. I'm sure she worried about the outcome, but she also knew that a little adventure might be good for all of us. The Endless Years probably felt endless to her, too.

When Lance answered back—via his caregivers—that he would absolutely love to meet a fellow iron lunger and could arrange to be in New York that day, I began to construct elaborate fantasies that involved the two of us falling desperately in love from the moment we met and being kindred spirits who, despite our physical limitations, would share an emotional bond so powerful that it transcended the corporeal. I tried to temper my expectations, but the fantasy was too powerful: Who else but a man in an iron lung would understand my futile hopes, my restricted world? Who else would ever fall in love with me? And despite my realization at the age of twelve that I would never have a romantic relationship, I let myself fall into a dream that culminated in a long, passionate glance. I wasn't sure our lungs would let us get close enough to kiss.

When the day came, we left for New York before dawn. I dozed the whole way as my father drove the van, but before we got to the city I asked my mother to put a little makeup on me. It seems pathetic now, but I wanted to look my best for a stranger in the overwrought hope that he might find my face attractive and want to spend time with me. We arrived at the hospital by 9 a.m., although it took until almost ten o'clock before they could safely transport my lung into the operating theater—one of the few rooms large enough to accommodate two iron lungs.

Lance's caregivers obviously thought it was sweet to have two iron-lung patients of about the same age and opposite sexes, and they had brought flowers for him to "give" to me. I was first in the room. They wheeled in Lance, who lifted his head a bit to smile at me. They parked us side by side but facing in opposite directions because we were both more comfortable turning our heads to the left.

"Hi, Lance," I said, giving him the most genuine smile I had used in the last decade.

"Hi, Vivian," he said. "Great to meet you. So glad you got in touch."

My heart jumped. He had a bit of rosacea and a prominent forehead, but his smile transformed his face from bland to almost handsome. One of the hospital administrators asked if she could take a picture, and we did our best to pose for the camera. The caregivers on both sides of our lungs began shaking hands and talking to each other, no doubt sharing stories of close calls and testing each other's tolerance for iron-lung humor. I didn't listen, because I was too caught up in Lance. I wanted him to speak again, so I asked him a question.

"What kind of music do you like?"

"You don't have to try so hard," he said. His smile was gone. His eyes held little more than hostility.

"I'm not. I'm just wondering if we have anything in common besides this," I said, nodding toward the lung.

"I agreed to this because it made my mom happy," he said. "Believe me, you don't really want to know me. I'm not in a good place right now."

"But that's why we could help each other," I said, so disappointed that he hadn't been sincerely happy to meet me. "I know exactly how you feel. I'm one of the few people in the world who could possibly know."

Lance's face softened a bit, but he didn't seem capable of pretending that he wasn't there under duress.

"Do you fantasize about dying every day?" he said. "Do you wonder how you can stand another twenty-four hours with your parents hovering over you?"

"I have good days and bad days. But I know what you mean. After all this time, it's like a contest to see how many days they can get out of us."

"Not a contest I want to win."

Before I could respond, the hospital administrator who had taken our picture decided to make a little speech about our incredible will to survive and the amazing advancements in medical care that kept both Lance and me alive when no one had believed we would live past childhood. Lance smiled again and turned his head toward his mother, who had approached him from the other side.

"Have you two had a chance to chat?" she said in a singsong voice that gave me some indication of why Lance was so desperate to escape. "I think it's just remarkable that you found each other."

Found each other, like this one-day meeting justified a life stripped of mobility, a life that subsumed other lives in its neediness. It made my fantasy—already juvenile—just sad. I called my mother over and told her I wasn't feeling well. All I had to do was cough a few times to end the conversations and congratulations.

Before the medical teams could regroup to move our iron lungs again, Lance asked if we could have a moment alone. Since we were in an operating theater and could be observed through the glass walls, our parents agreed. It took several minutes for them to all file out, during which time Lance rolled his eyes a few times and made me laugh.

"Watch this," he said, moving his right eyeball toward his nose with perfect control. "I'm not as good with the left, but I'm working on it. What else do I have to do?"

"Why did you send them out?" I said, confused about the sudden change in his attitude. "You've made it pretty clear that you've given up. Why even bother?"

Our faces weren't that far away from each other, maybe eighteen inches, so I could see the anguish in his eyes.

"I really like looking at your face," he said. "You're a pretty girl."

This was not what I had expected to hear from a man who had numbered his own days, but it was a compliment, and I took it.

"Thanks," I said. "You're not half bad yourself."

He laughed a little, but I could see that any emotion took its toll. His face was so pale, as if he never saw the sun, not even one day or so a month, as I did.

"When they're gone," he said, nodding toward the glass where our parents kept vigil, "or even before they're gone, you'll have to find some other reason to wake up in the morning. Something that motivates you."

"Like what?"

"I don't know. If I could figure that out, I wouldn't be where I am now."

Normally advice was easy for me to ignore. Who are you to tell me to hold a paintbrush in my teeth and "create" when you can't possibly imagine what it's like to have an unimpaired brain inside a body that might as well be made of wood? But Lance was different. He knew. He knew that I needed to find that motivation before I slipped off the ledge from which he had already fallen.

"I'll try," I said. I felt tears sliding down my nose, but I couldn't brush them away, so they dampened the sheet where my cheek rested.

"Please try," he said. "I want you to try."

Our parents had figured out by then that we were both crying, so they sent in the cavalry and pulled our lungs apart, steering us to different destinations.

"Good-bye, Lance," I said, turning my head to watch him for as long as I could.

"Bye," he said in a muffled voice, and I never saw him again.

As we drove away from the hospital, I pulled myself together long enough to glance through the windows of the van at the sidewalks packed with pedestrians and at the massive buildings, though I couldn't look up far enough to see how tall they were. The density of it all scared and thrilled me at the same time. At one point my mother got out at a street corner while my father drove around the block. She climbed back into the van with a giant pretzel crusted in salt and a bottle of Coke, a drink I wasn't normally allowed to have, because the caffeine kept me awake at night.

"A treat," my mother said, smiling. "What a very special day this is."

She broke off a small piece of the pretzel and placed it in my mouth, then let me wash it down with a sip of Coke through a straw.

A few weeks after the trip, we heard from Lance's parents that he had died. No explanation of how, just that he was gone. I wept upon hearing the news—both in grief for myself and in joy for him.

CHAPTER 18

After work, Holly decided to stroll by the gold shop to see if Racine might still be there. She had decided against calling him but thought he might happen to see her walking by and come out to say hello. But the door was locked and the lights were off, so Holly walked back to the office, kicking stones just in case Racine was still in the vicinity. When she reached her car, she felt foolish and drove home.

Once there, she made pizza for the kids and helped Connor with some homework before the boys went to bed. Then she spread out her bills on the kitchen table so she could calculate whether or not they could afford anything at all for Christmas. She had already solved the Thanksgiving dilemma by convincing the boys that they should volunteer at a soup kitchen, since Grandma wasn't going to be able to spoil them with a turkey and three kinds of pie anymore.

For the hundredth time, she added up the basic monthly expenses that weren't automatically deducted from her paycheck—the mortgage, the heating oil bill, the electric bill, the water bill, the car payment and the car insurance payment, the interest on the home equity loan, and the interest on her credit card bill. Then she looked at her income. There was a gap of about five hundred dollars a month even with the extra money she was making from Vivian, and even if she continued to have a job. Her retirement funds, as small as they were, had already been raided. She had shut off the cable and eliminated the landline. She bought the cheapest food she could find without sacrificing all nutrition. She bought as little as possible for herself, using Q-tips to dredge out the remains of her waning ChapStick and lipstick supply. Even if she could have sold her house—and that was questionable, given the market—it wasn't worth what she still owed to the bank between the mortgage and the home equity loan. And the bank was already circling, closing in.

When her mother was sending her monthly checks, she viewed her family as a tolerable kind of lower middle class. They couldn't afford much, but when one of the boys had a growth spurt and needed new jeans or a few dollars to chip in for a teacher's gift, she could always find it. Now she was one of those people she had always pitied—the ones who kept watching their credit card balances compound on a monthly basis, continually widening the chasm between financial stability and bankruptcy as the rope bridge across it stretched and frayed.

Being without money in a First World country had its parallels to being chronically ill, Holly decided. It hampered the ability to move freely. It meant exposure to unpleasantness, discomfort, even pain. It made the future seem bleak. It had even more parallels to Vivian's situation, Holly thought. If money were oxygen, she was the one flopping around like a fish outside the iron lung. Society expected people to have money. It really didn't know what to do with people who found themselves outside the norms of earning and spending and paying taxes.

And Vivian, who couldn't do much of anything that an able-bodied or even most disabled people could do, had all the oxygen she needed. She couldn't feed herself, but she could manage her own mini-empire from the confines of her iron lung. Holly was momentarily jealous. She almost wished she could spend a week or two inside the iron lung— detached from her body, no more or less than a cerebellum interacting with an adoring public and entertaining fans on the Internet. Never a worry about calls from a collection agency or Vince from the bank. She shook herself out of the fantasy almost immediately, but the shame of it stayed with her after she went to bed, chasing her into suffocating dreams of being trapped in the trunk of a car with the air running out.

ᗧ

Holly arrived at Vivian's house for her volunteer shift with two avocados. She somehow felt she had to make amends for wanting, even momentarily, to trade places just because Vivian didn't have to worry about money.

"Look what I have," Holly said, showing Vivian the avocados as she came in the front door. "A little something to brighten up your day. They need to ripen a bit, but when they do I'll make guacamole."

"Thanks, Holly," Vivian said, though she barely looked at them.

Holly walked around Vivian's head to sit in the chair to her left. Vivian smiled and turned her head toward the window.

"Is the sun in your eyes? I could close the shades," Holly said.

"No, it's nice," Vivian said. "I don't often get to feel the sun on my face anymore. It's been so gray lately."

"It has, hasn't it? Maybe we'll even have some snow."

Holly sensed some melancholy in Vivian, who occasionally succumbed but usually snapped out of it before long. She tried to think of something upbeat to discuss.

"So Marshall got back yesterday from his band trip to Disney World, and I think he might have a girlfriend. He's been on the phone constantly, and he's been mooning around the house, bumping into furniture, whistling. It's really pretty sweet."

"That is sweet," Vivian said. "I hope she's a nice girl who deserves Marshall. All I see on TV are these trampy girls who swear like sailors."

"I'm not even sure how to ask him about it. This is when I miss Chris the most. We would have talked about this for hours."

Vivian's face fell again. "Do you ever wonder, Holly, why God allows people to suffer? I've spent considerable time on that one, and I'm no closer to an answer. If you believe that God doesn't get involved in human affairs, then there's no point in believing in God. But if God does orchestrate anything at all, then why do nice, hardworking people suffer the way they do? Why did God take Chris from you at such an early age and leave your beautiful children without a father? Why is your mother hanging on—breathing effortlessly, I might add—when she doesn't even know what's going on around her?"

Holly, who was a nonpracticing Episcopalian, didn't know what to say. She knew Vivian had been raised as a Catholic but hadn't received Communion—which, in her case, required a personal visit—in years. They had talked about God before, but only in the context of the afterlife. When Chris had died, Holly remembered Vivian assuring her that there had to be a heaven for people who hadn't gotten a fair shake on earth.

"I don't know, Vivian," Holly said, looking down at her hands. "I rank that as one of the great mysteries of life."

"Most people don't have time to ponder life's mysteries, because they're too focused on their daily responsibilities," Vivian said. "I, on the other hand, have all the time in the world to wonder why God didn't just kill me off right away like my sister. What purpose did my suffering—my parents' suffering—have for anyone? The first time I overheard someone refer to me as an 'invalid' I was shocked. But that's what I am. Have you ever thought about the meaning of that word? In-*valid*. I don't count. I don't even register except as a burden to other people."

Holly was about to suggest that Vivian had, in fact, inspired many people to make the most of their circumstances, no matter how limited, when Vivian answered her own question.

"Any God I could believe in must have had some grand plan to use my suffering as a way to motivate others, right? But then I think of the poor souls like Chris, and I come right back to where I started. If there was some grand plan in killing him off, why do you and your kids have to suffer when so many other families don't? I don't buy into the idea that God doesn't give us more than we can bear. Sometimes I can't bear it, Holly, but I can't do anything about it."

In all her years as a volunteer, Holly had never heard Vivian speak of her condition that way. She felt compelled to counter her argument.

"You know what? We'll never really know why one person suffers tragedy after tragedy and the next person skates through life with all their relatives and friends dying in the right order with a minimum amount of grief. So we struggle. We wonder and we curse and we kill each other in religious wars, and we really don't get any closer to the answers, but we try. That's all we can do."

"I need a tissue, Holly. Can you . . . ?"

Holly was surprised to see a tear running down Vivian's temple, and she pulled a tissue from the box.

"Has something happened?" Holly said. "This isn't like you."

Vivian nodded almost imperceptibly. Holly dabbed at her damp face with the tissue.

"The one thing I could really take pride in was my economic independence," Vivian said. "But now I'm not sure how long that will last either. My accountant called me yesterday. He told me I'm now worth somewhat less than I thought. My stocks are all in the toilet." She sniffed loudly. "But I don't want you to worry about me. I've got other resources, and I have the gold store, which seems to be doing pretty well, right?"

Holly had never seen Vivian in such a vulnerable state. She really didn't know anything about the internal operations or even whether the store was making money, but she needed to say something reassuring.

"I can tell you that Racine is a huge draw," Holly said. "The place seems to have customers most of the time."

Vivian sniffed again and seemed to compose herself. Her face took on its business expression, one that said she was making mental calculations, adding columns of numbers and carrying the one.

"That doesn't surprise me," Vivian said. "But I'll need a better idea of when it will start paying off, so I can adjust my other investments."

Holly considered launching into her date night story but thought better of it. She now realized how foolish she'd been to go on a date, even a failed one, with Racine. Now it would be even harder to ask him for the information Vivian wanted.

"Just tell me what you need," Holly said.

"I'd just like a forecast for the year. Expenditures and expected revenue. He'll know what I mean."

"I'll track him down. Is there anything else I can do for you? Do you want a little snack, maybe some ice cream?"

Ice cream was the one food Vivian cherished, because it went down so easily and soothed her throat. She was a connoisseur of the high-end brands that were all about intense flavor.

"I wouldn't turn down some Häagen-Dazs," Vivian said, finally smiling. "See, I do have something to live for."

⌐∞

After her stint with Vivian and a few hours in the office, Holly decided to take a walk down the street to the gold store at lunchtime. It might be awkward to see Racine again, but now she had a job to do for Vivian. Along the way she turned in to the pharmacy, which had an extensive cosmetics counter with samples she had recently discovered. Once there, she was surprised to find Darla manning the register in a drugstore-issued smock.

"What are you doing here?" Holly asked. "Aren't you supposed to be back at the newspaper working for me?"

"Hi, Hol," Darla said. "They asked me to fill in for the regular cashier's lunch break. Most of the time I just work on the weekends. Didn't I tell you that Phil got laid off from the distribution center? You'd think beer would be the last thing people would stop buying, but I guess that isn't true."

"I'm so sorry," said Holly, wishing that her friend and colleague didn't have to wear a smock of any kind just to make ends meet. "I wish you'd said something."

"Why? So you could reach into your magic bag and pull out a job for Phil? Or a big raise for me? We all just do what we have to do to keep body and soul together. I was lucky to find this."

"I have a second job, too. I'm helping Vivian manage her gold store investment. In fact, I'm headed over there right now."

"Well, if you're going to see that Racine, you came to the right place. I'm gonna make you look like a movie star."

Ten minutes later Holly walked out of the pharmacy wearing a new shade of rose-colored lipstick, light brown eye shadow, and some blush, and thinking about what Darla had said: "We all do what we have to do to keep body and soul together." She wasn't sure that her body and her soul were even compatible anymore. The latter seemed like a luxury she could no longer afford.

A few customers were sitting at the back of the gold store having their offerings evaluated when Holly walked in, but she didn't see Racine right away. As she looked at the glass cases full of old jewelry, watches, and silver-plated brush sets, he emerged from the back room.

"Holly!" he said. "I was literally just dialing your number."

"You're making that up," Holly said, until Racine thrust his cell phone in front of her and she saw the first eight digits of her cell phone number. Racine came around to the front of the counter and put a hand lightly on her shoulder. He had a physical sureness that she envied and admired.

"I enjoyed our date," he said, now touching the top of his head. He touched it so often that she wondered if he was afraid of losing his hair. "I was hoping we could go out again."

Holly felt certain that he was just trying to be nice. What could he have enjoyed about paying for an expensive meal, then leaving before dessert because his date thought she might throw up? But she had to give him credit for trying.

"Sure, that would be great," she said slowly. "But I really came down here to get some numbers for Vivian. She wants a report on your expenses and projected revenues."

"Of course, of course. I'll get all that together and send her an e-mail."

"Soon, okay?" Holly said. "She's a little anxious about it."

"Nothing to worry about. Business is good, especially with the holidays coming. Everyone needs that extra cash."

Holly thought about the wedding ring again, wondering how many presents she could buy if she sold it. Somehow, knowing it was there in her jewelry box made her feel less poor, so she mentally put it back.

"So when can we get together?" he said. "Is there a good day this week?"

Holly felt another lurch in her stomach, knowing that she wouldn't fall gently if Racine kept pursuing her. It would be more like a cliff dive into rock-strewn waters, and then how would she get out of it intact once he was ready to move on?

"The boys are busy on Wednesday night with a band fund-raiser, so that might work."

"Wednesday night then," he said. "I'll come to your house around seven."

Leaving the gold store, Holly felt somehow as if she were walking on marshmallows, uncertain of how to step and overpowered by a sweet and expectant scent.

CHAPTER 19

Vivian's Unaired Podcast #7

I took Lance's advice and found a reason to open my eyes every day: investing in the stock market. I had received a small settlement as part of a medical malpractice lawsuit involving faulty catheters, so I had a small nest egg that wasn't earmarked for my medical care.

At first it was a game to me—could I beat the market? But then I realized that earning money meant that I could buy my parents some relief, and they needed it. My father's health was failing—all the years of hard labor had settled into his joints with a vengeance—which meant that my mother had to look after both of us.

It was around this time that technology began to broaden what I could do for myself. My mother found me a headset so that I could be on the phone without someone holding the receiver up to my ear. She still had to act as my operator at the beginning and end of the call, but I could talk to my stockbroker every day. I read all the stock market periodicals I could find and began investing in penny stocks (notoriously difficult, but I had a knack for it) until I had amassed a decent enough portfolio to buy blue chips. I did so well that I sent my parents to Virginia Beach—where they had gone for their honeymoon—on their first trip since polio killed Darlene and paralyzed me. Before they would agree to leave, I put an ad in the newspaper asking for volunteers to take some two-hour shifts with me—and luckily there were enough curiosity seekers in town that I ended up with a waiting list. I paid for nurses to take the overnight hours. Our roles quietly shifted: at forty, I became the breadwinner, and my parents allowed me to, at least occasionally, soften their lives.

One of my first volunteers was Marveen, who was just a young thing at the time, newly married to a somewhat older man, bored, and looking for a project. She found it right there on the top of my head.

"So nice to meet you, Vivian," she said after responding to my ad. Then she skipped all the phony chitchat and skipped right to what she couldn't possibly ignore.

"If I may ask a personal question, who does your hair?"

"My mother's used the same hairdresser for years—Sam Reynolds. He stops by every six weeks or so on his way home from work to give my mother a permanent, and he trims my mop when it gets too long."

"Now, I wouldn't use the term 'mop' exactly, but Viv, some shaping and a few highlights would change your life," Marveen said.

I glanced down at the iron lung just long enough for Marveen to get the point that it would take more than a new hairstyle to change my life. And yet I decided to let her try. I thought it might be fun to see a change in my overhead mirror that didn't involve identifying new wrinkles.

"Go for it," I told her. "I'm your guinea pig."

A few days later Marveen came back with a cart on wheels that carried her supplies from the few months she had spent in beauty school before marrying her husband, who had told her she never had to work again, so why bother with all those classes? My hair was difficult to cut because I couldn't hold my head up from the table for long, but Vivian found a way to prop it up on a foam rubber block just long enough to cut the back—which didn't matter much anyway since no one could see it. She gave me some long layers around the sides and then put in the foils.

"This will be stunning," she said. "Just wait till you see. You're going to look just like Kathleen Turner, the *Body Heat* version."

"I'll take it. Right now I feel like Ethel Merman."

I had my doubts, but after Marveen finished, I did look a little like Kathleen Turner from the neck up. When my parents came back, my mother gasped when she first saw me.

"Vivian, is that you?"

"Who's Vivian?" I said. "And who are you?"

My mother laughed and looked as rested as I'd ever seen her. In my parents' brief absence, I had realized that their lives would have been so much better without me. Yes, they would have grieved for both me and Darlene for many years, but they hadn't been too old to start over and have more children. They could have had perfectly comfortable lives without my medical expenses or the endless hours spent watching after me. They had essentially sacrificed their own interests, their own comfort, and their own health to keep my pitiful brain functioning day after day after day. And I had taken all of it for granted, even sometimes resented them for it. My mission became clear: make as much money as possible so my parents could enjoy whatever time they had left.

I studied the stock market, assessed the odds, and invested accordingly. According to my broker, I had the Midas touch. In the late 1980s, my parents were able to tour Germany, visit California, and spend winters in Florida, which eased my father's arthritis. But in 1995 my father developed pneumonia and died in a hospital in Fort Myers. It torments me still that I wasn't able to see him before he passed away. Just before he left on that trip, he told me how proud he was that I had found my calling.

"Who knew that my Vivi would run circles around Wall Street?" he said, gesturing with an arthritis-crippled hand toward my computer screen. "It's the darndest thing."

"I'm just glad you and Mom can get some time away," I told him.

"We only wish you could come with us," he said, wiping his eyes with the back of his hand. "But we'll be back soon."

After Daddy's death, my mother was done with her traveling. She seemed to want to care for me again, since it was the only role she'd had for most of her adult life, and yet I couldn't let her do it. She had become forgetful and weak sighted, and I had developed such a capable network of volunteers and aides who knew just how to make me comfortable and support my investment work. In the end, the medical staff and the volunteers took care of my mother as much as they took care of me.

At least I was able to care for her. That's what the money did. It softened the harsh corners, eased the aches, made us healthier with better food and medicine, let my mother sleep more comfortably on a softer yet more supportive mattress. Without it, the ticket counters closed, the lights dimmed, the temperature could not be regulated.

And yet . . .

And yet . . .

I would have given every penny I had ever made to spend a single day outside my iron lung.

CHAPTER 20

Holly sat down on one side of the red pleather booth at the diner next door to her mother's new nursing home in White Plains. Desdemona slid lightly into the bench seat opposite her, and Henderson shoved the table a bit to bump in next to Desdemona.

Holly picked up the laminated menu, which felt greasy. It had been a long morning of filling out paperwork and listening to Henderson carp about the monthly cost of the home, whose employees would care for their mother's body until it decided to join the rest of her on the other side of earthly cares.

"I'm sorry, but I can't believe," Henderson said, "that they're charging her an activities fee when she can't even communicate or move around on her own. Do they think she'll be playing pinochle in the rec room?"

Desdemona rolled her eyes for Holly to see, then looked down at her own greasy menu. "I'll just have some hot tea," she said. "I don't feel like I could eat anything."

"Well, I'm starving," Henderson said as the waitress approached. He looked up at her and launched in before she could offer her name in that pointlessly intimate ritual of American dining. "I'll have the chicken club, but with coleslaw instead of the fries. She'll have some hot tea. Holly?"

Holly glanced at the menu, a vista of landmines both caloric and financial. She only had six dollars and didn't want to risk having a credit card turned down in front of her brother and sister. In times past, she and Desdemona would have just assumed that Henderson would pick up the check. She missed those days.

"I'll have a bowl of the minestrone," Holly said, though she knew she'd still be hungry when she finished it. Maybe, she thought, Henderson wouldn't be able to finish his sandwich.

When the waitress left, Holly looked at Henderson and noticed for the first time that he looked about five years older than he had at Aunt Muriel's funeral just a few months before.

"Are you okay, Hen?" she said. "You look a little tired."

Henderson pressed the heels of his hands into his eye sockets. "Nobody's hiring. Everything has come to a standstill. I've never seen anything like it. I'm really not sure what to do next. I spent Thanksgiving Day sending out cover letters and résumés."

Desdemona patted Henderson's arm and told a story about her last dance performance, in which a new dancer high-kicked her legs right out from under her.

"And she'll be okay just like you'll be okay, Hen. You're a survivor. You'll figure it out."

Henderson's face darkened. "You both think I'll figure it out, but you have no idea what I'm up against. You can't just launch a new business once you've declared bankruptcy, and who would hire me? I've failed, girls. The condo's on the market, but I might lose money on it. I'm selling the Audi, and now all this with Mom."

"I'm so sorry, Hen," Holly said. "Is there anything we can do to help?"

Henderson put his napkin on his lap as the waitress set his chicken club and coleslaw down in front of him. He sighed. "Buy me lunch?"

Holly looked at Desdemona, who was dunking her tea bag with a spoon. Desdemona gave a tiny shake of her head, which Holly took to mean she had even less than six dollars in her wallet.

"I'll take care of it," Holly said, hoping that at least one of her credit cards wasn't completely maxed out. Spending money she didn't have felt like walking off a cliff and trying to find traction by pedaling in midair, and yet she couldn't seem to stop. "Listen, we'll all be okay. We're in a slump, but we'll come out of it. Mom would want us to help each other."

Both Henderson and Desdemona nodded. After lunch, the waitress had to try three of Holly's credit cards before one was accepted. Before they left the diner, they all stood in its brochure-lined foyer and agreed that their parents' money had served its purpose in getting their mother into a good nursing facility.

"She's in a good spot," Henderson said. "We did the right thing."

"We did, Hen," Holly said, hugging him. She imagined their father looking down on them, not ashamed exactly but surprised at how far all three of them had fallen. He had never been a sentimental man, leaving the emotional aspects of child rearing to Celia. But he had brought each of them to the bank to start a savings account, and he had lectured them on the value of setting aside a portion of each gift or each paycheck for the future. Now that the future was the present and the present the past, none of them had any savings at all.

⤳

The house was quiet when Holly returned from lunch. It took her a few minutes to remember that Marshall was at a Saturday band practice and Connor was at a neighbor's house to play video games. She noticed that she had a message on her cell phone when she took it out to check the time.

"Holly, it's Vince from the bank again. We've noticed that you've made another partial payment on your mortgage this month, and we're concerned. You'll be assessed a late-payment fee, as well as interest on the unpaid balance. Please give me a call to discuss the situation."

Holly put down the phone and sat on one of the rickety kitchen chairs that surrounded the small table for four in the center of the room. She simply had no way to make up the difference between what the bank charged her to live in the house she called a home and what she could afford to pay. As a good customer of fifteen years, she thought the bank would give her more than two months before it started harassing her at home. On top of that, it was almost Christmas. The boys had always had presents under the tree. When she was low on funds, her mother made sure she had some extra money to buy them gifts, and Celia gave them her own stack of presents as well. There was always some expensive electronic device from Henderson, too. But this year . . . she couldn't imagine giving them nothing. They weren't babies, and eventually they would understand, but nothing?

"What can I do?" she said aloud, rubbing her hands on her thighs. She felt a dull pain starting in her chest. Her breath suddenly became shallow, and her heart began to pound almost audibly. She thought momentarily that she was having a heart attack and might pass out. Her breath came in shorter and shorter bursts that reminded her of Vivian's frightening power outage episode. Just as she grabbed her phone to dial 911, Connor came in the door, and she felt her heart rate slow just enough to stop her from making the call. She didn't want to worry him.

"Hi, Mom," he said, going straight to the refrigerator, opening it and standing in front of its contents as if they might put on a show. "What's there to eat?"

Holly took a deep breath and braced herself against the table. She knew she would be able to function if she didn't look at her son.

"There's some leftover pasta in there," she said slowly. "And I bought some apples the other day. They're in the vegetable drawer."

Connor grabbed an apple and shut the refrigerator door. He whistled as he made his way through the living room.

A few days before, Holly had posted a short article about fuel assistance and realized—since she had depleted every other resource—that her salary was low enough to qualify for it. She had even driven over to the Town Hall food pantry, but while she was parking, she had seen Marveen unloading donations from the trunk of her car and couldn't face the shame of walking by her.

Holly put her head down on the table and tried to think of calming thoughts: *It'll be okay. You'll come up with something.* She lifted her head, wiping her face on her sleeve, and stood up, realizing she could wait no longer.

Holly took the stairs two at a time to her bedroom, where she fished around in her jewelry box until she found her wedding band. At the very least she had to see what it would be worth to assess the trade-off: wrapped boxes under the tree versus selling off the one object of value that memorialized her eleven-year marriage.

She called up to Connor. "I'm running out to do an errand, Con. I'll be back soon."

As she backed out of the driveway, she noticed the garish displays of Christmas lights on the homes in the subdivision above her house. Then she saw Marshall coming up the walk with his backpack and his trumpet case. She rolled down the window.

"Hi, sweetie," she said. "How was practice?"

"Okay," he said.

"Anything else on your agenda today?"

"Job hunting."

"What?"

"I know it's a 'cash-flow' situation, but I need some cash to flow into my wallet. I have some presents I need to buy."

Holly thought he was talking about her and Connor and almost told him they didn't need anything before she realized he probably meant his girlfriend.

"I saw a 'Help Wanted' sign at the Dunkin' Donuts next to the gold store," she said. "I was heading that way now, if you want to come along."

"That's okay. I need to put this stuff away and get something to eat. I also want to print out my stellar résumé of lawn-mowing and babysitting jobs. I'll walk over there later."

She nodded and turned her head before he could see the tears welling in her eyes. The palpitations began in her chest again as she finished backing out of the driveway, but she forced herself to calm down. She couldn't afford the co-pay in the emergency room.

She drove past the gold store looking for a parking spot when she saw the outline of Racine's head in the window and realized she couldn't go in. She couldn't bear the thought of Racine knowing she was desperate enough to sell her wedding ring, or worse yet, of watching him treat it like any other transaction. Instead, she drove past the illuminated Christmas bells on the streetlamps of Main Street to the section of town where the curbstones and sidewalks gave way to sad little clumps of low-rent commerce: the check-cashing store, the Salvation Army distribution center, and the furniture repair place that always had tarnished brass headboards propped up in front of it.

She pulled into the parking lot of the pawn shop across a bed of loose gravel. Next door was a liquor store with a grimy plate-glass window that Holly suspected had never been washed by anything but rain. She hurried inside the pawn shop as a man in a trench coat and sneakers—his hairy, bare legs visible between the hem of the former and the laces of the latter—came out of the liquor store clutching a paper bag.

She had never been inside a pawn shop, but it looked just as she had expected it would. A long glass counter in an L shape took up most of the room. Opposite and behind the counter were shelves crammed with all manner of items conferred in the vain hope that they might be redeemed, among them quite a few guitars and other musical instruments, including a nice-looking trumpet, power tools of all varieties, small framed paintings, heavy glass bowls of the wedding gift variety, silver-plated tea pots and serving trays, and neon signs advertising various types of beer. The items were all coated with a fine layer of dust.

Holly touched the wedding ring in the pocket of her cloth coat and was about to turn around when she saw a balding man behind the counter, looking at her.

"Can I help you, ma'am?" he said.

She walked over, pulled the wedding band out of her pocket, and slapped it down on the glass counter, making a louder noise than she had intended.

The man looked at the ring. "We've seen quite a few of these lately."

He gestured to a gray cardboard box in the glass case in front of him that appeared to have several hundred gold wedding bands inside it. Most of them looked pretty much like hers. She thought about how each of those rings had entered the market ensconced in velvet inside a hinged box—emblematic of new love and vows and the mingling of possessions and bank accounts—but would exit via cardboard and high heat.

"We don't have a huge demand for these," the balding man said. "So we can only keep them for about three months before we sell them on the gold market."

"I understand," Holly said. The thought of her wedding band joining the box of regret in the case in front of her made her sick to her stomach. But she had to find out, at least, how much it was worth.

The balding man took out an eyepiece like the ones used by the appraisers in the back of the gold store. He examined the ring and then placed it on a small scale.

"This is fourteen-karat," he said. "We have a standard rate that we pay by the gram based on the day's spot price. Some'll try to low-ball you—that new place over on Main Street doesn't pay as much as we do. You're here on a day when gold is up, so this would get you a hundred and twenty-five."

Holly's chin fell toward her chest. Was that all it was worth? All that mental energy and all the emotion she had invested in that one small gold band had added nothing to the scale, which only measured an inert element. It didn't seem fair. She picked up her ring with her right hand and laid it on her left palm. It was so light, and yet it weighed on her so heavily. It had been made to match her engagement ring—a sapphire set on a thin yellow-gold band that had once belonged to Chris's grandmother.

She remembered when Chris proposed to her, a year after they had met on graduation night from Syracuse. He had invited her over for pizza and a movie, but when she walked into his apartment, she noticed that he had actually cleaned up and set the small kitchen table with plates that matched. He did serve pizza, but it was homemade, and for dessert he asked her to sit in the living room while he cleaned up and fussed about in the kitchen. She was so irritated by the noise of him washing pans and loading the dishwasher that she got up to help just as he came around the corner with a cake ablaze with sparklers. Written on it with blue icing were the words "Marry Me?" She remembered looking up to make sure it wasn't a joke before she responded and finding Chris's eyes, which were stripped of any ego or fear and said so nakedly, *I love you.* She blew out the sparklers, screamed "Yes!" and threw her arms around him as he balanced the cake with one hand.

The engagement ring had never quite fit her properly. She had taken it off to make meatballs one day when the boys were little and had rested it on the edge of the sink. She didn't know it had fallen in until she was cleaning up eggshells and flipped the switch on the garbage disposal. When she heard the grinding sound, she knew what had happened and threw herself toward the switch to shut off the disposal, but it was too late. The twisted wreckage that came up amid the bread crumbs and goo wasn't recognizable as a ring. Chris had shrugged it off, but she had kept the once-ring in her jewelry box for years, until she had sold her small pile of jewelry several years before.

After that, she stuck to just the wedding band, which she wore on her left ring finger until a year after Chris died and then on a chain around her neck for another year. But it was time. She couldn't let Christmas go by without a few presents, and what good was the ring doing inside a jewelry box? It was no more than a blunt reminder that she and Chris had fulfilled their promises, because death—that unpleasant guest invited into marriage vows—had been the one to part them.

She nodded, watched the balding pawn-shop clerk put a twist tie tag on her ring, and took the thin envelope of cash from him, then sat in her car and cried. A decade ago, fiddling with her wedding ring during a school play or a movie, she could never have imagined being desperate enough to sell it. And now it was gone, which meant she had no cushion left, not even a paper-thin one. On top of that, her boys were almost grown. How was it that Marshall, who had trailed her around the house with his blanket, now asked her to buy razor blades? Or that Connor was already taller than she was? How could it be that they would both be leaving her soon—or worse, not leaving her if she couldn't afford to send them to college?

When the moment passed, she wiped her eyes and pulled her hair back from her forehead. It couldn't be helped, this growing-up thing, but no one had ever told her about the grief, the sense of loss as one phase of childhood morphed into the next, or how much she would ache in witness to their inevitable pain. No one had ever told her how much she would be willing to sacrifice to save them from even an ounce of it.

CHAPTER 21

Holly went into work on Monday feeling a little fragile after her weekend dose of fiscal reality. As soon as she sat down in her office, Marveen knocked on the door.

"Got a minute?" Marveen asked.

"Sure."

Marveen sat in the chair that faced Holly's desk and smoothed her jersey dress over her knees. No one else in the office wore dresses to work—Holly was often in jeans—but Marveen dressed for the job she wished to have, which was hosting and attending charity cocktail parties and lunches.

"I've been thinking about what Stan said," Marveen started.

"I've been trying to forget what Stan said," Holly said.

"I'd like to take a leave of absence. You could save my salary and put it toward keeping your reporters instead."

"But who would do the books? Who would make sure the advertisers pay their bills?"

"Any one of you could do it. It's not that complicated, and we have fewer accounts now anyway. You could split it up."

"Look, Marveen, Stan is worried, but it's not over yet. I don't want anyone to make that kind of sacrifice until it's absolutely necessary."

Marveen patted the pouf of hair that spread out from her head in gravity-defying radiance. The shape and whorls of it reminded Holly of a snail shell.

"The truth is . . . I wasn't sure I should tell you, but Arthur got a promotion," Marveen said. "He wants me to focus on our kitchen remodel, which will practically be a full-time job. We're adding three hundred square feet to the house, and it's a total teardown."

Holly nodded. It wasn't that she wanted to be Marveen—with her outdated bouffant hairdo and her bobbing chest and her fake nails—but for just a moment she wanted to be someone who could afford to leave a job so that her house could be enlarged.

"I thought Arthur's company just laid off a bunch of people," Holly said. "I think we had a story about it."

"You're right about that. Arthur had a terrible time with it. He was in charge of the downsizing."

Of course he was, Holly thought. She didn't doubt that Arthur had a "terrible time with it," but she imagined that his sleepless nights numbered far fewer than those of the laid-off.

Holly nodded and told Marveen to figure out when her last day would be, then she put her head briefly on her desk as Marveen left, only to find Portia standing right in front of her with her reporter's notebook in hand.

"What's up?" Holly said, pushing her hair behind her ears.

"We've got a three-car crash over on Walsh Road," she said. "Just wanted to let you know I was heading over."

"Fatalities?"

"One of the vehicles was a garbage truck, so maybe. They have Walsh blocked off, so can you post that on Facebook and Twitter?"

Holly nodded as Portia left. The *Chronicle* was only partially posted online, but they had recently embraced social media at Portia's insistence. Holly had become fairly adept at the Facebook postings, but she was weak on Twitter. She would spend too long trying to fill out all 140 characters she was allowed, because it seemed like an irresistible challenge to get the remaining character count to zero.

> *3-vehicle crash closes Walsh Road; ambulance called to the scene; garbage truck involved; stay tuned for updates from the Chronicle.*

Still eight characters left, and yet the whole story was there, Holly thought. Who needed newspapers?

⌐

Holly stopped at Vivian's house the next day to let her know that Racine would be sending along some numbers. The Sister Sisters were on their weekly shift, and they were just telling Vivian how they had sold their crosses at the gold store.

"Hi, Holly . . . So the nice young man—the one with the lovely smile—told us he would give us a great deal because we were using the proceeds for charity," one sister told Vivian. "We felt so special."

"We did," the other sister agreed. "And now we can afford the cow. Our African family will be so pleased, won't they, Sister?"

"They will, Sister," said the other one.

Holly had known them for years, but no matter how many mnemonic devices she tried, she couldn't tell one from the other. Both had faces that had gone from apple to pear shaped, with soft jowls covered in the fine fuzz that some postmenopausal women never seemed to notice, maybe because their eyes were simultaneously weakening. They both wore thick glasses and had similarly prominent front teeth. One had one green eye and one blue eye, but Holly could never remember if that was Eileen or Eleanor.

"I'm so glad for you both," Vivian said. "Eileen, how's your sciatica?"

The one with a green eye responded.

"So kind of you to ask, Vivian," she said. "It's much better. As long as I remember to do my exercises."

The sisters seemed to think that Holly was there to relieve them, though they still had twenty minutes left in their shift, so they gathered up their things and each made the sign of the cross over Vivian.

"Bless you, my dear," said the one with two blue eyes as they left in a blur of black fabric.

Holly put down her purse and took off her coat, since she would now have to stay until the next volunteer came.

"How on earth do you tell them apart?" she said. "It has baffled me for years."

"Easy," Vivian said. "Eileen is the one with the green eye. Two *e*'s in Eileen, and two *e*'s in green."

"Brilliant," Holly said. "Although they seem virtually interchangeable anyway. I'm not sure they even notice that no one seems to call them by name."

"You're wrong there. In fact, they can't understand why people confuse them. They're actually quite different. Eileen studied at the Royal Academy of Dramatic Art thinking she wanted to be an actress, but then she visited Eleanor on a missionary trip to India and decided she wanted that life instead. Still, she's the more dramatic one."

Once again, Holly felt a tiny knot of jealousy that Vivian had taken the time to learn the nuns' stories, when she was the journalist. She should have interviewed both nuns, and she should have known which one had the green eye. Instead, she was writing up police logs and putting captions on the winners of pet contests because her staff was so small now that these chores didn't get done unless she did them herself.

"So why are you here?" Vivian said. "You don't have a shift until Thursday."

"I just stopped by to say that Racine would be sending you the expenses and revenue projections by e-mail," Holly said, looking out the window, then back to Vivian. "And to let you know that he asked me out."

Vivian, who had been watching TV as Holly spoke, snapped her head around. "He asked you out? To do what?"

"I don't know. Dinner, I guess. Is that okay with you? I didn't know if it was all right, because of my status as your watchdog."

Vivian burst into laughter. "You mean, is going to dinner all right now that you've already been to dinner with him?"

Holly felt the blood run into her face. "Who told you?"

"Who do you think? But if it hadn't been Marveen, it would have been someone else. You seem to forget that I am the hub of Bertram Corners gossip, Holly. Everyone loves to tell me what's going on out there, since I can't see it for myself."

"Marveen has the biggest mouth on the planet."

"Oh please. She didn't mean any harm. She just thought it was sweet that you got all dressed up and went out with a good-looking man. She was trying to take credit for your makeover."

"Does it bother you that I didn't say anything? I didn't want you to think I was shirking my duties."

Vivian laughed again. "My dear, sweet Holly. Why do you think I gave you this job in the first place? When I saw Racine's picture online and spoke to him over the phone, I immediately thought, 'He'd be great for Holly.' Nothing serious, but a much-needed fling, which you haven't had since Chris died, or possibly ever."

"So you set me up? Who else knew? Am I the laughingstock of the whole town?"

"Of course not. I am the soul of discretion."

Holly walked to the window and looked out, wondering how she was perceived in the town where she had grown up. She really didn't know.

"Oh, look," Vivian said. "I just got an e-mail from Racine with the revenue projections."

"Are they good?" Holly said, walking back to look at Vivian's computer screen.

"Let me see."

Vivian told her voice-activated computer to open a spreadsheet and scroll down. Holly could see the numbers, but she wasn't sure what they meant."

"These are higher than I would have expected," Vivian said. "He's got a fairly big number in here for resale of estate items. Have you seen much of that happening?"

Holly couldn't remember any customers actually buying the estate jewelry and trinkets in the glass cases, but she wasn't in the store all the time.

"Not really," she said. "But don't you trust his numbers?"

"I should. But I'm a skeptic, which is why I'm a good business-woman. What I'd really like to do is go down there myself and see how it's laid out, then look at the books."

"So why don't you?"

Vivian shook her head. "You have no idea what a production that would be. It requires staff and renting a van with the right equip-ment, and then I'm not sure I'd be able to get inside the store. It's just too much."

"But it would be an adventure," Holly said, suddenly wanting Vivian to take charge of the gold store investment before she screwed it up. Holly worried that she would have the opposite of Vivian's Midas touch, sucking the value out of an otherwise successful business just as she had sucked the value out of her own house. "I could make all the arrangements."

"It would be nice to get outside," Vivian said. "I think it's been six months since I went to that concert in the park."

"What day do you want to go? Maybe Thursday?"

By then Holly would have had her second date with Racine, and Vivian's visit would give her an excuse to see him again without calling.

"What the hell," Vivian said. "Let's take this show on the road."

After work, Holly ran home to cook the boys some pasta for dinner, then brought them with her for a rare trip to the mall so she could see what they wanted for Christmas. They each needed a new white polo shirt for the school holiday concerts, which she figured she could pick up at J. C. Penney. Then she would follow them through the mall and see what they picked up and admired, hoping there were at least a few items she could afford. She would make a point of avoiding the Apple Store.

The plan went awry almost immediately after she found the polo shirts—on sale—for ten dollars each. Marshall saw a cluster of his friends and gave her a wave and said, "I'll meet you back here in an hour." She followed Connor as he made a beeline to the Apple Store, where he became engrossed in an online game.

"Go shop, Mom," Connor said without taking his eyes off the screen. "I'll be here when you're ready to go."

Holly patted Connor on the back and headed back out into the packed corridors lousy with garish lights and overheated shoppers with bags strung on their arms, evidence that other people could still afford the kind of Christmas she used to have. She had actually looked forward to taking the boys to the mall—a place they normally avoided—but now that she was here, it all seemed so pointless. The fear of rejected credit cards hung over her like a storm cloud. She wanted to pick out overpriced cashmere and holiday tins of peppermint bark and hat/scarf ensembles that would never be worn. She wanted that feeling of anticipation and that rush of adrenaline that comes from finding the perfect present which used to carry her through the season all the way up until the actual opening of said present and the response that never quite lived up to expectations.

But after the concert shirts, she still had a hundred dollars or so from the ring sale, which meant fifty for each boy. She picked up a plaid shirt in one store and looked at the price tag: $39.95. So that and a new pair of socks would blow the whole wad for one of them. She sighed and put the shirt back, wondering if she should head back to J. C. Penney, and then caught sight of Marshall in the way that a mother can pick out the slope of her own child's nose or his distinctive gait out of a large crowd. She looked again. Yes, that was Marshall, and he had his arm tight around the shoulder of a girl with jet-black hair and an eyebrow piercing. Holly pulled in a quick breath and put a hand instinctively over her mouth, shocked to see her son so casually intimate with a girl.

She maneuvered behind a rack of down coats to get a better look. The girl was petite and wore a short skirt with black tights and combat boots. She looked a little dangerous, which was probably what drew Marshall to her, but she wondered about the attraction in the other direction. Holly couldn't see any tattoos, but she somehow sensed their presence.

"Mom, what are you doing?"

Holly started. "Connor. Jesus, you scared me. I thought you were staying at the Apple Store."

"They have a time limit during the holidays, so I came to find you. Why are you spying on Marshall?"

"Is that his girlfriend?"

"I guess so," he said, crouching with her behind the rack of coats.

"What's her name?"

"Like Hannah or something."

"She doesn't look like a Hannah."

"If that's her name, then she looks like a Hannah," Connor said, and Holly couldn't dispute his logic.

"Why hasn't he said anything about her? They look very comfortable together."

"He's worried you'll freak out."

Holly turned to Connor, even at the risk of letting Marshall out of her sight. "Why would I freak out? I've been waiting for it to happen."

Connor buried his face in one of the down jackets. "It's just hard talking about stuff like that."

Holly stood up straight and turned back to the store. She waved a hand toward the racks of shirts and jeans and jackets and T-shirts.

"Anything you like in here?"

Connor shook his head. "If you can't plug it in, I don't want it."

Holly laughed and pulled him into an awkward hug. "At least you're honest."

When they met Marshall back in front of J. C. Penney, his girlfriend was nowhere to be seen.

"Ready to go?" he said.

"Sure," Holly said, for once forcing herself not to ask any questions. "I'm all shopped out."

CHAPTER 22

Vivian's Unaired Podcast #8

My mother died in her sleep. Marveen let herself in the door for a 6 a.m. shift and found the previous volunteer, Sid Mahoney, fast asleep—a fact she later shared with the entire town. She told me that she poked Sid in his "fat gut" before making sure I was breathing and then checking on my mother, who was not. She called an ambulance before she woke me.

"Vivian," she said, running a hand across my forehead. "Are you awake?"

"I am now," I said, still bleary-eyed and, as usual, wanting to stay inside a dream where I ran and jumped and drew air into my lungs without even thinking about it.

"Viv, I'm so sorry. It's your mother. The ambulance will be here any minute."

"What's wrong with her?" I said, now fully awake. "She was fine last night when she went to bed."

"Oh, Viv," Marveen said, stroking my hair. "She must have died during the night."

I didn't believe her. It wasn't possible. I thought it was some ugly attempt at a joke, despite the numbness creeping down my neck.

"That can't be true. She was fine last night. She was absolutely fine, I swear."

When I saw the look on Marveen's face and realized she was telling me the truth, I remember feeling that I had failed. I hadn't been there—or made sure someone else was there—when she most needed it. But Marveen reminded me that volunteers had been there through the night—she didn't mention right away how she found Sid unconscious that morning—and said my mother had gone peacefully.

"I thought she was still asleep," she said, shaking her head. "She looked so serene . . . Really, Vivian, it was just her time."

I cried long and loud, and Marveen let me. She mopped my face with tissues at appropriate intervals and nodded sympathetically.

"How could I have outlived both my parents?" I said. "They opened their veins and poured their blood into me, and for what? What did they get out of this life?"

"They did what they had to do, and you thanked them," Marveen said, as if she knew. "They understood how much you appreciated them."

I shook my head. I realized she could never fully comprehend what my life had been like, but I didn't want to be falsely martyred. I didn't deserve it.

"I was horrible to them for decades," I said, still crying. "I really was. You just didn't know me then."

"But I know you now, and I knew your mother, and she didn't regret one day at your side."

The EMTs opened the door and nodded sympathetically toward me while moving a stretcher into my mother's room. I cried like a child as they wheeled her body past mine in the only possible path toward the door.

"Wait," I said. "Just let me look at her for a minute."

They parked the stretcher next to my lung, and though my mother's face was several inches below mine, I could see clearly that she had, as Marveen said, died peacefully. There was no trace of pain or struggle on her well-lined face, the gray hair pulled into the long side braid she always wore to bed. I wasn't worried about what would happen to me—I had long since managed to direct my own care—but it did crash down on me that I was all alone in the world.

I was the end of the line, the last to survive in our immediate family. It made me sad that my parents had never experienced the joy of grandchildren. Their genes would never assert themselves in a generation down the road. Nor would mine, and all because I had been unlucky enough to contract a disease just before it became preventable.

I often thought about the nature of viruses and how they sought opportunity, just as people did. They had no moral code, of course. They didn't infect criminals or adulterers or racists any more than they infected kind, good-hearted people. They simply went where they could stake a claim and grow, just as families did. You couldn't blame a virus for doing what it was programmed to do from the moment one cell divided into two. But still, I found it difficult to reconcile my own loss of opportunity with the virus's success. Yes, it won. It took down my body and thrived for some limited period of time, but to what end? No virus walks away with a medal or a certificate or a bonus that buys an in-ground swimming pool. It seems like such a waste.

When I was born, no one could have expected that Darlene would die first, then Dad, then Mom. The invalid in the iron lung would be last.

CHAPTER 23

In the hours before Racine was due to pull up in his Jaguar for their date, Holly decided that the exterior of her neglected house needed an extreme makeover. She ducked out from work and ran to the hardware store to get a can of spray paint and some advice about the garage door from Nip, the owner.

"You checked to make sure nothing was stuck on the track? Like a rock or a stick or something."

"Nothing's stuck that I can see, but I can't get it to go up or down."

"Sounds like your wheels are off the track, or the track got bent somehow. I think you need a handyman."

"Nip," Holly said, looking around to make sure no one could hear. "I can't afford a handyman. I need a quick fix, even if it means taking the garage door off and propping it up against the house."

"Let me get my tools," Nip said. He called his daughter over to watch the register and followed Holly back to her house.

As Nip walked up the driveway, Holly could sense his dismay at how she had let the paint peel and the walkway crumble and the garage door rust into its present position. A man in Nip's business, Holly knew, could not comprehend how anyone could sleep until every hinge was oiled, every screw tightened, every air filter cleaned.

"I'm gonna help you out here, Holly," he said. "I just wish you had asked me earlier."

"What can I do?" she asked. "Just give me a job and I'll do it."

"Well, you can't paint the whole goddamn house in an hour, but you can spray those bare patches and tighten that wonky front rail while I deal with the garage door. What time does your boyfriend get here?"

"He's not my . . . never mind. Around seven."

"And I take it you need some time to freshen up," he said, giving Holly the feeling she needed more fixing up than the house.

"Like a half hour."

"Let's roll," Nip said, striding back over to the garage.

An hour and a half later, the garage door was down, the patches where the paint had peeled away were covered just enough in the waning light, and the railing was upright. Holly tried to give Nip a loaf of frozen banana bread she had in her freezer, but he refused it, which made her feel even more needy.

"Just enjoy your date," Nip said. "And when you're ready to take the plunge, I've got a great house painter to recommend."

Holly nodded, even as she knew it would never happen.

⌒

Racine arrived at her door promptly at 7 p.m. with flowers. She left him on the front steps and dashed inside and left the bouquet on the kitchen counter, still not ready for Racine to see the shabby carpeting and outdated furniture.

"Hi," Racine said when she returned, kissing Holly lightly on one cheek. "Don't you look lovely. I hope you don't mind, but after our first dinner experience, I thought we'd drive into the city instead."

The boys were both busy and had sleepovers planned, so she said, "Why not?" and climbed carefully into Racine's low-slung Jaguar.

An hour later they were zipping down the Henry Hudson Parkway at a speed she found disturbing yet exhilarating. Her city driving was overly cautious, which threw off the taxis and veteran drivers and labeled her an annoying and unpredictable tourist.

They parked in a garage in the Meatpacking District, a neighbor-hood into which she had never ventured, first because of its unappeal-ing name, and lately because it was too cool for middle-aged suburban mothers like her who mostly came to New York on school field trips and rarely ventured far from Fifth Avenue. Racine led her to a small doorway that had no sign on it.

He opened the door for her, and when it closed again she could see only about a foot ahead in the dark hallway. Racine squeezed past her and proceeded down a narrow flight of stairs, which led to a graffiti-covered door, behind which lay a cozy fondue restaurant with exposed brick walls and ten or so intimate tables that ringed a bubbling fountain.

The hostess offered to take her coat as she looked around at chic couples dipping chunks of bread and vegetables into bubbling pots of cheese or chocolate.

"This is charming," she said, catching her breath, which had left her suddenly. The place was almost too perfect, arrogant in its exclu-sivity. But then she chastised herself for being hypercritical. The point was that Racine had wanted to impress her. That in itself was to be appreciated.

Dinner turned out to be a rather brief affair, since the fondue pot had only so much cheese in it, so an hour later they were back out on the street, and Racine asked Holly if she wanted to take a walk on The High Line.

"What's The High Line?" she said. "I hope it's not some sort of code for drugs. My slang is way past its expiration date."

"No," Racine said, throwing his head back with a laugh. "It's a raised railway a couple blocks from here. The city has been converting it into kind of a long, narrow park where you can walk above the street level. You get great views of the river."

"I'm so out of it," she said, taking the hand he offered. "It's embarrassing."

"No, it's kind of refreshing. Most women I meet in the city are a little jaded."

She blushed in the darkness and felt delightfully warm and cheesy inside. They strolled down the sidewalk until they came to an iron stairway that led up to The High Line, which was aglow with lights on a crisp night. They walked south, gazing alternately across the Hudson on their right, which came into view like a painting every few buildings, and across the city streets on the left. Since they were elevated, it was easy to see inside many of the windows in the buildings to the left that were uncurtained and illuminated from inside.

"See, up there, a man playing a violin," Racine pointed out as they walked. "And over there, a woman putting spaghetti into a pot."

At one point a large hotel straddled The High Line, and as they were about to pass under it, Holly glanced up and let out a small gasp. A couple was performing some kind of bizarre sexual performance art in front of a well-lighted window. As she and Racine paused, they noticed that the act had generated a small crowd on The High Line, as well as on the street below.

"Now that would not happen in Bertram Corners," Holly said. "We don't take our clothes off with the lights on."

"You don't?" Racine said. "What a shame."

Racine then brought her hand up to his mouth and kissed the back of it. That simple gesture gave her such unexpected pleasure that she didn't know how to react. She wondered whether she should squeeze his hand in acknowledgment, and then how much pressure to return. She worried that her hand would start to sweat, and while she was assessing all the ways she could ruin the evening, Racine led her to a stairway that descended from the Highline.

"My apartment's right down this block," he said. "Would you like to see it?"

Holly was fairly sure that her answer would be a response to a more significant question. She wanted to sleep with Racine because he was beautiful and made her feel attractive again, but she had been celibate since Chris died, with the exception of one horrible night with a fireman who had responded to one of Vivian's crises and took Holly to his house for a "nightcap" that turned into a fumbling of sorts under green polyester sheets.

"Okay," she said, not looking at him.

He pressed her hand almost imperceptibly.

Ten minutes later they were at a plain brick industrial-looking building. Racine used his key to open an unmarked door and led her up the narrow stairs to a hallway on the third floor. Holly felt as if the hallway were getting more narrow and the air thinner as they approached a white door at the very end. Racine quietly unlocked the door.

Racine's apartment was small but impeccably decorated in masculine browns and beiges. Pieces of art that might have been original lined the exposed brick wall over the compact leather couch in the living room. In sum, it was the interior design equivalent of Racine himself—vaguely foreign and therefore appealing, but with an air of nonpermanence, as if it all came from the pages of a high-end catalogue.

Racine didn't bother to offer Holly a glass of wine or even turn on a light. He simply closed the door and faced her as the light of the city streamed through the windows. He kissed her gently and slid her coat off before she could even say a word about her fears, her reservations, why this might not be a good idea, or even how lovely his apartment was. It was hypnotic, how he knew exactly what to do, and so she let him, with a small sense of anticipation and curiosity.

He kissed her again and moved her through the door of what she presumed to be his bedroom. He guided her toward a bed with a snow-white duvet, the antithesis of the fireman's green sheets. As they shed their layers, she felt herself growing lighter, detaching from what was actually happening so that she could observe it and cut and paste it into her scrapbook of one-time experiences. Racine was a man who logged women—she thought of this even as he was caressing her hair—like entries into a spreadsheet.

She wanted to turn off the commentary in her head, but it didn't seem possible, even as he moved into her and she felt the perfect skin of his hips between her hands. She disassociated the sensations in her body with the cool dialogue she was already having with Racine in her head, a week afterward, when he would surely call to discuss the gold shop, never mentioning their liaison, which she was sure was how he would categorize it. Just two people intersecting on a given night.

But then he kissed her in the most tender possible way, and something broke open inside of her. She had to hold back tears, and she lost track of how it ended, because she was so engulfed in emotion. Racine rolled away, breathing hard, but she continued to stare at the ceiling, afraid to move. She chased the words to describe it, but they skittered away like forgotten names with only the first letter as a clue. She felt exposed—no, revealed. She was a cold egg cracked on the counter, the perfect yolk spilling out. It was all too much.

"I have to go," she said, sitting up.

"Not yet," Racine said, smiling and taking her hand. "It's still early."

"I have to go," she said, putting on the garments rapidly in reverse order of their removal.

Racine kept telling her she didn't need to leave, but that only made her dress faster. She hurried outside and flagged a cab, taking it to the Port Authority, where she found a bus that would take her home.

As she finally approached the driveway, she could see the patches of white spray paint, which glowed under the streetlamps with a different sheen than the rest of the paint. Her house looked like the surface of the moon.

⌒

Holly put down her purse on the hallway table and turned on the light in the living room to find a decorated Christmas tree in the corner. She could hear rustling in the basement and then saw Connor emerge with a handful of tinsel.

Connor ran to the bottom of the stairs. "She's home!"

Marshall came pummeling down the stairs, and the two of them stood grinning in front of the tree, which upon closer inspection was not precisely in the traditional conical shape. It was more like a fat cylinder that leaned a little bit to one side.

"Surprise!"

Holly wavered a little on her borrowed heels—she still hadn't returned them to Marveen—and felt faint. "What is this all about?" she said. "When did you do this? I thought you both had sleepovers."

Marshall started in. "We said we did, but instead we went to the park with my friend Brian, and he had his dad's handsaw—"

"And," Connor interjected, "we brought work gloves, so it was completely safe."

Marshall continued: "And we went way back into the forested part—you know, behind the dugout on the baseball field—and we found this perfect tree and cut it down and brought it home. We're not completely done with the decorations, but it's getting there."

Holly dropped to the couch and put her hands in front of her face. She knew she should tell them that chopping down a tree on public property was a criminal offense, but she couldn't. An avalanche of affection for her children swept her into a place of overwhelming gratitude.

"Boys, this is the nicest present anyone has ever given me," she said, tears running down. "C'mere, you two."

The boys sat down, one on each side of her, and she pulled each one toward her, alternately kissing them on the top of the head.

"Okay, Mom, jeez," Connor said, pulling out of her grasp, though Holly could see that he was pleased with her reaction.

"We know it's been hard lately," Marshall said. Of course they knew, she thought. She tried to hide it, but they were old enough to see her stress when the bills arrived. "We wanted to help out."

"You did," Holly said, wiping her face with a tissue. "So much more than you know."

CHAPTER 24

Holly put in a few early hours at the newspaper so that she could accompany Vivian to the gold store. When she arrived at Vivian's, she had to walk half a block because of all the cars and vans near Vivian's house. Inside, she was greeted by Vivian's medical team and a half dozen of her volunteers, all of them running into each other in the suffocating space of Vivian's living room.

"I've got the generator," one doctor was saying to a nurse. "I'm going to put that in the van first, and then we'll wheel the lung out."

"Holly," Vivian called to her. "I'm almost ready."

Holly made her way through the crowd as various technicians fussed around Vivian.

"What a production, right?" Vivian said, already looking a little tired. "It's like a circus in here."

"You're excited, though, right?" Holly said. "It'll be great to get you outside."

"Absolutely," Vivian said. "The only thing I'm worried about is Racine. He doesn't know I'm coming."

"I thought you were going to tell him."

"I changed my mind. I decided that he would behave differently if he knew about"—she looked around—"all this."

"But he'll know as soon as we squeeze you through the door."

"Right, but he won't have time to prepare. I'll see the operation just as it is."

A nurse put a straw into Vivian's mouth to give her a sip of water as Holly unwrapped one of the mints Vivian kept on a tray for her volunteers. She was now overly conscious of her breath around Racine, to whom she had not spoken since she ran out of his apartment. Holly stepped aside as the medical team approached to wheel Vivian's lung into the waiting van.

"Onward!" Vivian said as the wheels began to move.

Holly thought she sensed a slightly manic edge to Vivian's sudden cheerfulness, but she dutifully followed the iron lung out to the van and crouched inside as the other volunteers huddled in a group on Vivian's lawn, their arms wrapped around their chests, since they had left their coats in the house. A doctor stood next to Vivian's head monitoring her oxygen levels during the ten-minute ride to the gold store. At one point Holly heard a siren, which she assumed meant that the van had a police escort.

"This town would do anything for you, Vivian," Holly said.

"Oh, stop," Vivian said, though Holly could tell that she enjoyed it.

When the van pulled up in front of the gold store, the technicians had to perform a number of complicated maneuvers to set up a ramp and release the iron lung from the restraints that kept it from sliding around in the van. Holly wondered if she should go inside to warn Racine, but she sensed that Vivian wanted to make a grand entrance. The store's entrance was at street level, and fortunately the front door was fairly wide, which meant that Vivian could be wheeled inside on the gurney that supported her iron lung without too much banging and cursing. Holly followed at the foot of the lung and came inside just in time to see Racine emerge from the back room. He looked stunned.

"Racine!" Vivian called out as the technicians pushed her into the center of the room. "I'm Vivian. So nice to finally meet you."

Racine looked toward Holly, who gave him a slightly embarrassed shrug. Then he turned on the high-beam smile, as though he saw iron lungs every day, and opened his arms wide.

"Vivian! I'm so glad you're here! So what do you think?" he said, gesturing toward the glass cases and the three customers in the back of the store having their gold evaluated.

Holly could see that Vivian's vision was limited, so she said, much more loudly than necessary, "Vivian, can you see the customers?"

"Turn me around," Vivian said to the team of technicians. It required a three-point maneuver, but they managed to turn Vivian so that she could look toward the back of the store.

"Excellent," she said. "I apologize for dropping in like this, Racine, but I wanted to check the place out for myself. I like the way you've set up these front counters."

"Thanks," Racine said. "We've actually seen an uptick recently in our resale items because of the holiday."

As Vivian and Racine chatted, Holly took a moment to gaze into the glass cases and look at the watches, brooches, strings of pearls, and rings she could never afford. Jewelry had never consumed her the way it did some of her mother's housewife friends, who collected precious stones over the years as recompense for their boredom, but she appreciated the workmanship. Her eyes then fell on a black-velvet-lined case of engagement and wedding rings, which called to mind her recent trip to the pawn shop. She scanned the diamond rings, most of them standard solitaires, but then saw a large pear-shaped stone with emerald baguettes on each side.

Her mother's ring.

". . . so as I've told Holly, we're set to make all our targets this month," Racine was telling Vivian. "I think you'll be very pleased."

"Racine," Holly said. "Can I look at the rings?"

Racine looked reluctant to leave Vivian's side, but he walked around to the back of the counter and unlocked the sliding door of the glass display case, putting the rings on top.

"Are you in the market?" Vivian asked.

"I just saw one that reminded me of my mother's," she said, picking it up. Holly slipped it over her left ring finger and felt a chill. Her own hands—blue veined and almost translucent in the harsh fluorescent light—looked just like her mother's had looked when Holly had been a teenager. She was sure this was her mother's ring, but she didn't want to alarm Vivian until she could talk to Racine. She put the ring back in the box.

"Well, everything looks tip-top," Vivian said, sounding ready to leave. "I'm sure you can see now, Racine, why I hired Holly to be my stand-in, since I literally cannot stand. I hope I haven't startled you."

Racine shook his head. "Of course not, Vivian. You're welcome here anytime."

Holly admired Racine's composure, because she knew it was Vivian's intention to rattle him a bit. The thought of Vivian "dropping in" again would surely keep him on his toes more than Holly's occasional visits.

Holly stayed behind as the technicians prepared to move Vivian back out into the van.

"Do you have a minute?" she said to Racine.

"Of course."

"You told me once that the resale items come from different stores. Is there any way to trace them?"

Racine looked back at the case, but before he could answer, Vivian called from the doorway.

"Holly, let's go," she said. "I'd like to be back in time for *Judge Judy*."

"I'll stop back in tomorrow," Holly said, following Vivian, though she was reluctant to part from the ring, which now represented all that had been lost when her mother—her real mother—disappeared down the rabbit hole. At the same time, she had no idea how to tell Racine that her own mother's missing ring was in his jewelry case. He would surely tell her there was some mistake. Money, especially easy money, had a tendency to make people lie. She had seen it time and again while reporting on the larceny and embezzlement that happened even in a quiet place like Bertram Corners. And if she sensed he was lying, she wouldn't be able to trust him. She would never again be broken like an egg and revealed.

⌒

"So what did you think?" Holly asked.

The technicians and volunteers were all gone, *Judge Judy* was over, and Holly sat once again alone with Vivian.

"He was pretty much as I imagined him to be," Vivian said. "His voice is very much like his appearance. There's something incredibly smooth about him. Maybe a little too smooth."

"I meant the store. But I know what you're saying. It's tough to be around someone who is twice as charming and attractive as you are."

"I don't know about *twice*," Vivian said, smiling.

"What about the store, though? Is it what you envisioned? Do you think it will make money?"

"I think Racine will make money. The minute he walks out to start up a new one, it's not going to be nearly as enticing to go there."

"Does that worry you?"

"It'll be okay. The unemployment rate isn't likely to go down soon, so we'll have a decent base of customers."

Holly could not dispute the wisdom of that unfortunate statement. She changed the subject.

"Did I tell you that Marveen asked me for a leave of absence so she could renovate her kitchen? Some people aren't doing so badly in this economy."

"Some people always benefit from the misery of the masses. I guess I should include myself, since I'm the one backing this store . . . Still, I feel sorry for Marveen sometimes. She's married to that house like it's a living thing. If she had children, she wouldn't care about having the latest nickel-plated faucet. And what does it get her in the end? How does society benefit from an overdecorated home?"

Holly had never heard Vivian criticize Marveen in quite that way. She agreed completely, but something made her want to stick up for Marveen, since she wasn't there to defend herself.

"At least she's keeping the kitchen people employed," Holly said, though she didn't mention that Marveen's husband had gotten promoted by laying people off.

"This is true," Vivian said, suddenly sounding tired again. "Marveen should do what makes her happy."

"Not having to pay her salary might give us another few months of life at the *Chronicle*," Holly said, trying to sound cheerful. "Maybe it was meant to be."

Vivian's eyebrows pulled together in a look that Holly had seen only once before, when one of her volunteers accidently threw out her telephone headset.

"Nothing is ever 'meant to be,' Holly," she said. "It's nothing more than an excuse. I'm the perfect example of that kind of thinking—everyone's always telling me I was spared for a reason, and I'm getting too old for it anymore."

Like most people, Holly wanted to believe there was some lesson to be learned in her own misfortune, some developmental pain required to reach a gentler phase of life. If she didn't subscribe to that notion, she would have a hard time putting one foot in front of the other. And yet she knew that Vivian was probably right.

She said none of this to Vivian, who, she suddenly realized, might secretly hold the opposite point of view. Otherwise, how could she go on?

↜

Holly found a letter from the bank in her mailbox when she got home later that night. This one wasn't from her old friend Vince but from

susan schoenberger

some corporate official, who told her she had until January to submit her missing mortgage payments. If she failed to do so, foreclosure proceedings would begin. She had no idea if foreclosure took a month or year, but the thought of closing the door to her house one last time and being out on the street with her boys and all her belongings gave her another panic attack—which is what a WebMD search told her she had had before—as she sat alone in her kitchen. She put her head between her knees and tried to breathe. When the attack subsided, she went into the living room and saw the fully decorated Christmas tree, its white lights aglow in the semidarkness. Connor was on the living-room couch doing some homework. She sat down and put her arm around his shoulder.

"The tree is beautiful, honey," she said. "It really makes me happy that you boys thought of it."

"Everything's going to be okay, Mom," Connor said. "Really, it will."

"You think so?" she said, squeezing his shoulder. It made her simultaneously sad and proud that he would try to comfort her.

"My band director says hard times make us appreciate the good ones, and you may never know why you're being tested," he said. "Some things are just meant to be."

Just as she could not dispute Vivian's logic, she couldn't dispute Connor's either.

"I'm sure your band director is right, sweetheart," Holly said, rubbing his head.

She sometimes wondered how her boys might have turned out had she been able to give them whatever they asked for. Entitlement had its own pitfalls.

"He's absolutely right," she said. "Now go to bed."

CHAPTER 25

Vivian's Unaired Podcast #9

I was one of the first to use a long stylus between my teeth that let me manipulate a cursor. I would work at it for hours, because it gave me something I had always craved—direct connection. I could write— write!—without dictating to someone else, just by pressing letters with the stylus on my customized overhead keyboard. It was painstaking, but I was so grateful to eliminate the middleman that I didn't care how long it took.

As far as the online world was concerned, I was no longer a medical anomaly trapped inside a machine; I was the equal of everyone else with a computer—just as whole, just as nimble, just another seeker, no longer in-valid. My screen name was VBucks—genderless, ageless, without disability, suggestive of wealth. I was a complete person who could navigate the world and its resources without moving more than my head.

It would be years before the rest of the world reached my level of Internet obsession. I was one of the first to start an online diary, which later evolved into a blog and eventually into my weekly podcast. I felt like a prisoner who finally emerges from captivity, blinking into the daylight.

Of course, connectivity had its downside. I repeatedly fell in love with people I met online and always had to tell them eventually that a face-to-face meeting would never happen. Once I let it go too far with a guy named Dennis (screen name: Indie D). We met in a forum devoted to independent films, one of my passions, and began corresponding via instant message:

> *VBucks: Can't believe Steven Soderbergh is willing to direct Andie MacDowell in another movie.*
>
> *Indie D: He's in love with her. Can't you tell from the long, lingering close-ups of her face?*
>
> *VBucks: You must be right. There's no other explanation.*
>
> *Indie D: I'm definitely right. Mark my words, they'll be married within a year and divorced six months later . . . You ever been married?*
>
> *VBucks: No . . . you?*
>
> *Indie D: Once, but it didn't last much longer than what I predict for the MacSoderberghs . . . You know, it's been so great talking to you. I feel like we have so much in common.*
>
> *VBucks: Me too.*
>
> *Indie D: I hope this doesn't sound weird, but would you send me a picture?*
>
> *Long pause.*
>
> *VBucks: OK, but you'll have to send me one, too.*

I knew it was risky, but I didn't want to lose contact with Dennis, so I had Marveen take a picture of my face without showing the iron lung. When he sent me his, I almost cried. He was a lovely man, probably in his midforties—a little tired and lonely around the eyes. We talked every day, sometimes for hours. He finally said he would be in New York for business and wanted to know if I'd meet him in the city.

I had to end it there. I couldn't bear to tell him about my condition online, and I certainly didn't want him to see me. I did the cowardly thing. I switched my screen name and never went on that forum again. I didn't respond to any of his IMs or e-mails. In the moments before I fell asleep each night, I pined for Indie D the way I had pined for my fellow iron lunger Lance and for an end to my life when I was seventeen.

I never talked about these crushes with my caregivers, though, because of the inevitable questions. No, I could never have a physical relationship with another person, or at least not from the neck down. But that just proves that love is primarily a mental connection. What we truly crave—at least from what I understand of it—is a reflection of ourselves. People can't walk around with a mirror in front of their faces all day, so they seek out someone who reflects back their own self-worth. Love, when you think about it, is a value proposition, much like the stock market, which is probably why I never quite gave up on it.

⌣

As the Internet became more accessible and more people bought home computers, my list of volunteers grew exponentially. Everyone wanted to get my advice about what kind of computer to buy, how to set up an e-mail account, and to ask me what a gigabyte was. I was the Steve Jobs of Bertram Corners.

It was around that time that I met Holly, who had come back to live in the town where she grew up. She was newly married and working as a reporter for the local weekly, but she had some time on her hands and volunteered to sit with me a few times a week during the unpopular 11 p.m. to 1 a.m. shift. We clicked instantly. Holly seemed like the kind of person I would have become had it not been for the polio. She was bright and funny, open and caring, attractive but not obsessed with her looks. She loved a good pun. She was one of the few caregivers I was always sad to see go at the end of her shift. "I really admire you, Vivian," she said once, after we'd known each other for about a year.

"Why?"

"Because you say what you think. I've never been able to do that. I usually say what I think people want to hear."

"But you're a reporter. Don't you have to challenge politicians and dig up dirt on people?"

"I'll let you in on a little journalism secret. Most of what I do could be categorized as PR."

"Why did you go into journalism then?"

"You can't know what it's like until you're actually doing it. And maybe it would have been different on a big-city daily, but Chris and I wanted to live in a small town. I loved growing up here. So you take what you can get. And I won't be doing this forever."

I recall being a little disappointed in her attitude. You don't just take what you can get when you're young and able-bodied and reasonably intelligent. You set lofty goals, climb the ladder, fighting for every step. You scoot up to the wall between the sane and the insane and at least look over. Does anyone have an excuse to live an ordinary life? Not when you have all the resources you need to succeed. Not when it's just about motivation.

It wasn't long before Holly was pregnant with Marshall and settled into a fixer-upper that would never get fixed up or outgrown or paid off. Connor arrived three years later, and despite her new-mother responsibilities, Holly never took a leave from her schedule on the rotation. Sometimes she even brought one of the boys with her in a car carrier.

"Do you ever wish you could be alone?" she asked me one day. "The kids need me constantly. Sometimes I just fantasize about renting a cheap motel room and bringing a stack of paperbacks so I don't have to interact with anyone at all. Just for, like, a day."

"I don't think I've ever been left alone for more than a few minutes," I told her. "I guess I can't crave what I never had, although it does get tedious sometimes when some of my volunteers want to chat and I'm worn out. Sometimes I just close my eyes and pretend to be asleep. They eventually shut up."

We bonded, Holly and I, because she asked me those kinds of questions and because she came back week after week, year after year, as others got too busy and dropped off the list or couldn't handle being close to someone who represented their worst medical fears. No one but Holly thought I would want to talk about the obvious difficulties, but I did. A part of me wanted everyone to know just how hard it was to be me.

CHAPTER 26

Holly ate an aging apple from the fruit bowl on Marveen's abandoned desk before walking down to the gold store. The apple sloshed around in her otherwise empty stomach as she passed the pharmacy where Darla would be ringing up customers. The economy, as broken as it was, still chugged on for most people, she realized. Even with high unemployment, the vast majority of people had some kind of job, squeezing every last benefit for all it was worth. Only a small minority would be spit out altogether by the economic engine, she thought as she approached Dunkin' Donuts, the aroma of which almost made her faint. She hadn't had a good cup of coffee in ages. She stopped in front of the plate-glass window at Dunkin' Donuts and put on a quick coat of the only lipstick she owned that didn't require a Q-tip. She pressed her lips together and noticed how the cold air accentuated the lines around her eyes.

The gold store was busy when she came in, so she waited until Racine finished with a customer.

"Can we talk?" she said.

"We need to," he said, leading her toward the back room.

She put her purse down on a small desk next to which was a single metal folding chair. She noticed that Racine had done nothing to personalize the space in the months the store had been open. Besides the desk and chair, there was a laptop, a phone, and a power strip. The walls were bare, more evidence that Racine would vacuum Bertram Corners for its gold and leave it with nothing but a trace of cologne and the memory of his magnetic smile.

"Why didn't you tell me?" Racine said. He ran a hand over his hair and then dropped it down by his side.

Holly had been so focused on her mother's ring that she forgot about Vivian's surprise visit.

"I had no idea what was coming through the door," he said, his voice strained. "I've never even heard of an iron lung before. I had to look it up online after you left."

"I'm sorry, but Vivian asked me not to say anything," Holly said. "She said her business partners get nervous when they know about her disability."

"Then why did she show up?"

Holly paused, not wanting to tell Racine that Vivian mainly wanted to ogle him like the rest of the town. She wondered if he understood just how much he stood out in Bertram Corners. To the residents of a small town, he was like the okapi at the zoo—so unusual that it drew a crowd.

"I think she just wanted an excuse to get out," Holly said. "She spends all her time in one room, and she gets bored sometimes. I think also she wanted to shake you up a little."

"Mission accomplished," he said, running a hand over his hair again.

"Really? Because I thought you handled it so well. You were completely on."

"On?"

"The charm. You turned it right on, like you do for all the customers."

"It's not something I'm conscious of turning on and off," Racine said, pulling his shoulders back.

"Don't get upset. It's a huge asset."

Racine let his shoulders drop and looked down. "I just wish you had warned me. I thought we had something more than a business relationship."

Holly wasn't sure what to say. Part of her was relieved to hear Racine use the word "relationship." Another part of her thought he was being unfair. She still had to do her job for Vivian.

"We do," she said. "And you're right. I should have warned you. But the reason I came over today has nothing to do with that, or with Vivian."

Racine sat down on the desk. "What then?"

"You know that ring I asked to see yesterday?"

"The diamond with the emerald baguettes."

"Yes. Do you know where it came from?"

Racine ran a hand over his jawline, which had a day's worth of stubble on it. He looked like he hadn't slept much the night before.

"We get most of our resale jewelry from the stores in New York. Why?"

"It's my mother's ring."

Holly was sure that Racine would deny it, but instead he began shuffling through a pile of papers on the desk.

"Are you sure?"

"Positive. She's in a nursing home in Connecticut now, but it went missing a few months ago from her rehab place right after she had a stroke. The staff said we shouldn't have brought in valuables, so there's nothing we can do. We've been hoping it would turn up, but I never expected to see it here."

Racine continued rifling through papers until he pulled one out. "It came with a shipment from New York last week."

"I guess I can't really prove it's my mother's ring. It's unusual, but I'm not sure it was one of a kind."

Racine walked out of the back room, unlocked the cabinet, and came back with the ring. "This one, right?" She looked at it again in his palm and nodded, reaching out to take it. Racine closed his hand before she could. "I'll try to track down what happened. Don't worry, though. I'll keep it safe and get it back to you as soon as I can."

Holly nodded again. If she couldn't trust him, she needed to know that now.

"I'm sure it's my mother's ring," she said. "And I do need it back."

"I won't let you down," Racine said. He squeezed the ring and held up his fist. "You might not believe it, because of the business I'm in, but I don't put things before people."

Then Racine kissed her in a way that could have meant *Can't wait to see you again* or *Good-bye*.

⌣

On the way back to the office, Holly stopped into Radio Shack to see what she could buy her boys for Christmas. The cell phones they wanted were far too much money and required monthly payment plans. Anything else was either too expensive or essentially worthless to them—accessories for the phones and game systems they could never have.

She left empty-handed, then walked idly into a used-book store that was closing. She wandered the crammed aisles, examining the titles, when she came upon a hardcover of *Where the Red Fern Grows*. She pulled it out and examined the worn jacket. This had been Chris's favorite book as a child, one he'd never had a chance to read to the boys. She started to put it back but changed her mind.

"Do you have a basket?" she asked the ponytailed man at the counter.

He nodded and handed her a plastic container with a handle. She spent the next half hour pulling books from the shelves and CDs from the dusty bins in the back. She pulled anything she thought that Chris would have liked and would have wanted the boys to have: *Treasure Island* and *Catcher in the Rye*, CDs of Miles Davis and Nirvana and the Beastie Boys. She filled the basket, and the total came to $89.49, which left her enough money to buy them some candy for their stockings. She left the store feeling that she had hit upon the one gift that wouldn't be obsolete or out of fashion by January. The one and only thing that would matter.

On Christmas Day each boy had a stack of presents under the tree. Holly watched them open each book and CD and read the inscriptions telling them about Chris's connection to that story or that music. They took turns reading aloud from *The Hobbit*, inside which Holly had written "This was your dad's favorite book in middle school. He used to say he couldn't wait to read it with the two of you." In the glow of the tree her sons had cut down illegally just to show her how much they loved her, she thought that she had never had a more perfect Christmas.

⌒

Stan knocked on Holly's office door as she was putting together the four-page holiday edition that came out between Christmas and New Year's. It was always the smallest edition of the year so that her staff could take a break over the holidays. Stan looked as if he had eaten some bad clams.

"God, Stan, you look awful," Holly said. "Sit down. What's wro . . . oh."

Holly was certain that the bad-clam expression was now on her own face.

"We're closing," said Stan, who nodded, then left his head down.

Holly felt as if she had been punched in the abdomen.

"I'm so sorry, Holly," he said, finally looking up. "You have until the end of January. The directors were hoping the holiday ads would pick us up, but they didn't."

"Is there any hope?" she said, panic starting to rise in her chest again. "Any chance they'll change their minds?"

"I don't think so," he said, slumping down in his chair. "No one's buying anything. No one's advertising anything. They're all just waiting to see what happens, and waiting kills newspapers."

"Marveen took a leave of absence," Holly said. "Won't that buy us a little time?"

"It's over, Holly. We can offer people the vacation pay that's coming to them after we close. They have the option to buy into the state insurance plan for up to a year, but essentially everyone should start a job search as soon as possible."

"In an economy where no one's hiring."

"You don't have to remind me. I'm out, too. My last day is the same as yours."

"But your kids are in college."

Stan put his elbows on Holly's desk and put his head in his hands. He looked up with a sad smile. "Remember when we were idealistic young journalists who thought we could make the world a better place? We wanted to chase out corrupt politicians and uncover fraud and investigate murders. It turns out we were just filling space around the ads, and nobody really cared that much about what we wrote."

"I'll let you in on a secret. I never really wanted to do the hard stuff," Holly said. "I wanted to write stories about the school plays and the Eagle Scout awards and the town budget. I thought that was the important part."

"It was, Lois," Stan said, his voice thick. "It was all important. Every word you ever wrote. And don't forget that."

"So put on your Superman cape and spin the world backward to turn back time, Clark," she said, with her own sad smile. "That should fix the problem."

Stan let out a tired laugh. "The cape's at the dry cleaner's, Lois," he said, "which I can no longer afford."

~~

By New Year's Eve, Holly had gotten a few uninformative texts from Racine, but he wasn't returning her calls. The gold store was opened each day by the appraisers, but she saw few customers inside.

"You've tried his cell phone?" Vivian asked her as the clock ticked toward midnight. Vivian's regular Thursday night volunteer had had New Year's Eve plans, so Holly had stepped in. The boys were both at parties that involved sleepovers, and she didn't relish watching the ball drop by herself, nursing a cup of weak tea. Vivian, at least, was good company.

"Of course I've tried his cell phone," Holly said. "He just texts back and says he's working on something, and he'll be in touch when he can."

Holly had told Vivian all about her mother's ring, but Vivian wanted to talk to Racine before she tried to extricate herself from the investment. Holly worried that the gold store made its real money from stolen merchandise, and if it did, she wondered how Racine could have been unaware of it. From the beginning, her confidence in his sincerity had an inverse relationship to the length of time they were separated.

"Another year," Vivian said, sighing. "Every year at midnight I'm absolutely sure that I won't be around to see that damned ridiculous crystal-covered ball drop, and then here I am, watching the whole spectacle again. Have you ever been in Times Square on New Year's Eve?"

"Are you kidding? That's the last place I'd want to be, packed into that crowd like a sardine, freezing cold, no place to go to the bathroom. It's my worst nightmare."

"And yet they all look so happy."

"That's the alcohol."

"That reminds me. I had Marveen get me a bottle of champagne. Should we open it?"

"I thought you weren't supposed to drink."

"I'm not. But I break the rules every now and again. What do you say?"

"Why not?"

Holly went to the kitchen and found the champagne in the re-frigerator. She popped the cork, then poured hers into a water glass—Vivian didn't own wine glasses—and Vivian's into one of her plastic cups with the attached straw.

It was almost midnight. The ball had already started inching its way down, which always seemed to Holly like the coward's way to sneak up on the new year. By all rights, she thought, the ball should free-fall and shatter into a million pieces.

"Ten-nine-eight-seven-six-five-four-three-two-one," Vivian said, surprising Holly with her enthusiasm. "Happy new year!"

"Happy new year, Vivian," Holly said, clicking her glass with Vivian's plastic one. She held the straw to Vivian's mouth and let her take a sip of champagne before taking one of her own. She had eaten early, so the alcohol hit her almost instantly.

"Nice," Vivian said. "I feel like a grown-up, even drinking out of a straw."

"It's lovely," Holly said, closing her eyes. "It takes me momentarily out of my mess of a life."

When Holly opened her eyes again, she could see Vivian staring at her. Once again she felt guilty about calling her life anything less than perfect in Vivian's presence.

"Tell me what's going on," Vivian said. "Well, give me another sip of champagne first, then tell me what's going on."

Holly put the straw in Vivian's mouth and watched her suck down half the glass in one pull. She then took a long sip of her own, feeling the bubbles rising through her brain.

"You really want to know?" Holly said, taking a deep breath. "Well, the bank is about to foreclose on my house because I can't pay the mortgage anymore—my mother was helping me, but now all her money is tied up in the nursing home. The newspaper is going under at the end of January, so I won't have a job or health insurance. My rich brother, Henderson, went bankrupt, so I can't ask him for money, and my sister has even less than I do. And Racine, as you know, is a question mark at best."

"Oh, Holly," Vivian said. "Why didn't you tell me before?"

"What could you do, Vivian? You're already paying me for a made-up job."

Vivian nodded at the cup with the champagne in it, and Holly held it up to her again. She drained it.

"We need a plan," Vivian said. "And as long as we're telling the truth here, I should tell you that my accountant says that most of my investments are basically worthless right now. I was heavily into growth stocks that have completely tanked, so my only hope of climbing back right now is the gold store. I haven't even told him about the ring situation."

"Vivian, no. That can't be. What if the store goes under and we can't get your money back?"

Vivian let out a long shuddering sigh. "I won't be destitute. I own the house free and clear, and I get my medical disability checks every month. My medical bills are covered. Lots of people live on less. I just wanted to have something to show for all those years my parents sacrificed. I was hoping to make a big charity donation in their names when I died—you know, like those secretive cat ladies who stash money in the mattress and endow a library or something."

She looked at Holly. "But you're much more important to me than a library. We'll figure this out. I'm not going to let you and your boys suffer."

Holly drained her own champagne. She told Vivian about the boys and their Christmas tree and about the gifts she gave them after selling her wedding ring.

"They deserve so much more," Holly said, now weeping champagne tears. "I can't even keep a roof over their heads."

"You've done everything you can. Now it's time you let someone else help you out."

For an hour Holly resisted. She wanted to keep her house. Yes, it was falling apart, but it still held their memories, and she didn't want to give up on Chris's dream of adding to its history. She thought about his plans to renovate the bathrooms and his stubborn refusal to replace the crushed-stone driveway even after the pebbles, always in the boys' pockets, ruined their washing machine. But Vivian finally convinced her that holding on to the house would only drag her down. They decided that Holly would send her keys to the bank and move in with Vivian. That would take the pressure off the mortgage situation. When the newspaper closed, Holly would use her unemployment checks to buy into the state's health insurance plan while she looked for another job.

When the nursing aide came at two in the morning, Holly left Vivian's feeling simultaneously relieved and tortured. She couldn't be more grateful to have a free place to live, even if it meant leaving her cherished home behind, but how would the boys react? If she couldn't find another job, she might end up even more in Vivian's debt. And what about Racine? She thought he was basically decent, if a little misguided. She never would have pegged him for the kind of man who would run off with stolen goods, especially after she told him what the ring meant to her. And if he had run off, why was he texting her?

As if to respond to the query she threw out to the universe, Holly's phone rang as she was driving home, and she let it go to voice mail. When she pulled into the driveway, she took the phone out of her purse to see that she had a message.

"Holly, it's Racine. I know you've been trying to reach me, and I'm so sorry. It's kind of a long story, but I still have your mother's ring. I'll give it back as soon as I can. Please don't forget about me. I'll be in touch soon."

Don't forget about me? Holly couldn't get over what a strange thing that was to say, especially since she could never forget what it felt like to be unearthed and turned inside out after being entombed in her worries for so long. She was not in love with Racine—at least she didn't think she was—but she wanted to be. She wanted to lie awake in bed thinking about the way he touched the small of her back when they walked into the Bertram Corners Inn, drop his name into conversations, moon over his smile or the way his suit jacket fit his shoulders. But she found it hard to sigh when she couldn't breathe. Too many anxieties crowded her every thought, leaping and pushing each other as they shouted for her attention. She had no time for love or even lust when every day was a marathon of maneuvering just to keep from slipping further behind.

CHAPTER 27
Vivian's Unaired Podcast #10

The online world was hot and dense through the '90s, but then the Internet exploded like the Big Bang into billions of particles of potential energy. Most of them went flying off into space without consequence, but some connected and grew and changed the world at an exponential rate.

It wasn't just me and my geek friends chatting on message boards anymore; the entire population of the First World was suddenly typing and sharing every thought that had ever entered their excitable little heads. I was a little annoyed at first that everyone suddenly seemed to have a computer and could use it without much, if any, specialized knowledge. But then I realized that my sphere of influence had expanded once again. I e-mailed back and forth with an iron-lung patient in Ireland, and I contributed to a polio study being conducted in Ukraine. I was able to download more and more movies to my computer and watch them whenever I wanted instead of waiting for them to arrive on the cable channels or network television.

My investing took another leap forward as information went online at an accelerating pace, and in turn I purchased the best, most powerful personal computer I could afford. I had become so adept at using my voice-recognition device that I could send an e-mail almost as fast as a typist with ten working fingers.

But as the Internet opened doors for me, it also took a jackhammer to Bertram Corners and left jagged holes in its economy. The small paper mill that employed a quarter of the town closed down because envelopes and paper became a quaint notion associated with prior centuries. Many of the local shops couldn't compete with the new online retailers and closed their doors, leaving sad little orphaned storefronts that no one loved anymore. The schools and the churches and the institutions like Holly's weekly persevered, but they had to fight for every dollar. The Internet revolution—which should have eased our lives—instead threw a pall over the town, which couldn't seem to adjust to a new way of thinking.

I tried to help. I volunteered my services to the library and recorded tutorials so that the little old ladies of Bertram Corners could sign up for e-mail accounts and learn how to check a website when they wanted to book a flight to Las Vegas. Holly called me the Cyber Siren, claiming that I wanted to lure everyone to my own dark side.

"Sometimes I just get tired of these blogs and these long e-mail strings where you have to hear about every random thought that ever crossed someone's mind."

"You don't get it," I said. "I spent decades, Holly, with only my mother around, and she wasn't much of a talker. If you want to tell me that you're drinking coffee or that you just mowed your lawn or that your kid lost a tooth and that made you cry, I'm all ears. I want to know everything. I am the definition of living vicariously."

"Really? Because it all just seems like oversharing to me."

"Well, you're living it," I told her. "But you're also reporting and writing about Bertram Corners, so maybe none of it's new to you."

"I could say that about you," Holly replied. "You've got the whole town circulating in and out of here on a weekly basis. You know more than I do about what's happening."

Holly was right to some extent. But what I knew wasn't posted online; I knew the scars and the scabs underneath the makeup. I was the one who told Darla to leave her first husband after he came home drunk one night and gave her a black eye.

"What happened to you?" I asked her when she came for her volunteer shift.

She touched the bruised, yellowing skin under her eye, and burst into tears.

"I'm supposed to say that I walked into a door," she said. "That's what Harry told me to tell everyone."

I looked at her with pity. I was completely vulnerable to anyone's abuse, and yet I had never been mistreated. I didn't really know what it was like to be punched or kicked, but I did know what Darla needed to do.

"Do you have a suitcase with you?"

"I can't leave," she said. "I have nowhere to go."

"You do. You can stay right here with me. In the morning you'll go to the police station and report him."

Darla put a hand over her mouth and stifled a sob. "He'll find me. He'll make me pay for reporting him."

"So he gets away with it? He gets to beat you up whenever he wants?"

"You don't understand."

"You're right," I said, holding her gaze. "I can't understand at all. He's a monster, and you need to leave him and start a new life. Look inside yourself and find the strength to do it."

Darla stayed over that night, and in the morning she reported the assault. Eventually, she divorced him and got the house and the dogs when the bastard moved to Florida. Then she met Phil and had a real marriage, the kind where the only battles were over the TV remote.

I was the receptacle for all the subterranean drama in Bertram Corners because I listened. I was a captive audience, and I needed my volunteers, but I paid in lost sleep and free therapy. Maybe that's why I didn't mind the online chatter about the quotidian stuff. It seemed like the best part of the life I never had.

CHAPTER 28

Years later Holly remembered that first week in January as the dividing line between one phase of her life and another. She had to tell her newspaper staff that they would be shutting down in a few weeks, and she had to tell her boys they would be leaving the only home they had ever known.

"But why so soon?" Portia asked when Holly broke the news at the *Chronicle*. "Can't they give us a little transition time? A few more months to find new jobs?"

Darla began to cry, and Les, who for once wasn't out covering a high school game, put an arm around her. Les, Holly suddenly realized, had aged significantly in the ten years they had worked together. He had a paunch now from eating too many vending-machine dinners in overheated gymnasiums and much of his hair was gone, circling the drain with his dignity. Les, who had once covered the State House for the daily paper in Albany, had been a victim of the great contraction of the American print media, a vicious game of musical chairs in which more than half the chairs were eliminated with every round, leaving the remaining few reporters grappling over what was left.

"Did Stan say there was any hope?" Les said. "Maybe someone will buy the paper. It's happened in other places."

"It's remotely possible, but I wouldn't pin my hopes on it," Holly said. "The strange part is that we still make money, although the margins are smaller than they used to be. Apparently we just don't make enough to keep the owners happy."

Darla wiped her eyes on the sleeve of her drugstore jacket, which she had forgotten to remove when she came back from lunch.

"I can't go home and tell Phil," she said, sniffing loudly. "I just can't."

Portia was the one to finally ask the question Holly knew was coming. "What will you do?" she said.

Holly looked around at the cluttered office and saw the desks piled halfway to the ceiling with back issues of the *Chronicle* and old phone books, the empty water cooler in the corner that they kept even after they couldn't afford to refill it, the hole in the suspended ceiling where Les had punted a football one day while demonstrating the exciting finish of a high school game for a group of visiting Cub Scouts, the line of Smurf figurines that Darla had set up on the edge of her cubicle, targets for Portia's remarkable skill in launching a rubber band. It was a scrap heap, a landfill, but in the articles long yellowed and the notebooks filled with the quotes of widows and widowers, science fair winners and grieving parents, school superintendents and principals, mayors and police officers was the history of Bertram Corners. The sum total of a town.

Holly shrugged and tried to smile, but the corners of her mouth trembled. "We'll be okay," she said. "I'll find something. And Vivian has offered to let me and the boys move in."

"You're selling your house?" Les asked.

"More like giving it back to the bank. That was inevitable even without this news. This just puts us on the sidewalk a little sooner."

Portia put her hands up to her face. "Holly, no."

"Look, guys," Holly said, "this is not the end of the world. We're all going to figure out how to move forward from here. In the end we'll probably all be grateful that we weren't stuck here until retirement. Try to see it as an opportunity. I do."

Holly guessed that her optimistic sentiment might be true for at least a few of them. But she knew that this would break one or two of her colleagues, perhaps permanently. They would drift around, writing freelance for too little money and taking on short-term projects, sending out résumés and going to interviews until one day they just gave up and folded themselves into a small corner of the world they once knew, biding their time until Social Security kicked in. That might be her story.

⌒

At home the news did not go down any easier.

"How will I get to school?" Connor said. "Vivian's on the other side of town."

"I'll still drive you," Holly said. "It really won't be much different. You'll have to share a room, but Vivian has a basement we could fix up."

Marshall looked down at his hands and rubbed them together. "I hate this, Mom," he said, his voice hoarse. "I do not want to move into that freak show, with all the volunteers coming and going every hour of the day and night."

Holly rubbed her temples. She hated to disappoint her kids in any way, but this seemed so primal, so essential. She felt like she had let them down, and yet she had to hold it together. Someone needed to be in charge. Besides, she thought they were being unfair to Vivian, who was saving them.

"It's not a freak show, Marshall," she said at a volume that surprised even her. "We're very fortunate that Vivian is generous enough to give us a place to live rent-free. I know it's not ideal, but we don't have too many options right now."

Connor left for the basement without saying another word. Marshall looked like a young child trying to hold back tears.

"I have a girlfriend now, Mom. Did you know that?" he said. "And I haven't even invited her here, because of how everything's falling apart. Don't you think the whole town is going to find out that Vivian took us in like charity cases? How do you think that makes me feel?"

Holly looked around the living room. The Christmas tree was half brown, but she hadn't been able to bring herself to take off the ornaments and remove it. The couch—secondhand to begin with—was now so worn and frayed that most of it was draped with throws. She turned the cushions to their slightly better side on the rare occasions they had company.

"You have every right to be upset, Marshall," she said. "But in some ways this is going to be better for all of us. If I don't have a mortgage to pay, maybe we can find the money for your driving classes."

"Don't even say that, Mom. You're losing your job, too. There won't be any money for driving classes . . . I just want to graduate from high school and start my own life."

"Marshall," said Holly, who felt her son's pain as keenly as her own, "I'll find a way."

"No, Mom," he said. "I'll find a way."

꜒

As difficult as it was to accept, the plan to move in with Vivian gave them all purpose, things to be checked off a list, which required forward motion. The first thing Holly did was organize a yard sale so that she could pare down the belongings they would be cramming into Vivian's small Cape. Since it was January and their yard was covered in snow, she called it an "estate sale" in the classified ad she snuck into the paper for free. That had a better ring to it, although she was afraid it might attract people looking for things of actual value. She invited Desdemona and Henderson, who both wanted to sell a few things of their own, and she got the boys to plaster the upscale subdivision near their house with signs and flyers.

In preparation Holly and the boys set up folding tables borrowed from the newspaper office in the living room and kitchen. They all scoured the house looking for items they could live without. Holly told the boys they could keep the proceeds of whatever items they sold, so they were highly motivated to part with their possessions. Maybe too motivated.

"What's this?" Holly said. She was putting white sticky strips on each of the boys' items so they could determine a price.

"It's the Xbox Uncle Hen gave me," Connor said. "And all my games. Maybe some kid will want them."

"But you love these. This is your favorite form of entertainment."

Marshall heard them as he was dumping two old tennis rackets on a table. "Who would want that anyway?" he said. "It's ancient technology."

"I've outgrown it," Connor said.

Holly had to turn away so the boys wouldn't see her face. "Help me with this," she said, pointing to an empty bookshelf from IKEA that she had dragged up from the basement. "Over here."

They moved the bookshelf, then Holly slapped a sticker on it and wrote "$10." She had no idea how much to charge people for her worn and practically worthless possessions, but she had to start somewhere. She put a sticker on the beat-up couch that said "Move it and it's yours" and went on to the kitchen items, which included a hot-air popcorn popper and a blender with a cracked lid.

Desdemona soon showed up at the front door with a canvas bag full of scarves, old costume jewelry, and some tutus and ballet skirts she no longer used.

"This is great, Des," Holly said. "We'll set you up over here with your own table. Girls will love this stuff."

"All right," she said, sounding tired.

"What's wrong?" Holly asked. "You look like you haven't slept in a week."

"It's the collection agency for Aunt Muriel's casket. They're calling me day and night. I'd turn off the phone, but I'm always afraid I'll miss a call about Mom, or maybe a dance company call. It's horrible, Holly."

Aunt Muriel was gone, Holly thought, and yet she still owed money on her final home. Death, apparently, was no escape from bill collectors.

"Why are they calling you?" Holly said. "Henderson picked it out."

"I guess my name was first on the documents or something. They'll probably hit both of you next."

"How much do we owe them?"

"Close to eight thousand."

"What were we thinking?" Holly said. Looking back on that day at the funeral home, she had trouble believing they hadn't even discussed the price tag of the casket.

"We thought Mom would pay for it. Or Henderson. That was back when at least some people in our family had money. Poor Aunt Muriel. She'd be mortified to know she was buried in a stolen casket."

"Luckily, she won't ever find out."

Holly looked around her living room at the dozens of items displayed on tables and draped on racks, the detritus of her life, which would be sold piecemeal to others who might repurpose it, give it away, or sell it eventually at another tag sale. She needed very little of it. She wasn't sad to lose the items themselves, but she was sad to lose the memories they embodied: the antique rocking chair was the first piece of furniture she and Chris had purchased together; the toboggan made her think of snowy afternoons when the boys were too small to walk through the snowdrifts without losing their Velcro'd boots; the silver-plated teapot had been tarnishing in her mother's basement until she rescued it a few years ago. Each triggered other related memories, a whole vast canopy of intertwined branches. Her sale was like the gold store—forced amnesia in the name of profit.

Henderson arrived with his carload of boxes, and Phoebe got out of the car with her trombone case.

"Phoebe," Holly said, giving her a hug and kiss. "I haven't seen you in ages. Look at you."

They all looked at Phoebe, who was slightly overweight and sported wire-rimmed glasses that gave her face a pinched look. She was wearing her school uniform of a white blouse and plaid skirt even though it was a Saturday.

"I surprised Phoebe," Henderson said. "I picked her up at her brass ensemble rehearsal and came right down here."

"Well, we're happy you came," Holly said, shooting Henderson a look. "Let me find Connor and Marshall."

"I'll find them, Aunt Holly," Phoebe said, looking resigned. She walked into the house with her trombone case as Henderson and Holly followed her in.

Connor was putting prices on his individual Xbox games.

"Hey, Phoebe," he said. "I didn't know you were coming."

Though Connor was thirteen and Phoebe was twelve, they looked like they came from two different eras. Phoebe had the battered air of a retired schoolteacher, while Connor still seemed like a child and sometimes watched cartoons on Saturday morning. Holly could attribute some of the difference to gender, but both had had to deal with adult issues like death and divorce, foreclosure and bankruptcy. She didn't know why Phoebe had the kind of fatigue and resentment that wasn't supposed to settle in until at least forty.

Henderson pulled Holly aside as Connor showed Phoebe around the display of sale items.

"We're in trouble," he said, pulling on the collar of his crew-neck sweater. "It's Aunt Muriel's casket."

"I know. Desdemona told me she's been getting calls from a collection agency."

"We've got to find the money. They can't come after me right now because of the bankruptcy, but I know this kind of company. They won't rest until they get it out of one of us."

"And there's no way to get the money from Mom's estate?" Holly said, wishing she didn't sound so desperate.

"It's too late. We should have thought about it before she had a stroke."

Holly looked around at the tables piled with the junk she hoped to sell that day. One table was completely filled with old music books that Marshall and Connor had been required to buy while learning their instruments.

"I'm looking at bringing in, what, a hundred bucks today?" she said. "I don't think that'll make much of a dent."

Phoebe came up to Henderson, still holding her trombone case. "What do you want me to do," she said, sighing.

"First, put that down somewhere," Henderson said. "Then ask Connor if you can man the money box or something. Look, here's Aunt Desdemona."

Desdemona walked up to Phoebe and draped a gauzy scarf around her shoulders.

"You look lovely, dahling," Desdemona said.

Holly was surprised to see Phoebe smile, but Desdemona had always had a special connection with her. Something about Phoebe's awkwardness brought out Desdemona's entertaining side.

"Keep it," Desdemona said. "It suits you."

A car pulled up, and Holly looked out the window. She thought her first customer had arrived well ahead of the 10 a.m. start time in her ad, but a teenager got out and waved the car off. It was the girl she had seen with Marshall at the mall. Marshall came bounding down the stairs and ran outside to bring his girlfriend into the house.

"Mom," he said, "this is Emily. We'll come back up when it's time to start selling stuff."

"Hi, Emily."

Emily, whose jet-black hair now had a bright pink streak in it, nodded at Holly and gave her a quick smile, then followed Marshall down into the basement.

"Believe it or not, that's progress," Holly said to Henderson and Desdemona.

Right then the first customers rolled up to the house, still well before the advertised start time, and the line of people in and out the door didn't stop for several hours. Holly's initial humiliation at having strangers pawing through her shabby belongings disappeared when she realized that the pickers made no connection with the people selling the goods and the goods themselves. They were simply looking for a bargain in whatever form it might take. When a bearded man asked her how much she wanted for her faux–Pottery Barn floor lamp, which wasn't even for sale, she said "Fifty." He peeled the cash off a large roll, unplugged the lamp, and walked out the door without even looking at the rest of the merchandise.

In the early afternoon, she made sandwiches and a pitcher of lemonade and gave everyone turns in the basement to eat, which flushed Marshall and his girlfriend back into the light. He and Emily stood behind the table with Marshall's possessions on it, looking as if they wanted to hold hands but couldn't. Holly found it both sweet and sad that her son had moved into this painful stage of life, especially without a father to guide him. She worried about how he would react when this Emily broke his heart, which seemed inevitable, though she knew there would be other Emilys in quick succession.

In the late afternoon, just as things seemed to be winding down, Holly heard another car pull up. Henderson looked out the window.

"That's a pretty nice Jaguar," he said, snorting. "This guy doesn't look like he needs any secondhand furniture."

Holly saw Racine coming up the walk just in time to run upstairs and shut the bathroom door. She needed a moment to prepare, to sort out her reaction, and to pull her hair out of its frazzled ponytail.

"Holly," Henderson called up the stairs. "There's someone here to see you."

"Be right down," she called, trying to sound nonchalant, though her voice broke in the middle of "down." She couldn't imagine why Racine had chosen this moment to reappear, especially without giving her some warning.

CHAPTER 29

As Racine walked in the door, the scene of strangers rifling through her family's things receded into soft focus for Holly. Racine was smiling, and this alone made her feel better, despite all her questions, despite losing her home, despite how miserable she felt about the boys. She realized all at once how much she had missed him and how he energized the air in a room.

"Holly," he said, kissing her lightly. Though she had never noticed it before, she saw that Racine, too, had lines around his eyes when he smiled.

"What are you doing here?" she said. She sensed that she was smiling, but she seemed to have no control over her face.

"I needed to see you," Racine said. "Can we talk somewhere?"

"Let's go for a walk," she said. She ducked into the hall closet and emerged with a long coat, a scarf, and a hat over one arm, then noticed that Racine was only wearing a suit jacket. "Never mind. Follow me."

She led him to the kitchen, which was at least outside the line of sight for all of the family members and estate sale stragglers in the living room. She offered him one of the four wooden chairs that surrounded the small kitchen table and took one of the others.

Racine reached into his pocket and pulled out a small ring case. He placed it on the table. After a brief moment of displacement when she thought he might be proposing, Holly picked it up and opened it. It was her mother's ring.

"It's yours again," he said. "I'm sorry it took so long."

Holly took the ring out of the box and let the yellow kitchen light bounce off the facets of the diamond. The ring looked as if it had been cleaned.

"I did some research, then I brought it to my boss and told him that the ring had been stolen," Racine began. "From a rehab hospital of all places."

Holly looked at Racine, whose brow was raised enough to show her he was sincerely troubled. She realized very suddenly, sitting in the unflattering light of her own kitchen, that he was not some wheeler-dealer who descended on small towns to suction up their gold without a look back. Maybe it was his slight accent that had given her the wrong impression. No, he was a middle-aged man with a smile that had made it a little too easy for him to get women. So easy, in fact, that he didn't have to pick a place, a time, a relationship in which to invest. But she also sensed that he was searching for something more than what he had.

"He denied it, of course, but I kept asking him to show me the paper trail," Racine said. "So finally he admitted that his resale sources didn't always have the paperwork to back up their merchandise, but he wanted the ring back, so I threatened to call the police. That's when he fired me."

"No," she said, putting a hand over her mouth.

"I would have quit anyway. But when he heard me say I was going to the police, he suddenly decided that I could keep the ring. No questions asked. As long as I keep my mouth shut."

"So now we're both unemployed."

"What happened to your job?"

"The chain is shutting down," Holly said, her mouth a straight line. "We're apparently not making enough money to keep the investors happy. That's what this sale is all about. I'm losing my house. I didn't want to tell you, but the boys and I are moving in with Vivian. We have nothing left."

Racine shook his head. "Don't say that. You'll figure this out. It's only a temporary setback."

The words fell to the floor, burdened with uselessness. They both looked down.

"What will you do?" she said quietly.

"I'll be fine," he said, whisking away their seriousness with a wave of his hand. "I've saved a fair amount of money. I'll look for another business to invest in, but I'll run it myself this time."

Holly looked at the ring again, wishing she could put it back on her mother's finger but knowing what had to be done. "How much do you think this is worth?"

"We'd have to weigh it and have the appraisers look, but that's a large, high-quality diamond. My guess is ten to twelve thousand."

"Enough to cover a casket that's already in the ground. With a little left over."

"What?"

"Never mind," Holly said, racing out into the living room. She showed the ring to Desdemona, who sank into a chair behind her sales table with relief.

Henderson nodded his head and said, "Aunt Muriel won't be re-possessed. One debt paid."

Holly had left Racine in the kitchen, but when she returned to bring him out for introductions, he was already standing by the back door.

"I really need to get back to the city," he said. "I have a lot of business to wrap up."

"Of course," she said. "I understand."

Racine nodded, gave her a quick kiss on the cheek, and then left. Holly, who didn't really understand, watched him walk down the sidewalk in his thin European shoes, which must have allowed him to feel every pebble. *He'll look back*, she thought, *and if he does, he's not walking away from me forever. It's meant to be.*

But Racine didn't look back. He kept walking, his head bowed against the cold.

⌒

A week after the tag sale, Holly sent her house keys to the bank in a padded envelope with a note explaining that she couldn't keep up the payments. Dropping the envelope into the mailbox was both wrenching—failure and loss in equal measures—and freeing, since it meant she didn't have a mortgage anymore. The hardest part was that she had let Chris down. She hadn't managed to hold on to his dream. But then again the house was never really them. The boys were them, and their future mattered more than any inanimate structure, even one with great bones. She made six trips back and forth to Vivian's house with the family's pared-down belongings stuffed into her Subaru.

Vivian smiled broadly as they came in the door with the first batch of belongings. "Look in your room, boys," she said. "I have surprises for you."

"You didn't have to do that," Holly said. "You're already keeping us off the street."

"I know. But I wanted to see their faces. They need a little joy right now."

Marshall emerged with tears in his eyes holding an envelope.

"She gave me driving lessons, Mom. The whole package. All the classes and everything. I can get my license."

"Vivian, it's too much," Holly said, caught between gratitude and frustration that she couldn't provide the classes herself.

"Hush now," Vivian said, smiling at Marshall. "He's a young man. He needs to get behind the wheel of a car and cause mischief. That's what teenagers do."

Holly put an arm around Marshall, who sat down on the couch, clutching his envelope. Connor emerged next, holding a large box he had unwrapped.

"It's a PlayStation," he said softly. "I can't believe it."

"I want you to be happy here," Vivian said. "I want you to feel like this is your home. Your friends are welcome anytime."

Both Connor and Marshall gave Vivian awkward pecks on the cheek as Holly wiped away tears.

"You are too much," Holly said.

"No, I'm just enough," Vivian said. "Just barely enough."

As Marshall and Connor left to haul another load of bags and boxes from the car, Holly and Vivian talked about Racine's revelations.

"I've already been looking into selling my interest," Vivian said. "I can't do business with a thief."

"I feel like it's my fault," Holly said. "If I hadn't seen the ring, everything would have been fine."

"Holly, in no way is this your fault. It's a sign of how little you can trust people in the business world anymore." Vivian sighed and turned her head so that she faced the window. "With the exception of you and your boys, I'm feeling very negative about humanity right now. Sometimes I just get tired of all the terrible things people do to each other, as if disease and the wrath of nature didn't cause enough suffering."

Holly could have countered her with all the generosity she herself had just shown to people who weren't even related to her, but she mainly agreed with Vivian. Sometimes the pain people inflicted on each other in the name of money or fame or random willfulness was just too much.

"You're right," she said. "People suck."

Vivian smiled and turned her head back to face Holly. "I love that you know when I can't be talked out of a mood, no matter how irrational. We're all going to get along just fine."

⤚

After a few days of settling into Vivian's house, Holly arrived at the office with several large tote bags. The newspaper had two more weeks to operate, but she knew it would take her that long to sort through her office, which was a storehouse of memorabilia from all the stories she had covered over the years.

She picked up a dusty eggplant-shaped ceramic dish, which she had bought at the opening of the Bertram Corners Farmers Market a few years ago, when farmers suddenly realized that people living near them might actually want to buy their fresh fruits and vegetables. She placed the dish carefully into the bottom of a tote bag. She threw a stack of old newspapers into the recycling bin and behind them found a round campaign-style button from when she had covered a wheelchair-rugby tournament. She remembered getting choked up behind the camera as the men in wheelchairs clashed and sweated harder than professional athletes, so determined were they to prove they had not lost their masculinity. She put the button into the tote bag, too, afraid to lose the triggers that held up her memory like magnets on a refrigerator. The tight weave of Bertram Corners was the only thing that kept her from complete despair, even as the shuddering economy might have pitted its residents against each other. And there was Vivian, their most valuable municipal project, and the spiritual center of a town that otherwise might have lost its way.

"Holly, do you have a minute?"

Darla came into her office with the Sister Sisters following close behind.

"The sisters heard we would be closing soon," Darla said. "And they wanted to stop by to show their support."

"We brought you muffins," one sister said, placing a small, cloth-covered basket on Holly's desk.

Finally, Holly thought, after all these years, she was now the muffin recipient, the object of pity for two elderly nuns.

"Thank you so much, Sisters," Holly said. "We really appreciate the gesture."

"It's just so unfair . . ." both sisters started. They looked at each other and laughed.

"We're always doing that," said Eileen, the one with the green eye, whose name Holly could finally remember. "We start and finish each other's sentences."

"Anyway," said Eleanor. "We just think it's terrible that your newspaper won't be around anymore. We rely on it. How else would we know about the deaths and the births and when people are in need? It's absolutely essential to the town."

"That's so nice of you to say," Holly said. "We feel the same way, but it's all about the bottom line these days. The company doesn't think it's making enough money."

"We also heard you were selling your house," Eleanor said. "We hope you're not moving out of town."

It was a perfectly innocent remark, but Holly almost couldn't find her voice to answer. She didn't want the sisters' baked goods, or Vivian's extra bedrooms. She wanted desperately to be the giver—the dispenser of muffins and the owner of a much-used guest room with clean, crisp high-thread-count sheets and thick, warm blankets.

"Vivian is giving us a place to stay," she said slowly, opening another tote bag to avoid seeing the sisters' faces.

"Oh, that's marvelous," one of them said. "She'll love the company. I do think she gets a little tired of seeing the same faces on rotation. A little more activity in her house will do her a world of good."

Holly nodded, hoping the sisters were right. She tried to imagine the boys and their friends detouring around the iron lung on their way to play video games in the basement. It didn't feel right.

"Well, we must be off," the sisters said in unison, laughing again. Darla suddenly appeared again as they made their way toward the door. Once they were gone, she came back into Holly's office.

"Black buzzards," she said. "That's all I can think of when I see them. They're always on the trail of death and destruction."

"Come on," Holly said. "They're lovely people. Did you know one of them wanted to be an actress?"

"Which one? Oh, forget it. I can't tell them apart anyway . . . So you're packing up already?"

Holly looked around the room. She couldn't imagine it empty, soulless. She wondered what these offices would become. A yoga studio? Another coffee shop? An orthodontist's office? She pictured a tween in a glitter slogan shirt sitting in a dental chair getting metal brackets glued onto her teeth.

"It's going to take a while, so I thought I'd get started," she said. "Did you schedule the photo with the high school robotics team?"

"I did. I'm headed over there now. Then I'm talking to the drugstore manager about picking up some more hours."

"Ask him if he needs anyone else."

"Are you serious?"

"Dead serious. I can't stay with Vivian forever, and I've got to find something."

"I'll ask him," Darla said, pausing as if she couldn't decide whether to say something. "You're not alone, you know. We all want to help."

"Thank you, Darla," Holly said, welling up again. "That means more to me than you know."

ᔈ

When she left the office that night, Holly instinctively took a left turn at Main Street instead of the right she should have taken to drive to Vivian's. She found herself in front of her house before she realized that she didn't live there anymore. In the few days they had been gone, the house had taken on an air of abandonment. A light snow had fallen the day before, and no one had shoveled the path to the front door or the sidewalk. In the falling darkness, the spray-painted patches glowed—a whiter whiteness on white.

She turned off the engine, took off her gloves, threw them on the passenger seat, and rested her head on the cool plastic of the steering wheel. It wasn't just the house that she had to let go, it was Chris. It was the whole story of the life they had expected to have. Saying good-bye to the stone foundation and the Dutch colonial roof meant finally accepting that she had a different life now, one that had veered down a dark, winding road. She had been living as if she could keep everything intact, as though Chris could walk in the door any minute and spruce the place back up in no time. But that wasn't going to happen. Now she could only see as far ahead as her headlights would allow.

She felt as though she were in a Frank Capra movie, about to either jump off a bridge or meet an angel. But neither happened. She put her gloves back on and restarted the car, driving back to Vivian's in silence, feeling the slip of her balding car tires on the snow.

CHAPTER 30

It was after seven when Holly finally made it back to Vivian's and found the boys eating pizza from TV trays in the living room. They were all watching a James Bond movie on the flat screen above Vivian's head. Marveen came out of the kitchen with a two-liter bottle of Coke as Holly put her tote bags and a small grocery bag down.

"Hi, Mom," Connor said through a mouth crammed with pizza. Marshall nodded at her and kept eating.

"Hi, guys," Holly said, turning to Vivian. "What's all this?"

"There's a James Bond marathon on," Vivian said. "I told Marveen to order some pizza so we could make it a little party."

Holly had stopped at the grocery store on her way back to Vivian's. She had chicken breasts, broccoli, and brown rice in the bag. Her plan had been to make, retroactively, the meal she had told Connor to lie about on his Health questionnaire. Without the mortgage to worry about, she felt she could actually afford better food now. And here they were eating pizza.

"It's from Luigi's," Marshall said, pulling off another slice. "Not that cheap stuff from Village Pizza. Look, this one's got ham and pine-apple on it."

Holly smiled and put the groceries away, then pulled up a chair. "You really don't have to feed them," she said, though Vivian was intently watching the movie.

"I know," she said. "I just thought it would be a nice treat. I want them to feel at home."

Marveen nodded toward the kitchen, and Holly followed her, grabbing a slice of the ham and pineapple pizza to bring with her.

"Something's wrong with her," Marveen said in a low voice. "She's completely bipolar all of a sudden. One minute she's wailing about the injustice of humanity, and the next she's ordering new curtains for the boys' room from QVC."

"She ordered them new curtains? They're boys. They don't even know that curtains exist."

"That's the least of it. I have never seen her so erratic."

"Maybe it's just the disruption of having us come to live with her. She's not used to having so many people around."

"That's not it. She's thrilled to have you here. She told me she loves feeling like she's living in the middle of a busy family. She never had that growing up. It was just her lying there and her parents hovering around her."

Holly hadn't really thought about what the arrangement would do for Vivian. It pleased her to think she wasn't the only one benefiting from it. She poured herself a glass of Coke, but it tasted too sweet. Her inability to afford soda for the last few years had probably been a blessing.

"What do you think I should do?" Holly asked. She took an apron from a kitchen drawer, tied it around her waist, and started washing the few dishes and cups in the sink.

"I don't know," Marveen said as Holly scrubbed a dish that already looked clean. "But I'd love to leave at eight, and Darla can't get here until ten. Do you mind covering?"

"Of course not," Holly said, even as she realized that this would happen more and more frequently. Vivian's volunteers would come to think of her as backup every time they wanted to trade or skip a shift. "I'm here anyway."

susan schoenberger

"You're a lifesaver," Marveen said. "The tile guy is coming in the morning, and I still need to choose the final pattern for the backsplash. Arthur has been working such long hours that we haven't had a chance to talk about it, and he cannot keep his eyes open past nine thirty."

Holly had a sudden revelation that money didn't alleviate worry, it simply transferred it to a different class of consumer goods. If you didn't have to worry about whether you could afford Luigi's versus Village Pizza, you worried about your tile backsplash and your pool lining. And if you didn't have to worry about your tile backsplash and your pool lining, you worried about your private plane and the exchange rate in euros.

Marveen dried the last of the dishes and put them away.

"And now you're going to tell me about Racine," she said. "What's happening? I heard that he wasn't in town anymore."

Holly walked to the doorway to check on Vivian and the boys. All were glued to the TV screen. "It's complicated," she said. "He did leave town, but he came back. But then he left again. Maybe he's lost interest. I really don't know what to think."

"Why? Because he hasn't called in a few days?" Marveen said. "You're past the games, so it's okay to call him now. Have a little fun in your life."

Holly looked down at her shoes, black ballet flats that were so worn and scuffed she couldn't have put them in a Goodwill bag without being embarrassed. "I can't do that. I'm just not one of those women who can sleep with someone for fun."

"For God's sake, Holly. Life is too short to insist on true love."

Holly knew Marveen had a point, but she couldn't acknowledge it without betraying what she had felt with Racine. She had taken to remembering their evening in New York in minute detail. Something had happened—whether it was inside her head or not—that had raised sex to a different plane. They had had some spiritual connection, maybe touching upon the holy, and she couldn't pretend that she only wanted to sleep with him before he left again. She would rather have their one time together as the clean and perfect union it had become in her memory.

"You go home and work on your tile," Holly said. "We'll be fine here."

⌒

Holly thought Vivian might be dozing when she came back into the living room, but Vivian opened her eyes as the credits for the James Bond movie rolled.

"Can I get you anything?" Holly asked. As Vivian shook her head, the boys took their cue and grabbed the empty pizza boxes to bring into the kitchen.

"Thanks for the pizza, Vivian," Marshall said on his way to the room he shared with Connor.

"Yeah, thanks," Connor said.

"You're very welcome, boys," Vivian said, smiling at them, her chin suddenly quivering.

"Is anything wrong?" Holly said, putting a hand on Vivian's forehead as if she might have a fever. It worried her to see Vivian's emotions so close to the surface. "You seem upset."

"I'm not upset. Could you get me a tissue?"

Holly grabbed the box on Vivian's tray and dabbed the corners of her eyes. "Do you need to blow?"

"A little."

Holly held the tissue firmly under Vivian's nose as Vivian weakly pushed air through her nasal passages. When Holly took the tissue away, Vivian sniffed loudly.

"They're such nice boys," Vivian said. "When Connor came home from school, he told me all about his science project, and Marshall played me a little song on his trumpet just before we got the pizza."

"That's so nice to hear," Holly said. "They're not always so polite, so it's nice to know they can behave when I'm not around."

"You have so much," Vivian said, sniffing again. "You think you don't, but you do. I hope you realize that."

Lately, she had been so conscious of her own sense of diminution—a husband who didn't live to see forty, a house she couldn't afford to keep, a job she loved disappearing out from under her, the sense of sliding down the chute after her parents had climbed the ladder—that she hadn't been able to appreciate what she still had. "It's all relative," her mother used to say.

"I know," she said, tearing up herself. "I'm a very lucky woman."

Then Holly's phone rang. It was a number she didn't expect to see. "It's Racine," she said.

"Take it," Vivian said. "I'm fine. You should talk to him."

Holly checked Vivian's eyes, which were dry, and took the phone, still ringing, to the corner of the room near a window that looked out into Vivian's side yard. Snow was falling again, and trees were starting to bend and wave in the wind.

"Hello," she said quietly.

"Holly? It's Racine."

"I didn't know if I would hear from you again. When you left my house, you didn't look back."

"I thought you needed that time with your family. I felt like I was intruding."

"You weren't intruding, Racine. You really weren't."

A silence ensued, and Holly briefly wondered if Racine had put his phone down and walked away. Then she heard a sigh.

"I really need to see you," Racine said. "Can you meet me at the diner?"

Holly looked at her watch. It was close to nine.

"I'm in charge of Vivian," she said. "I can't leave the house before ten."

"I'll come over there. What's the address?"

Holly didn't want to have a private discussion with Racine in Vivian's presence and didn't want to sneak him into her bedroom with the boys in the house.

"Can it wait until tomorrow?"

"No, it can't. I leave in the morning for New York."

"But everyone's here."

"I'll meet you right outside. The snow's falling. It's a beautiful night."

"I can't talk for more than a few minutes."

"I'll make it fast."

Holly gave Racine the address. Vivian had her eyes closed and appeared to be drifting off. Holly walked down the short hallway and knocked softly on the door of the boys' room.

"Marshall," she said, opening the door. "I need to have you sit with Vivian for a few minutes. I'll be right outside, and she's asleep. You just need to make sure she doesn't choke or anything."

Marshall was sitting on his bed surrounded by open books and note cards. He had an old laptop his friend had given him propped on his outstretched legs.

"Mom, I've got a history paper due tomorrow, and I'm right in the middle of it. Can't Connor do it?"

Connor was lying on his stomach reading a gaming magazine. He got up reluctantly and followed Holly back to the living room.

"Now, all you have to do is sit here on the couch," she said. "If Vivian starts to choke or make noises, you run right outside and yell for me."

"Okay," he said, flipping the magazine open again. "I'll find you."

Racine called again to say he was outside. Holly put on her coat, changed into old snow boots, and added mittens, a wool hat, and a scarf. As she opened the door, she could hear the wind, which sounded like a tin whistle. Racine was a shadow in the distance, the only moving object in her field of vision.

She walked down Vivian's front path and met him on the sidewalk.

"It's fantastic, isn't it? All this snow?" he said, winding her scarf once more around her neck. "Are you cold?"

"It's the wind," she said, inexplicably out of breath, struck by how serene his face looked in the moonlight with the snow catching on his eyelashes. "Where's your car?"

"I walked over from the diner. It's just a few blocks."

"Let's go sit in the bus shelter. It's right there on the corner. At least it's out of the wind."

Holly looked back toward the house and in the light from the living-room window saw the outline of Vivian's iron lung. They walked to the corner and sat on the bench inside the shelter, which was painted on its three sides with murals done by the middle school art students. Holly herself had covered the story of its creation.

Racine took Holly's mittened hands in his bare ones. "The thing is," he started, "I thought I was ready to move on, now that I'm free of the gold business. I thought I'd do what I always do and look for a new town, a new state, maybe even a new country. In my whole adult life I've never lived anywhere for more than a year or two."

Holly reached out with one of her mittens and brushed some snow from Racine's hair before it could drip onto his face. She nodded for him to continue.

"But there's something about this place. I don't feel that itch to start over again. I feel at home here. People are actually nice to each other. Look at how you all take care of Vivian. You don't have to do that—she's not related to you—but you're committed to her. I find that remarkable."

The wind had gone from tin whistle to bassoon. Holly saw several porch lights come on as people looked out at the storm from the warmth of their houses. She felt oddly exhilarated to be inside the storm—in the eye, as it were—as the snow and wind blew around them.

"So," Racine continued, "I did something I probably should have told you about before, and that's why I needed to talk to you tonight."

"What did you do?"

"I talked to Vivian, and we canvassed her caregiver network. Then we created a website so that people in town could contribute to a fund to buy your newspaper from the chain—for a song, by the way. They jumped on it. No one wanted the *Chronicle* to close. I can help you get it up to speed with an online presence, but it's yours to run. As long as it breaks even, you can keep publishing."

Holly looked out at the snow, which made her dizzy as she viewed it through a prism of tears. Did the universe suddenly decide she deserved a break? That she would be allowed to stay employed, at least, instead of facing the vast, black unknown of a paycheck-less future? That she could keep her kids housed, clothed, and fed?

"Do they realize," she said, "that this business has no future? That's what everyone says anyway. And if you'll help me, does that mean you're going to stay?"

Racine blinked and leaned closer so she could hear him over the wind. "I just bought the Dunkin' Donuts franchise on Main Street," he said. "You're stuck with me."

Holly pulled his face closer to hers, a mitten on either ear. "Are you sure you want that?" She felt warm inside, even as the tip of her nose froze in the cold night air.

Racine kissed her. "You let me in here. You made me feel like part of this. And the time we had in New York. I don't know what it was, but I can't stop thinking about it. That's all anyone wants, Holly. To find that . . ."

As Racine searched for the right word, Holly suddenly heard a voice cutting through the wind. She got up from the bench and ran outside the bus shelter to see that the lights were now completely dark on Vivian's street. Her view had been blocked by the mural.

"Mom! Mom!"

Connor was leaning outside Vivian's front door, screaming into the snow and the wind and the dark night.

"Help! The power's out! What do I do?"

Holly took lunging footsteps to cut across the snow on the lawn to Vivian's front door, with Racine right behind her. When she came inside, she heard Marshall on the phone with the police. It somehow seemed darker inside than it did outside.

"No, the generator didn't come on," he said, his voice rising to a frantic pitch. "And she can't breathe."

Holly ran to a drawer in the kitchen that she knew had a flashlight.

"Oh my God," she said. "How could this happen?"

Holly shone the flashlight onto Vivian's face, which looked contorted and blue. Her eyes were shut tight.

"The generator," Holly said. "It's brand-new. Why isn't it working?"

She looked toward it and saw that the cord had been pulled out from the wall. She ran over to plug it back in. Before she inserted it, she looked back at Vivian, whose eyes were now open wide. Vivian shook her head deliberately, her eyes pleading with Holly. The message was clear, but Holly turned back to the outlet, her hand hovering, shaking, just above it with the plug.

"I have to, Vivian," she said, crying. She looked back at Vivian. "I have to. I can't let you go."

Vivian let out a strangled cry. "Please," she said, her voice just a rasp. "I can't."

Holly shook her head, pushing the plug halfway, then she stopped. She hung her head, defeated, and pulled it out again, dropping the cord.

Vivian gasped for air, and Holly ran over, taking Vivian's head in her hands. Vivian looked up at her. Her face was pinched and contorted, and yet her eyes told Holly that she needed a way out.

"Thank . . . you," Vivian said, hoarsely expelling the last of her breath. She closed her eyes, and her face finally relaxed as Holly stood sobbing, tears dripping down onto Vivian's now-slack cheeks.

The sirens cut through the sound of the wind as police cars, ambulances, and fire trucks all converged on Vivian's house. The paramedics came in first and put a portable oxygen mask on Vivian's face, though Holly knew that was pointless without the machine pumping at her lungs. The firemen went right to the generator.

"It's unplugged," one of them said. "Jesus."

One of the firemen went to plug in the generator, but Holly shook her head, speaking through her sobs.

"She's gone, okay? It's too late."

The fireman dropped the cord. The room, full of first responders, fell silent. Connor buried his face in Holly's coat.

"What happened, Connor?" Holly said. "You need to tell me."

"She woke up when the lights went out," he said, now crying convulsively. "She told me to unplug that machine over there, the red one, because she said it could short out her iron lung when the power came back on. I didn't know, Mom. I just did what she asked, and then she started gasping. She told me not to get you, but I was calling for you anyway, and I got Marshall to call 911. You didn't hear me, Mom. I kept calling, but you didn't hear me, and I couldn't see you."

"It's my fault," Holly said, putting an arm around Connor. She turned to the firemen. "I left them for a few minutes, and I didn't know the power went out. He didn't have the training. It's completely my fault."

Racine was standing with the cluster of policemen, who were all looking at Vivian.

"It's what she wanted," Racine said quietly. "She told Connor to unplug the generator. She was ready to go, and he was her chance. No one else would have done it."

A policeman came forward with a clipboard in his hand to begin the paperwork that would usher Vivian from the world.

"But I wasn't ready," Holly said, knowing as she said it that her readiness didn't matter. Racine put a hand on her shoulder. "I still needed her."

Then Darla, who had heard the ambulances on her way to Vivian's house, pushed her way through the crowd.

"Oh my God," she said, her voice quivering. "She can't be gone."

Holly slowly nodded her head, though it took what she noticed was a surprising amount of effort.

"I'll take care of everything," Darla said to Holly. "I'll get the rest of the crew together and we'll manage. You take care of the boys."

Holly nodded weakly. She turned to Racine, who looked confused.

"Special edition," she said. "If anything ever justified it, this is it. We'll want to have them printed by morning and delivered to every house in town."

He nodded.

The paramedics worked around the lung, detaching cords and un-latching the rubber collar, as one of the policeman ushered the boys and Racine into the kitchen. Holly stayed to see them remove Vivian from the lung. Her body, dressed in one of the loose white hospital gowns that had become her only wardrobe, looked so small and frail as they placed her on a stretcher that was half the size of the one that held up her machine.

The machine now looked forlorn, stripped of its purpose. Holly walked over to it and closed it back up so that it didn't look so exposed. She wondered what would happen to it. Surely, no one else would use it, but where would it end up? In a junkyard? A scrap heap? A museum of antiquated medical devices? She couldn't imagine. She touched the smooth enamel surface and silently thanked the machine for keeping Vivian alive for so long.

CHAPTER 31

Vivian's Unaired Podcast #11

I'm fascinated by this new company called Facebook, which allows me to live vicariously to an unprecedented degree. I'm trying to get Holly and Marveen to join, but they keep saying they have better things to do.

"You would love it," I told Marveen after I discovered it. "You can share your photos with friends and find out what everyone's doing. It's like gossip on steroids."

"C'mon, Vivian. It's nothing more than a bunch of kids talking about getting drunk and a bunch of bored moms telling you about every single poop little Jimmy has ever taken. Who has time for that?"

"You don't know what you're missing," I said. "You get on this thing, and I guarantee you'll be hearing from old boyfriends and reconnecting with your best friend from nursery school."

I, in fact, was able to track down Timmy Gallagher, the boy I hadn't seen since elementary school. And, remarkably, we were able to talk as if we had lived next door to each other for decades.

"I remember that day my mother took me to your house to see your new television set," Timmy wrote to me. "After she pushed me out the door, she couldn't stop talking about how terrible it must be for you, trapped inside that machine. The thing is, you seemed fine.

What she really meant was that it made her uncomfortable to see you that way."

"And you never came back," I wrote back, not to make him feel guilty but just to state a fact.

"I missed you, though. You were the wittiest girl in school."

Timmy, I found out, later went by Tim. A few years after our television party, his family moved to Houston, where he graduated from high school before joining the navy. He married young, at twenty, and had four children, who had all gone on to liberal arts colleges, the kind I had always wanted to attend.

After we caught up, we talked rarely, but I liked knowing what had happened to Timmy. I liked knowing that he was a good citizen with a solid family and less heartache than most. And I liked that his recollections of our school days gave me a different impression of my own past. I liked being called "the wittiest girl in school."

⌒

It wasn't long before Holly, Marveen, and the rest of Bertram Corners had Facebook profiles, and it meant that I could schedule the volunteer rotation without having to send out e-mails to a long list of people and wait for them to reply.

It was Facebook that gave me the idea of investing in the cash-for-gold business. I saw a few people talking about how they traded in broken jewelry for cash and comparing the best ways to do it. I had already decided that I wanted a solid investment right here in town so that I could adopt one of those orphaned storefronts and bring some little segment of the town center back to life. The cash-for-gold idea just seemed like a good investment, too, with investors getting skittish about the stock market and pushing up the price of gold.

Here's the thing about investing: all the information is out there in the market coverage, prospectuses, annual reports, and the like. But almost no one takes the time to read any of it. They'd rather work at pointless dehumanizing jobs to make tiny paychecks than sift through a spreadsheet and figure out which stocks to buy. Money makes more money. It's really not that hard to understand.

Bertram Corners has its comfortable residents, the ones who drive a Lexus and use "summer" as a verb. But in the twenty-plus years I've lived here, I've seen a generation lose ground—people like Holly, who grew up in a manor house and now can't afford to put her kids through college. I've tried to talk to her about it, but she acts like she can't do anything about it.

"I can show you how to invest, Holly," I told her. "You're a smart woman. You'd get the hang of it."

"Vivian, I barely made it through algebra," she said.

"Why does everyone think there's high-level math involved? It's more logic than anything else."

"I'm just nervous about the stock market. If it went down and I lost that money, I'd never forgive myself. To me, it's like sticking money in a slot machine."

The Bertram Corners of twenty years ago wasn't the most progressive place on earth, but I feel it contracting in its worldview. People seem to move here out of resignation. Decent but not outstanding schools. High but not outrageous real estate prices. Crumbling but not completely deserted town center. It's like the Wendy's of towns—a notch above McDonald's but still fast food. I want better for Holly and her kids, so I keep trying, because it's what keeps me going.

More and more, though, I have days where I'm not sure why I continue to wake up or what I contribute to this planet. I find myself reading the obituaries and feeling strangely envious. The struggle is over. "Is" becomes "was." No more pain, no more sorrow, no reason to fret about that extra ten pounds or the drug-addled nephew. Just peace.

~

Holly, I assume you'll be the one to find these podcasts—which I recorded when my nurses were here and otherwise occupied. If you have, that means I found a way out. Like Lance, I just couldn't stay motivated anymore, and once I knew your family would have a stable future I decided it was okay to leave.

You more than anyone in my life besides my parents were able to look past the ghastly machine that kept me alive and see into my soul. You didn't judge me, you didn't try to minimize my predicament, and you didn't find an excuse to leave me, even when you had enough problems of your own. You mostly just listened, and for that I will always be grateful.

I'm sure you know by now that I left you my house so that you never have to worry about having a roof over your head. I didn't leave you the rest of my money—what was left of it—because I believe so strongly that you will find your own way. I didn't want you to feel that I bailed you out, or that you wouldn't have succeeded on your own.

Good-bye, my dear friend. Know that I am in a better place—or no place, which is still better.

—Know that you helped me.

—Know that you are a beautiful person and a devoted mother, and that your sons are growing up into fine young men.

—Know that you have resources deep within you.

—Know that you are loved.

CHAPTER 32

Holly put on the only dress she owned with flowers on it. Even though it was February, Vivian had decreed in her will that everyone should be asked to wear spring colors and "cheerful" clothing to her memorial service.

She had also specified that she didn't want a funeral with a traditional casket.

"I've been laid out in front of this whole town for decades," she said in her instructions to Holly, whom she had named as executor and to whom she had left her house, free and clear. The savings she had went to establish a new computer lab at the library. "I want my memorial service to be the opposite of a funeral. I want people to move, since I never could."

Holly had hired the DJ Vivian requested, and he was setting up in the high school gym, the only place in town large enough to hold the crowds expected. As per Vivian's instructions, people were asked to donate balloons instead of flowers.

"How's it going, boys?" Holly called to Connor and Marshall, who came into her room in their stiff new blue blazers and khakis. Since Vivian had not dictated what the boys should wear, Holly had decided they needed to look presentable.

They were ready long before they needed to be, so all three went into the living room to wait for Racine. The room looked empty without Vivian's gurney and iron lung taking up most of the space. Holly hadn't had time to think about buying any furniture, with the newspaper establishing its online operation. But she would eventually. She would make their new home warm and inviting, a place the boys would be proud to bring their friends. And being there would keep them close to Vivian. They would never forget how she had cushioned their fall.

Connor sat down on the small couch that used to be pushed up against the wall for Vivian's visitors. He sighed.

"What's wrong, honey?" Holly said, coming over to feel his forehead. "Feel okay?"

"Everyone's going to look at me funny," he said. "She could still be alive if it wasn't for me. I still don't understand why she asked me to unplug the machine."

Holly sat down on the couch and put an arm around Connor, who looked like he might cry. Marshall, to whom Vivian had left her state-of-the-art computer, parked himself at the small desk in the corner to continue saving her podcasts and files to an external hard drive so he could free up some memory.

"You're wrong, sweetheart," she said. "You were her salvation. Remember what I told you? She still had time when I came inside, but she asked me not to plug the generator back in. She thanked me, Connor. Those were her last words."

Holly placed her chin on top of his head, pulling him toward her so that they fit like puzzle pieces. She felt him relax against her but realized she would have to reassure him for a while longer.

The doorbell rang. It was Racine, who was dressed in a slim-cut tan suit with a pink-and-white-striped shirt underneath. Holly marveled at the fact of him standing there. The fact of them, a couple.

"I'm early," he said. "I didn't know what to do with myself this morning."

"I know what you mean," Holly replied. "I guess we could head over early. Are you ready, Marshall?"

"Wait a second," Marshall said. "She left something for you, Mom."

They all gathered around the computer screen as Marshall pointed to some files. "These are all podcasts that she made in the last few months," he said. "But none of them have aired. And the file names all say 'For Holly.'"

"Click on one," Racine said.

Marshall opened the first one, and they all listened, wide-eyed, as Vivian's voice emerged from the speakers and spoke of the day she came down with polio. Holly drew in a breath so loudly that everyone turned to her.

"It's her story," she said. "What's the date on them, Marshall?"

"Looks like she started them in September of last year."

"That was right after the storm knocked out the power to her generator," Holly said, remembering how terrified she was that day. She wondered, now, if Vivian had been planning her exit ever since.

⟿

Holly drove slowly, with Connor solemnly holding the balloons through an open window, since they wouldn't fit inside her Subaru with everyone in the car. On the way to the high school, they drove past the gold store, which had closed, and the Dunkin' Donuts, which was thriving, since Racine had convinced the town to allow him to put tables with umbrellas on the sidewalk. As they approached the gym, they could see dozens of cars with balloon bouquets being held outside of windows, and dozens more with so many balloons inside the car that the occupants couldn't be seen. The gym itself looked like a carnival, full of balloons and bright colors. Bluegrass music—Vivian's favorite— blared from the sound system.

"Holly!"

She looked around and saw Henderson moving through the balloons, dressed in a dark blue suit and red tie, looking like the successful businessman he used to be. Phoebe trailed behind him, carrying a giant

Mylar balloon in the shape of the letter *V*. She was wearing a white sundress with flowers on it and no glasses.

"Phoebe," Holly said, putting an arm around her. "You look spectacular."

"Contacts," Phoebe said. "They have changed my life."

Holly smiled at Henderson, who tugged at the cuffs of his shirt, each one in turn. He had taken a job with his ex-father-in-law, who was looking to expand his business overseas. Henderson had told Holly that he hoped to be running the show in another year, since his ex-father-in-law was being robbed blind by his staff. She had always been sure that Henderson would land on his feet, but she had been slightly surprised to see him bury his pride and join up with his ex-wife's family. Then she saw Henderson glance tenderly at Phoebe, who was talking to her cousins and waving up at the balloon-plastered ceiling. *This*, she thought, *is why we do what we have to do.*

Desdemona, whose angular features and thin frame seemed at odds with all the balloons in the room, slipped through the crowd toward them in a floor-length, hot pink dress. Holly feared that Desdemona's elbows might pop some of the balloons.

"What a scene," she said as a man came up behind her and put his arms around her tiny waist.

Holly looked at the man behind Desdemona, wondering where she had found him. Her rap on the men in New York was that they always wanted the women they couldn't have.

"Holly, Hen, this is Jerome," Desdemona said. "He's my podiatrist . . . or was my podiatrist. I hope you don't mind that he came along. I was telling him about Vivian, and he wanted to pay his respects."

"An amazing woman," Jerome said. "I read her obituary in the *New York Times*."

Holly shook Jerome's hand and wondered how long he'd be around, since Desdemona tended to fall in and out of love like a teenager. Still, she was glad to see Desdemona at least momentarily happy and Henderson back on his throne of privilege, where he belonged.

Holly spied Marveen arranging chairs on the platform that had been constructed to form a stage and excused herself to join her. The Sister Sisters, who were wearing their traditional black robes with Hawaiian leis, waved to her as she walked by.

"Holly, thank God you're here," Marveen said. "The DJ says he doesn't have 'All Shook Up.' Do you think Vivian would be upset if he played 'Jailhouse Rock' instead?"

"I can pretty much assure you that Vivian would not mind," Holly said.

Marveen began to walk away, then turned back around. "Everyone understands, you know," she said, looking Holly directly in the eye.

"Do they?" She found it hard to believe. It was human nature to want to blame someone for a death that might have been prevented.

"I told them," she said, "that Vivian asked me to unplug the generator before I left, but I refused. She knew the storm would get worse. She knew she might have a chance to get out. She was counting on the fact that you loved her enough to let her go. That's what I told them."

Holly smiled at Marveen, who was a better friend than she sometimes gave her credit for. She unfolded the notebook paper she had in her pocket. She hated public speaking, but Vivian had asked in her extremely detailed will that Holly give her eulogy.

When the service began, Holly looked out over the crowd. The *Chronicle* staff was there taking photos and video. Her boys were sitting with their friends from school, and Racine was standing in the back with Darla, who gave Holly an enthusiastic thumbs-up as she caught her eye.

After the pep band played the Notre Dame fight song, "Victory March," which Vivian had loved ironically, Holly stepped to the podium. Her hands were damp and her stomach unsettled, but she was determined not to show her nerves. She smoothed out the paper and looked up at the expectant faces of Bertram Corners.

"Thank you, everyone," she said. "We are all here today to honor a remarkable woman, Vivian Eunice Markham."

A murmur rippled through the crowd. She heard a few "Here, here's" and an "Amen" from a member of the choir.

"Truth be told, Vivian didn't want the kind of recognition she has in her passing. She would have preferred to have led an unremarkable life like the ones that most of us have, lives in which we walk and breathe and eat and hold our children without even pausing to consider our good fortune. But Vivian was tapped by the hand of a higher power—or maybe just fate—to live a very public life, one in which she inspired all of us with her perseverance, her sense of humor, and her honesty. I'm sure many of you remember what she used to say: 'If you can't say something nice about someone, come here and sit next to me.'"

Holly could hear Darla's laugh above the rest.

"For fifty-seven of her sixty-three years, Vivian survived only because a machine kept her alive. It was a machine that she both loved and despised. It was both an amazing feat of human ingenuity and an outdated piece of technology, but we all loved it, didn't we? If it hadn't been for Vivian's iron lung, none of us would have had the privilege of getting to know her, of hearing her wisdom, or of seeing the cold night sky pierced with stars as we left her house after a volunteer shift.

"Vivian changed us. Bertram Corners has its problems—empty storefronts, a depressed housing market, unemployment, no good sushi—but we came together around Vivian. We embraced her. According to her, we kept her alive, both physically and spiritually.

"This wasn't a selfless act. We did it"—and Holly paused to take a long breath to stop her voice from breaking—"because we loved her."

The crowd in the gym applauded.

"According to Vivian's wishes," she continued, "this memorial service is a celebration without mourning. Vivian wanted whatever comes next or doesn't come next, and she wanted us to liberate her both literally and figuratively. With that in mind, we have paper balloons outside that each contain some of Vivian's ashes. Before the dance party in the gym, we ask everyone to file outside, where you will be split into small groups to launch the balloons."

Holly was one of the last to emerge into the weak February light. She found Connor, Marshall, and Racine, who were about to light the base of one of the devices, which worked like miniature hot-air balloons. All around them, one by one the balloons went aloft, floating into the morning sky. Some were red, some were pink, and some were white. Each one wobbled at first, then found its way upward, onward, drifting off into the distance until it was a speck on the horizon.

Holly watched as Connor steadied their balloon and waited for it to fill with warm air before letting it go. Before letting *her* go. Holly watched the sea of rising balloons, now absolutely certain that this was what Vivian had pictured and wanted for so long. Instead of grief, she felt gratitude. The hollow places in her soul felt less hollow because she had been useful to a remarkable spirit whose every breath—as forced as it was—mattered.

ACKNOWLEDGMENTS

In 2009 I read a remarkable obituary in the *New York Times* about Martha Mason, a North Carolina woman who had contracted polio at eleven and lived the rest of her life in an iron lung, dying at age seventy-one. The poignant story, written by Margalit Fox, mentioned that Martha Mason had written an autobiography. I ordered it immediately, read it over a few days, and grew even more fascinated. Martha somehow lived a long and useful life from within the confines of an eight-hundred-pound machine.

The Virtues of Oxygen and the character of Vivian emerged from that true story. Though she is gone, I'd like to thank Martha Mason for her inspiration, courage, and character. My story would not exist if she had not told her own.

Thanks to my editor, Lindsay Guzzardo, who also edited my first novel, *A Watershed Year*. Lindsay has the ability to coax emotion out of my writing and to identify where I've glossed things over or taken the easy way out. My gratitude goes out to my agent, Jessica Regel, who sold this book to Lake Union and who has been with me from the beginning. She's a professional with a heart, and I owe her much.

Thanks as well to agent Laura Biagi, the team at Amazon Publishing, and copy editor Marcus Trower.

Friends and family continue to support me, and I appreciate each and every person who has listened to me talk ad nauseam about the intricacies of the publishing business. Among them are Karen O'Brien, Theresa Sullivan Barger, Adele Angle, and Marge Ruschau, who read early versions of this novel.

I owe a big debt of gratitude to my friend Adam Sapiro, who let me hijack one of his jokes and bend it for the purposes of my story. I'd also like to thank my former colleagues at Patch.com, who influenced how I viewed the job of covering local news. It is a noble and sometimes thankless calling.

Finally, I'd like to thank my family. My children—Andrew, Jenna, and Claire—have been incredibly supportive of my writing. They inspire me with their own creative endeavors. My husband, Kevin, to whom this book is dedicated, is my rock and my partner. He gives me the space to go off into my own world whenever necessary, and I love him for it.

ABOUT THE AUTHOR

Susan Schoenberger is a writer and editor who lives in West Hartford, Connecticut, with her husband and three (almost-grown) children. Her short stories and essays have appeared in *Inkwell*, *Village Rambler*, and Bartlebysnopes.com, among other publications. A longtime journalist, Susan has worked for the *Baltimore Sun*, the *Hartford Courant*, and many other newspapers and online publications. Her first novel, *A Watershed Year*, won the gold medal in the William Faulkner–William Wisdom Creative Writing Competition. Please visit her website at susanschoenberger.com and follow her on Twitter @ schoenwriter.